DATE DUE

The Girl with the Botticelli Face

Also by W. D. Valgardson

Novels and Short Stories

What Can't Be Changed Shouldn't Be Mourned
Gentle Sinners
Bloodflowers
God Is Not a Fish Inspector
Red Dust

Poetry

In the Gutting Shed
The Carpenter of Dreams

The Girl with the Botticelli Face

W. D. Valgardson

Douglas & McIntyre
Vancouver/Toronto

Douglas & McIntyre
1615 Venables Street
Vancouver, British Columbia
V5L 2H1

All the characters, events and places in *The Girl with the Botticelli Face* are entirely fictional. Any resemblance they may bear to real persons, experiences and locations is purely illusory.

Canadian Cataloguing in Publication Data

Valgardson, W. D.
  The girl with the Botticelli face

  ISBN 1-55054-030-0

  I. Title.
PS8593.A53G5 1992   C813'.54   C92-091461-6
PR9199.3.V34G5 1992

Cover design by Tania Craan
Cover illustration by Bernice Eisenstein
Detail from *The Birth of Venus* by Sandro Botticelli
Printed in Canada by Best Gagné Book Manufacturers Inc.
Printed on acid-free paper ∞

The Girl with the Botticelli Face

1

PISSING DOWN. A COLD, STEADY DRIZZLE. Like you feel you're standing under a downspout or got into the shower with your clothes on before driving home after a party. Drizzling for months. Drizzling for so long I'd forgotten what it was like to wake up to sun, to blue sky, to bluebirds on my window sill. Every day the clouds were low and heavy and looked like roadside snow in April. That's a poetic way of saying dirty. Filthy, actually. The kind of day the tourism department never mentions in their glorious, four-colour brochures filled with Victoria's charms.

After weeks of rain, water seeps under doors, through basement walls, down minuscule cracks in shingles. The sheets are clammy. I've been sleeping with my socks on night after night. Some nights I don't bother taking off my clothes. I just roll myself in a comforter and graze the channels looking for a sign.

At two in the afternoon it's so dark I have to stand under a street lamp to read the personals. The parking lots have turned into lakes of drowned cars. Camaros hydroplane through red lights. Store owners scowl at rivers running down the sidewalks, rivers that threaten buildings filled with toupees, exercise machines, elaborate Valentine cards, pants with thirty-inch waists. The whole city is depressed. Somebody told me he's heard of an entire apartment block on Valium.

That's not me in the Tilley hat. I can't afford a Tilley, not with what my wife spends on bodice rippers and Szechwan on the run. I'm the guy with the Greek fisherman's cap and the worn pea

1

jacket pulled up high at the neck and my walking shoes with hardly any sole left. I'm thinking about Costa Rica, palm trees, possible assumed names, sipping rum through a straw, when I hear some-body yelling, or I think I hear somebody yelling. This is when it's hard to get the memory right, you know what I mean? I think I hear somebody yelling help but I'm not sure, I only sort of hear it between thinking about the taste of rum punch drunk from a coconut and the feel of the sun and the sound of a slight breeze through the palms. I stop right in the middle of a puddle and listen, looking around like a goof, but there's nobody on the street. Everybody with any brains is inside, sitting with their feet in the oven, fighting off dry rot.

I am just starting to think about the sand and the palm trees when I hear the yelling again and I turn around in a complete circle. I look up at the apartment block behind me. There's this guy standing on one of the balconies and I wonder if he thinks he's fishing for salmon. I wave to him but he's got his back to me. If he wasn't up so high, I'd figure he was doing a B and E. It crosses my mind to say something to the super, punch the button at the door and tell him some poor bugger has been locked out by his wife, but the yelling distracts me, makes me start looking for who's making all the noise. Nobody is breast stroking across the parking lot on the other side of the street. Right beside me is hoarding, I think that's what you call it, you know, plywood fencing set up around an excavation. They dug an excavation there when every-one was still optimistic, before the Kurds were driven into the mountains, *glasnost* turned to chaos, and the divorce rate reached fifty per cent.

I wade over. There'd been an outdoor art competition years before. Artist wannabees paid twenty bucks and got to paint on a sheet of plywood. The plan was to add some humanity to the city. The painting in front of me shows a bloodshot eye with a knife shoved through it.

I stand there looking through one of those holes they cut for sidewalk engineers. Have you done that? Ducking your head this way and that, trying to see around corners without looking like an idiot. The excavation runs right to the next street. In the bottom,

2

a strange flooded city. Concrete pilings rising out of the grey water. Rusted steel rods sprouting out of the concrete. Off to one side, on a mound of earth, there's a green construction shack. I take my eye from the hole and put my ear to it.

That's when I hear people fighting. A man and a woman. Her voice higher, like nails on a blackboard, and his deeper, more like a dog barking.

I shuffle along the fence until I come to a place where the panels have twisted and pulled away from each other. I grab a two-by-four post and step onto the other side. There's a three-foot grassy ledge, then the excavation starts. It's maybe thirty feet down. I hang on to the two-by-four and lean over.

The bottom, I can see, isn't flat. Around the outer edge there's a mud road. No ramp, though. No place for trucks to get up or down. And just below me there's this guy and some woman. They're facing each other and yelling. While I watch, she picks up a piece of scrap two-by-four and throws it at him. He hops sideways but still gets hit on the shoulder.

She's a tall blonde. He's shorter and even from here you can see his hair is dyed black. Because of the odd angle from which I'm looking, everything is distorted and unfamiliar. There's the top of his head and then his potbelly, but from here it looks as if he's got a wash basin in his pants.

"Stop it, stop it, stop it," he starts yelling. He swings at her but misses because he slips in the mud.

"What's going on down there?" I yell. They both look up. I take a firm grip of the two-by-four and lean farther out.

"Bob," the guy yells back. "Is that you?"

"Dr. George?"

"Bob? Thank God! Am I happy to see you."

Shit! This guy used to be our marriage counselor. He's the last person in the world I want to see.

The wall isn't quite vertical. There's a bit of slope. The m.c. runs to where I'm standing, close to one corner, and now I can see that someone has gouged steps in the clay. Not steps like stairs but indentations just deep enough to get your toes into. The rain's eroding the holes but he starts up. His wife—I hadn't recognized her with her bouffant plastered down by the rain—starts swinging at him with her bare hands. When he keeps climbing, she picks up a piece of concrete and throws it at him, hitting him in the back. He gives a short, sharp yell but doesn't stop. He keeps slipping on the wet clay, losing his grip, sliding down. That gives her a chance to find more things to throw. She throws in that awkward, broken-arm way women have, and the bits of steel and concrete miss more often than they hit. Each time he's hit, he screams at her to stop, but it doesn't do any good. She keeps throwing and he keeps climbing, sometimes stopping to scoop water out of the holes.

"What the hell's going on?" I yell. "What're you doing down there?" His wife throws a piece of reinforcing rod at me but it falls back and nearly hits her on the head. "You live under a mansard roof with a double garage and a purple Jacuzzi."

"Tax shelters," he screams back, "flow-through shares, junk bonds, anal retentive tax agents." He's raving as if he's not really connected. Everything's got to him and he's spitting it out like bits of barbed wire. "We came to check on this investment and the ladder broke."

I look across the excavation. A wooden ladder has pulled away from the bank and has fallen so that the top's jammed on some pilings. The pilings are in the water. He'd need a boat and two strong men to get the ladder tipped back up.

It takes him a while but he finally struggles to the top of the hard clay. I lean farther out to see why he can't climb any higher. There's a three-foot band of topsoil. When it's touched, it disintegrates. If he manages to lunge, all he'll grab is grass and the grass'll come out like hair from a nervous wreck and he'll lose his balance and fall or slide to the bottom.

He's wearing one of his good suits. I remember when he bought it at Straiths. Maybe British Importers. But probably Straiths. Sixteen hundred on sale. It's soaking wet and smeared with clay. There are snags where he's been hit with things. His tailor, if he could see this, would weep. Tailors in this town are so professional that when they fit a suit, they ask which side you carry your balls. He's wearing a nice silk tie but it's ruined. There's a button off his tailored shirt. I can't bear to look at the mess his shoes are in. He never buys anything but genuine lizard, bison or antelope. Patients taller than him he always refers to other psychologists. This has cut so deeply into his practice that he's had to have a local cobbler add a discreet half-inch sole to give him a little extra height. Instead, I look at his face. There's a bruise on one cheek and a long scratch down his forehead.

"God," he breathes. He's so out of shape he has to catch his breath after every word and there are high-pitched sounds between the words, like somebody who's just finished a marathon and come second. "Am." Wheeze. "I." Whine. "Glad. To. See. You."

"You said that," I remind him.

He swallows a few times and sucks in air. "Give me a hand. Up." He lets go with one muddy hand and reaches towards me.

His wife has quit throwing things. Instead, she's getting ready for his return. She's scouring the bottom, gathering weapons. As I watch, she reaches into the water and pulls out a board. She holds it with both hands and practises swinging it. It has a nail in one end.

"Not getting along?" I say.

"Help me up. Just give me your hand. I've made it to here a dozen times but I'm not strong enough to get out on my own." Speaking exhausts him. He leans his forehead against the wet clay. I feel sorry for him. He's usually so fastidious. In his desk drawer he has a magnetized brush for lifting lint off his suit.

"You tried negotiating?" I ask.

"Fuck negotiating," he says. I'm sorry about that. But I'm trying to get it right. Just as I experienced it.

I haven't seen him for close to a year. When I used to go to his office every Wednesday, he never talked like that. He sat in his big, black chair and nodded a lot. He was a great nodder. He had, I believe, a postgraduate course in nodding. He also made steeples with his fingers. Just the tips touching. He never, ever said fuck. Not once. Not even when I ripped open my wounds and bled on his white British India carpet. Although he did keep spot remover in his desk. If anyone got a spot on his carpet, he'd take out the spot remover, sprinkle it on, then brush it off into a crumb tray, which he'd bought from my wife.

5

"Give me your hand," he whines. "I've gotta get out of here. I've gotta get a hot shower and a meal and some sleep. Then I'll be okay." He pauses and swallows again. The rain's running through his hair, streaming in muddy rivulets into his collar. That shirt was hand sewn in Hong Kong. It has his initials embroidered on the pocket in a pale, understated blue.

Gotta! That shocks me. More than fuck. Fuck's sort of instinctive. Even old maids and ministers who don't say it, think it. Even the best people let it slip out occasionally when they're agitated. But I'd never heard him use gotta. It had always been got to. Or necessary. Or inevitable.

"Will you come back and help her get out?" I ask.

"I don't know." He sounds impatient. If I'd had a pencil and a notebook, I'd have written that down. *Impatient. Unable to deal appropriately with stress.* And underline it twice. Seeing my disapproval, he adds, "Of course. Sure I will."

"You loved her once. You married her. For better or worse."

"I know my marriage vows," he says.

"In sickness and in health," I tell him. I try to remember his words of advice. Usually they were more than words. More like paragraphs or even speeches. Some sessions he made such long speeches that I wondered if he was Castro's illegitimate brother. "Are you meeting her needs? Maybe if you went back and took your time and got her ready and had good sex, she'd quit throwing things. Good sex is the glue that holds people together. I help you get out of there and run away, then what? Your life's not going to get any less complicated. You can't shrug off your history together. At your age anybody you meet's going to have a history. You've just made love to somebody and you're lying there with her head on your arm and she whispers that she's got five kids and a jealous ex-husband. Or she'll look like she's twenty. Tennis shoes and a ponytail. But it's a mirage. She's had a bum lift and a tummy tuck, been married three times and all her husbands have been married twice to women who have been married before. Marry her and you'll be related to people who kiss snakes or eat baby mice."

I lean farther out. Lower my voice. Repeat back to him the

advice he's given to me. "Stay with what you've got. Deal with reality. Don't run away from what is."

Instead of paying attention, he's desperately trying to dig a handhold in the topsoil. It's like trying to sculpt sawdust.

To change the topic, I ask, "Does this belong to you?" I wave my free arm to take in the entire excavation.

"We had plans," he snaps.

"Renew them," I counsel him. "Seek inside yourself for those early hopes and dreams."

Below us his wife is balancing bits of concrete on the end of the board. She's using the board like a catapult. She's able to throw higher but is hopelessly inaccurate.

"Don't do this to me," he cries.

"There's lots of ways of being married. Work out a compromise," I suggest. "Make it your unique way of being together. Don't become a statistic. Increase her credit limit. Generosity is always appreciated. Send her flowers. Take her out for dinner. Go on separate vacations. Give each other a little leeway for romance as long as it's discreet. Make her fantasies real."

"I can't stand the pain any more," he shouts. His shirt has pulled open. On his pale, hairless chest there's a cross-stitching of old scars. In all the time I've known him, I never suspected. He'd kept them carefully hidden under the starched shirts and college ties.

"A younger woman isn't going to make you happy," I remind him.

"I don't want a younger woman," he protests. "I want to sleep. I want to wake up alone in bed. I want to quit arguing. I want to sit and do nothing. I want silence."

I glance at my watch. It doesn't seem like it but, from the time I'd first heard his voice, it was fifty minutes.

The table at the back of the Green Café is always reserved for me on Wednesdays at this time. The waitress with the green running shoes, the pink socks and the Botticelli face will be watching for me. Across the street there's the travel agency with its posters of Costa Rica, which I study regularly. My weekly lottery ticket is in my pocket and it's Wednesday afternoon. The draw will be held shortly. My waitress never asks what I want anymore. When I come in and sit down, she makes the cappuccino, strong, the way I like it, dusts it with chocolate, puts it down in front of me and says nothing, not even hello until I've had a chance to settle. Only then will she read the menu from her hand and ask me about my writing, or comment on the ballet, or mention some show that is coming to town. On my bad days she says nothing, leaving me to silently recite my lottery numbers, willing the coloured balls out of the distant machine, one after the other, while I stare through the doorway, through the window, across the rain-swept street at the posters of palm trees, white beach and blue sky. Thinking of that, I reach down, put my toe gently on the m.c.'s head and give him a little nudge, not hard, not unkind, just enough to throw him off balance and start him sliding.

2

Let me tell you about the waitress with the Botticelli face. She wears short dresses. Until a year ago, she wore long dresses to cover up her bruises. Once when she caught me staring at her bruises, she said she had a blood disorder, nothing catching. Nothing anyone else had to worry about. Her cheek was blue. It's not likely to be fatal, she said. I'm doing something about it. And sure enough the bruises faded and didn't come back. What did appear was a young man with long, untidy hair, a permanent day's growth of beard and fingerless gloves. He often met her when she got off work.

After the bruises faded, she seemed happier. Her smile was no longer forced. Her face was fuller again, more angelic, with her wide-spaced dark eyes and red lips. When she left work, she mounted her old-fashioned blue bicycle with an energy I had not seen before and pushed off into the traffic, her collection of tips secure in an empty coffee bag.

The café is tiny. The tables minuscule. Two people sitting facing each other can't avoid touching knees. One has to eat delicately not to crash the plates together. Some of the tables only have one chair. My table is one of those. Dining, unless you are like me, alone and brooding, is intimate, even with a stranger. Most of the time I'm not up to conversation and yet I like the feeling of closeness, this silly idea of a café, unable to hold more than a dozen tables at the front, another dozen at the back, with its high old ceiling, its lamps suspended on brass poles, its green paint, its walls hung with an ever-changing display of paintings of indescribable ugliness. Paintings of blotches and blobs, landscapes identifiable only by the names of the cards tacked under them, completely uncompromising in a marketplace that loves gentle cats, wide-eyed, improbable native children, perfect daisies, irises, roses and cottages in which tragedy is inconceivable. The paintings are appropriate. No one minds their ugliness. On the contrary, we all applaud it. Socially realistic, figurative representations would be distracting, would mute the defiance of the café's mood.

There is a bizarre silence that occurs when people speak without making a sound, their lips and hands moving, their eyes touching, but silent because Pachelbel's Canon fills up everything. Since the café opened six years ago, the chef has insisted on its being played constantly. Without it, he descends into immobility, sits staring blankly at the counter, uninspired by lettuce, feta, olives, lentils, pineapple, grapes, Brie, crusty croissants. Demytro, the owner, has worn out one hundred and nine tapes keeping the chef inspired.

Strangers, dropping by, sometimes find the music irritating and ask that another tape be put on. The waitresses comply, take the tape off the recorder and put on a fresh tape of the Canon played by a different musician. I find the sameness soothing. The music provides certainty in an ever-changing world. Here the music stays the same but the menu always changes. The menu is created by the whim of the weather, the transportation system, the pricing system, the mood of the chef as he visits the wholesalers in the early morning.

Some people who have come once and not returned claim the café is busy only because it is close to the mental hospital. It is true that the owner has stayed there on occasions, and it is true that is where he met the chef, a small, sad Frenchman who once cooked in a four-star restaurant but finally could no longer stand the strident demands of the public. He had nightmares in which he was forced to inject goose fat and butter directly into the veins of his patrons.

The waitresses, not all of them, but some, have come to the café directly after being released from the hospital. Some are on day passes. Safe within the close confines of the hospital at night and the café during the day, they wear their plastic wristbands with the same pride as the m.c.'s wife wears her many gold bracelets. Not everyone is a patient or former patient. There are those, like me, who heard of the café while visiting a patient. I was skeptical of the praise but once inside I found the deep green walls, the music, the dim lighting, the unheard conversations soothing. Since that first tentative visit I have become a regular.

The food is cheap. No one minds if I linger over a cappuccino for an hour. I sit at my table, my back to the wall, thinking, trying to figure out what has happened to my life. When I have papers or tests to grade, I bring them with me. At the college there are endless interruptions, constant, unpredictable demands, a chorus of whining with which I can no longer cope. At home, my wife never stops complaining. Here, there is just Pachelbel and privacy. The patrons seldom speak. It is too painful. But we know each other. The woman in the red hat. The blind man who always orders a café latte for himself and a bran muffin for his dog. The nervous real estate agent who sometimes brings clients and when, as usual, he doesn't sell them anything, returns to sit with his head gripped in his hands.

And me. If you go by, someone will point me out as the Captain. I'm not really a captain, not even a sailor. I hate the sea. It is too unpredictable. Both times I agreed to go sailing, I did nothing but watch for clouds, listen for wind. They call me Captain because of this cap I bought cheap one day at the back of a salvage store, a Greek sailor's cap, and also this peacoat, which is heavy, excellent for keeping out the cold and the rain. Some days, especially those on which I don't shave, I give the impression of being an unemployed sailor. The kind of person who has no friends and stays in a rooming house owned by an irascible landlord.

Demytro used to close the café on holidays, but the effect on his staff and regular customers was so terrible—all these people with no place to go, sitting alone in their rooms or the hospital and he himself feeling the loneliness so keenly he'd plucked all the leaves off his precious African violets by the end of the day—that he always keeps it open longer than normal on holidays. On

Christmas and New Year, Mother's Day, Valentine's Day, Thanksgiving, he sometimes stays open all night. When he has an ethnic waitress, he stays open for her national holidays. He's been open late for Hanukkah and Ukrainian New Year. He works the waitress whose holiday it is harder than anyone else, giving her more tables, extra duties. On my birthday he hired me to work in the storeroom, sorting and piling and bagging and boxing until I was so tired I fell asleep curled around a box of mangoes.

On holidays he lowers his prices to attract customers, puts on specials, keeps every table full. He will go to heaven for this. I've assured him of that many times, I know what he is up to, but he only gets embarrassed. He is one of those large men who was large when he was still a child, clumsy and awkward, standing a foot or more above his classmates. It has made him shy. He walks through his own restaurant as if he is intruding and is going to be ordered out. He has grey hair and a grey beard. I've never seen him without his apron. His shyness inhibits the giving of compliments, so little gifts accumulate along the counter. They are from his staff and customers. A single daffodil in a Perrier bottle, a rose, probably picked in the park or some home owner's yard, but no less precious for that, a special stone found on the beach, a bit of driftwood, a beautiful shell.

The soup is like the music. Always the same. The menu proclaims soup of the day in bold black letters with two exclamation marks, but it is always borscht. The menu is quite handsome. It was done by a regular who spent years learning calligraphy only to discover his skill was no longer needed because computers now contain all the alphabets ever known. He fell into despair and the despair turned to such bitterness that he has become a politician. When the waitresses hand you a menu, they will point out the beauty of the calligraphy, but when you try to order, they will make other suggestions. They never actually admit that nothing on the menu, except the soup of the day, is possible. Instead, they consult their left hand and read off what is available. When something runs out, they wipe the item off their palm. When one of them brings fresh ingredients, they pass around a pen and write in the new dish. On a day in which the chef is inspired they may have a list halfway to the elbow.

When strangers drop in and insist upon an item from the menu, the kind of customers who are referred to as yuppies or preppies or dinks, the kind who know who they are and their position in the world, the waitress, whichever one it is, in her brightly coloured skirt and blouse, her blue or green hair, will be solicitous and understanding, will write down the order and show it to the chef, as is a waitress's duty, and the chef will abandon his chopping and cutting and blending and will leave his small enclosure where he prepares the finest light meals in the city. He will study the customers until he feels he understands them. Then he will return to his kitchen and make something he thinks is appropriate for them. It is always something with lentils.

My wife has heard of this place but she has never come here. I'm grateful for that. She'd fill the place up until everyone else was squeezed out, until everyone, the owner, the chef, the rainbow-coloured waitresses, the sad real estate agent, all of us, would be pushed out onto the street with nowhere to go. She worships reality. She'd suggest to Demytro that he get a more compliant chef, that he do a survey of customers' food preferences, that he advertise, that he buy out the beauty parlour next door so he can expand, that the waitresses wear uniforms, that he raise his prices and set a minimum charge and put up little signs that say be considerate, someone is waiting for your table. She'd offer her advice unasked, with the finest intentions. She admires success, believes in maximizing potential, reads books on time management and attends seminars on motivational psychology.

Every time she finds me sitting in my study doing nothing she says, "Baths are good for relieving depression but have a shower, they're more ecologically sound."

I've quit trying to explain to her that I can't stand getting water on my face. It's just water, she says. Quit being a baby. Just because your mother got water on your face when she washed your hair or something is no reason to hate showers when you're an adult.

She has no use for the past. She believes nothing she cannot experience in the present. It was during her stay in the hospital that she also discovered reality. For a long time after she rejected fantasy, she went around doing things like pointing at the oak in our front yard and shouting at me, "This is not a sacred oak. The old gods are dead. They never were alive. They were just a fantasy. This is just a tree. There is no magic in it. If I chop it with an ax, it will fall down and can be cut into lumber. The lumber would be worth one hundred and sixty-five dollars."

Six months after embracing reality, she discovered feminism. She has become, she says with fervour, reborn. Her new religion teaches that the world's problems are created by men. The world's solutions are created by women. If we'd kept worshipping a female god, the world would be a sensitive, gentle, kindly place. I will not enter into a dialogue with you. I will, she says, instruct you in the truth. She refuses to discuss Catherine the Great, Margaret Thatcher and Indira Gandhi. Her new political awareness hasn't shaken her loose from four years spent in a boarding school run by nuns. It's just changed her focus. Her dozen plaster statues of Christ she resculpted, leaving his long hair, sanding off his beard and adding plaster to form breasts. She then painted his robe pink. Now she goes up and down the stairs on her knees, prostrating herself to the daughter of God.

This is what I'm thinking as the waitress with the Botticelli face finishes her shift and mounts her blue bicycle and rides away. She's wearing a bright yellow slicker and a cloth cap with a plastic bag snugged around it by a rubber band. Painters should be fighting to capture her likeness as she takes the bike away from the tree, puts one foot on a pedal, turns towards the window and waves. There is the flash of her pink socks and green runners and then she is gone. But only momentarily, I think. Tomorrow is another day. She'll return with the dawn. All will be right with the world.

Before she left, she refilled my cup, put her hand on my shoulder and said, "I'll see you tomorrow."

Something in her voice gave me the courage to do what I hadn't dared do for nearly a year. I said, "I've got two tickets for the ballet. Would you like to go tomorrow night?" I said it quickly, quietly, so that if she wanted, she could pretend she hadn't heard me.

Instead, she squeezed my shoulder and said, "Yes, that would be nice. Let's organize it when you come in for coffee tomorrow."

But the next day, she wasn't there with my cappuccino, and the faces of the staff were white and yellow and hung in the air like stones.

3

I CHECKED BACK AT THE CAFÉ twice more, then waited for an hour over coffee but Sharon never turned up. I couldn't bear the ballet alone, with an empty seat beside me, so I finally went home. I'd expected to retreat to my room but my wife wouldn't hear of it. She was having guests for dinner and insisted that I be at the table for appearances' sake.

We were sitting around the dinner table, eating roast beef and baked potatoes, when the accountant asked what was it like to be a writer and I said I didn't know any more. Why was that? he asked and I said because I no longer was a writer. I used to be a writer. I could, I said, tell him what I used to think and feel about writing and the theories I used to believe B.M.C. What's B.M.C.? he asked. Before marriage counseling, I said. My life is divided into B.M.C. and A.M.C. Just like B.C. and A.D. except B.M.C. and A.M.C. were different in that Christ brought eternal life and marriage counseling brought death.

"Rather melodramatic, isn't it?" he asked. He didn't seem capable of making a statement. When he was a child, someone praised him for asking questions and he was still doing it.

"Don't pay any attention to Bob," my wife said. "When he has to deal with reality, he gets into these moods."

"What do you do? When you see this counselor, I mean?" the accountant asked. Everyone is born with a finite number of question marks and one day he'll use all his up. It will be a crises of monumental proportions.

Everyone at the table leaned forward like pussy sniffers in the front row of a strip joint. His wife said, "I can never figure out what they do for all this money they make. Harold has some psychiatrists for clients. Two hundred and fifty thousand a year and all they do is sit in an office and talk. For that kind of money I'd talk all day."

"Do you lie on a couch?" the accountant asked. "Isn't that what they do in all the movies?" He had a high, slightly bulbous forehead with a triangular indentation over his left eye. It looked as if he'd been hit with something very sharp. At least, I hoped he'd been hit with something very sharp

"That's Freudians," my wife said. "Bob doesn't need a Freudian. The marriage counselor is also a psychologist. His specialty is reality. He helps people deal with reality. You've got an illusion, he kills it. You get too big for your britches, he deflates you. Bob should still be going to him. Reality is exactly what he needs. I don't approve of this new one. I think his credentials are mail order."

"I thought writers needed fantasy," my wife's brother said as he attacked the roast again. "That's their *raison d'être* or something."

"Writers," my wife announced, "can write about reality. As long as it's not offensive to women and children. Or the disabled. Or minorities. Besides, fantasy is for children before the age of six. After six they know the difference. After that it's lying."

She'd invited the accountant and his wife because she was looking for someone to do her books and she wanted to find out if he was realistic about deductions.

"How would you describe therapy?" the accountant's wife asked. She was a junior high school phys. ed. teacher who also taught spelling and health and guidance. Two periods a week, she was the school maturation counselor. She specialized in helping preadolescents explore their wakening sexual identity. She was particularly proud of her innovative strategies. Her latest innovation was an inflatable rubber penis, which she pumped up to show girls the effect they had on their classmates by dressing provocatively. She admired Arab culture and for a time had taken to wearing a *chador*. She had given it up when she found out that Saudi women were not allowed to drive cars.

"Psychological vandalism," I replied. "The therapist runs around inside your head smashing things. Good things, bad things. He digs up the dead so they roam about your life like half-rotted corpses in a Hollywood B movie."

"Nonsense," my wife said. "Anyone can see you're better adjusted. You don't rant and rave over items in the newspaper that don't concern you." She shook her head slowly and scrunched her lips together. "He used to be impossible. He'd get so upset about the way life is. You just have to accept life. He was always trying to correct injustices. We were always donating money to some cause or other. Idealism is fine until thirty. After that it is just neurotic delusion."

"Cultural imperialism is all it is," I said, raising my voice. "They destroy all ethnic values and beliefs and replace them with pseudo WASP middle-class values and then try to brainwash the victim into believing he's happy being a coconut or an apple or whatever kind of fruit he might be."

"Would you like this slice?" my wife's brother asked. "I prefer mine rarer."

"Woody Allen goes to an analyst," the accountant's wife declared. "He's very creative."

"What I don't understand," the accountant said, "is what good creativity is if you can't depend on it? Didn't I learn to be an accountant so people can depend on me to do accountant things every day? What good would it be if I only could do someone's books when the mood struck me?"

My wife's brother was a vegetarian except when he came to visit. Then, in a gesture of family solidarity, he betrayed his principles and forced himself to eat spare ribs, roasts and steak. When we visited him, we lived on a diet of celery, carrots and tofu. He was proving his love for his sister with a half-inch slab of rare prime rib.

"You're resisting again," my wife said. "You'll never adjust to reality if you keep resisting."

"Therapists," I said, savagely burying my fork in my baked

potato, "are the priesthood of the secular age. Before religion lost its authority, the church earned its keep by policing the thoughts and feelings of the lower classes. The upper class supported the church in return for the protection it provided the privileged. Now, the church has lost its authority. We live in a secular age and the lower classes still have to be kept under control. That's why we have psychiatrists and psychologists. They are priests and their god is mediocrity and their creed is adjustment." By the time I finished my speech, my potato was in tatters.

I put down my fork and knife and picked up a piece of prime rib with my fingers. I ripped the meat off the bone with my teeth. Waving the bone at our guests, I said, "That's how us lower-class types do it. No forks, no spoons. Just hands and knives. Catch the animal in the field, rip off a leg and eat it right there. Three-legged animals all over the place." I put the bone down and wiped my fingers on my purple napkin.

"Writers do such unexpected things," the accountant's wife declared. She often had small parties to which she invited a local artist or two in hope that they would do something outrageous to liven things up. Her greatest social coup was when a local poet, after a bottle of Scotch, got into an argument with a lawyer and bit him on the ankle. The lawyer threatened to sue but never went through with it. The poet had no money and the lawyer had no use for five hundred copies of a book of poems no one wanted to read.

"You feel counseling has robbed you of something valuable?" the accountant asked.

"My identity," I replied. "This idiot kept saying, Don't think of yourself as a writer. Think of yourself as a person. Think of yourself as a person who writes. Every bloody moron who is semiliterate is a person who writes. Writers don't have diplomas that make them writers. Not like doctors or accountants. Writers have to struggle all the time just to maintain their identity, to believe in themselves. Lower your expectations. He's got this tape in his head. Lower your expectations. Then you'll be happy. If that's all it takes, every bum with a bottle of cheap wine is living in bliss."

"One of my students made a breakthrough," the accountant's

wife said. "She accepted the idea that oral sex is all right if you find yourself without condoms."

"You haven't told us what you thought about writing before B.M.C." the accountant said.

"I thought it the most important thing in the world. Nothing was more important. Now, I feel as if I've been wasting my time."

"Male menopause," my wife interjected. "The next thing you know he'll be talking about working at the food bank. I told him, don't get involved in other people's problems. It just leads to unpleasantness."

"Would you say you're in a depressed mood?" the accountant said as he wiped his face with a blue napkin. It was embroidered with the letter *N*. His wife had a pink napkin with the letter *K*. My wife, in spite of her liberation, kept to certain conventions. Both were good linen. The reason the colours and letters were different was that my wife had picked them up as odds and ends at garage sales.

"Don't pretend you aren't," my wife said. "His favourite waitress has run away. Eloped or something."

"A waitress?" the accountant's wife said.

"How is it you described her?" my wife asked. "Wasn't it the girl with the Botticelli face?"

"She's very reliable." I was trying to keep my voice under control. I pressed my fork hard against my plate. I didn't want to start shouting. "She's been there for the past two years. She's never missed a day. She fills in when other waitresses are ill."

"People in these jobs come and go," my brother-in-law said. "They flit from restaurant to restaurant. If she was a good waitress, some other employer may have snapped her up."

"I know exactly how you feel," the accountant's wife said. "I felt the same way about my hairdresser. He knew exactly what to do with my hair. I felt absolutely safe. And then he up and ran off to Edmonton."

"Good help is hard to find," my wife's brother said. "Does anyone want this last piece of roast?"

"There are always lots more people entering the service industry, aren't there?" the accountant said.

"I miss her green shoes and red socks," I said. "And her yellow shoes and blue socks. She always wore cheerful combinations."

"We have apple pie with ice cream," my wife said. "Everyone for that?"

"Cheer up." As he spoke, the accountant pointed at the pie. My wife pointed at the ice cream, the accountant shook his head, pointed at his stomach to indicate it was too large, which it was. "The odds are that she's fine. People appear and disappear at an alarming rate but they nearly always turn up, don't they?"

My wife pointed at the tray with lemon slice, butter tarts, chocolate torte and rum balls. When the accountant still shook his head, she sighed with disappointment.

"Not like the people down the street from me," my brother-in-law interjected, stopping eating for a moment. "We knew there was trouble there. Nobody home for days and when we looked in the window there was blood everywhere. Not thin, watery stuff, either. Dark blood. Brain blood. I could see it from the back door."

I was shocked to hear him say that. I hadn't heard that expression since my son had watched a woman jump in front of a car twenty-seven times. He hadn't seen all twenty-seven suicide attempts, only the last, successful one. I told them that. I told them twenty-six drivers had been wary enough, defensive enough, alert enough, to keep the woman from succeeding. With each try she became more cunning, more practised. Her first attempts were pathetically naive. She simply walked into the middle of the highway and trusted drivers to run her down. All she got were waved fists, curses and a trip to the hospital. There, she met some of the future waitresses of the Green Café.

When she was released, she'd tried lying down on the road. Her theory was that she wouldn't be seen or, if seen, would be mistaken for something else. A log or a shadow or a piece of cloth dropped from the back of a passing truck. She was returned to the hospital. Her next attempts were made by running in front of approaching cars but she couldn't judge distance. She would run out far too soon. The cars would stop, then inch around her as she stared, bewildered. As she adjusted to reality, she managed a broken arm. A broken leg. Concussion. I knew her because, between hospital recuperations, she came to the Green Café to drink espresso and eat croissants and Brie. Most of the time she just sat, staring at her cup, her hands wrapped around it. Sometimes, when she was more animated, she'd wave her cast, or point out her bandages and say they were lessons, that she was getting more in touch with how things worked. And, finally, she did. She chose the bottom of a hill with a blind curve, rush hour, wore tan clothes, hid behind a telephone pole with the sun behind her and did not run but dived into the asphalt and death. One wheel of the car ran over her head.

My son saw the whole thing. Although he was only twelve, he stayed and directed traffic until a police car arrived. When he told me about it, I asked if she was really dead. He said she must be because there were two kinds of blood. Light blood on her jacket and dark blood around her head. Brain blood, he said, and when there's brain blood you're dead, Dad. He said it with such absolute conviction that I believed him.

A certain heaviness had settled over the table. Not that any of them knew the woman who committed suicide or the waitress. They were not the kind of people who would ever set foot in a place where a customer could help himself to coffee, where no one was offended if you cleared a table for yourself or, if you came often enough, cut yourself a piece of pie.

To lighten things up, I said, "Their soup of the day is always borscht," but they didn't understand how funny that was. Thinking of the extra cream the waitress always added to my borscht made me melancholy. I wasn't used to someone being so thoughtful. I excused myself and went and sat in the bathroom for a while. When I came back, the conversation had veered towards welfare rip-offs and the need to bring back the death penalty.

4

"YOU CAN'T GO ON LIKE THIS," my wife said. "It makes no sense. She was nothing to you. A waitress. She brought you coffee. There are thousands of waitresses leading tragic lives. That's the reality of being a waitress. What would the world be like if customers brooded about their fate? Unless, of course," she said, suddenly suspicious, "there was more to it than you're telling me."

"Don't be absurd," I answered, fidgeting with the music box I'd bought at the auction. It was exquisite. It was delicately made, a porcelain castle set on a green hill that nestled in a blue ocean. Just inside the castle door was a large cauldron. Because it didn't work, I got it cheap, but I knew that there wasn't much wrong with it. I'm careful about that, precise, always visiting the auction at least twice, inspecting every item for cracks and chips, questioning the auctioneers but finally trusting only my hands, counting the number of knots on the back of a Kerman, feeling for tiny angels' heads and feet that have been broken from Dresden. A quick glance never reveals the damage. People are very clever at hiding it, making repairs, covering them with paint, fitting furniture with bits of wood, filling gashes with sawdust. From a distance, everything looks perfect. God's in his heaven, all's right with the world. I never go anywhere without a jeweller's glass and a sharp penknife.

It all started as a hobby. No, that's not true. Before that, it was necessity. We'd moved here and there, kicking about Canada and the United States, leading a sort of academic gypsy life, renting houses, making do with furniture we could borrow or buy at the secondhand shops. When we moved to Victoria, we decided it was time to stay in one place. After we bought a house, we had only fifteen hundred dollars left and no furniture or appliances. We visited the local stores and discovered that to buy the basics we'd have to go ten thousand in debt at fourteen per cent. My wife's memories of family stories about my great-aunt saved us. My great-aunt was the only financially astute member of my family, making a fortune during the great depression, buying up houses and renting them out in anticipation of better times. She also bought furniture cheap from people who had fallen on hard times. Gradually, she developed an eye for the good but unappreciated. Things that had been discarded but were still sound, even exquisite beneath their coat of paint or dirt. She hired unemployed cabinetmakers to restore these pieces so that people coming to one of her houses in answer to an estate ad in the local paper paid well for them and gave them a place of honour in their homes. She was, she said with some pride, a resurrector. She took in the homeless, the unwanted, and gave them new life. What Christ did for people, she did for furniture, she claimed.

She cultivated a better class of person, that is, those with money. Her husband, a humble barber by trade, left her to her own devices. Her devices were many. She took pieces on commission and sold them from her living room. It was said that everything in her house was for sale. If you liked the cup in which she served you coffee, you had merely to turn it over to see what it would cost you to take it home. Once some visitors took away the couch upon which they had sat for the evening. When we visited her, we never knew what to expect. In the midst of tea and sandwiches, someone might come for the table, someone else for a chair. My mother swore that once she was drinking her tea when my great-aunt took away her cup, emptied the tea into another cup, took the emptied cup with its saucer into the kitchen, washed them, wrapped them up and handed them to someone who'd come to the back door.

When I was a small child there were two family tragedies but what is remembered and remarked upon is my great-aunt's conduct during each of them. My grandfather fell ill with cancer when he was still young enough to have both a grandchild, me, and a second family with children younger than me. His prolonged dying was out of time. On the final night, my great-aunt sat at his bedside with increasing anxiety. Members of the family were cheered by this unexpected example of sisterly devotion. When he finally died at six in the morning and they had closed his eyes and drawn the sheet over his head, she took the handmade comforter from his bed, saying he had promised it to her, and left. She did not return for his funeral but she did return the next year for the funeral of two of my great-uncles. They were drowned in a boating accident that claimed five lives. She took photographs of the funeral and sold them to the city paper. She could not, she said, defending herself to someone who criticized her, bring them back to life, and if she hadn't taken the pictures, someone else would.

Because of her I had an antipathy to auctions. Say auction and I had a vision of Great-aunt Matilda leaving empty spaces behind her as she filled her hearse. She'd bought the hearse secondhand from a bankrupt mortician. When anyone commented on it, she said it suited her admirably. It had a beautiful ride, heavy suspension for carrying loads and lots of room. She was a regular at the old folks' home. People forced to go there always brought more than they could fit into their closets, or store under the beds, and she helped them out by taking the surplus and providing them with a bit of cash. She even double dipped before double dipping became a term. She scooped their excess belongings when they moved in, and when they died, she was back to snap up the rest. Since the closest mortician was thirty-five miles away and he had only one hearse, she sometimes took the body with the belongings, dropping it off at the funeral parlour before she went on to the city.

Thinking furniture, my wife remembered her, and remembering her, she thought auction and, after I'd got over a nervous attack, she got me to take her around to the nearest auction house. For fifteen hundred dollars we bought everything we needed. Our lives remained normal but two events then occurred, which, at the time, seemed insignificant. When we got the couch home, my wife found four dollars and ninety-seven cents under the cushions.

That excited her. I should have been warned. She chattered about it the way someone might who'd panned gold nuggets in the local ditch. Later, when I'd received three or four pay cheques and we could afford something better, we cleaned and repaired the auction furniture and put it up for sale. We doubled our money. That was the second event.

Our lives took a sudden turn. What had been a humiliating necessity became my wife's passion. She attended auctions with fervour. Two nights a week she bought toasters and irons and vacuums and tea sets. She stacked everything in the basement until we finally had to make paths in order to get to the freezer or the washer and dryer. She held garage sales every Saturday until the neighbours, fed up with the traffic, especially the early birds who sometimes mistakenly knocked on their doors instead of ours, complained to city council, charging that she was running an unlicensed business.

I thought that might slow her down. Instead, she moved her operation to the local rec centre where there is a flea market every Sunday. She quickly formed a network of informants and pickers. She'll talk to anybody, bag ladies, people at bus stops, grocery clerks, receptionists. She once talked for three minutes to someone sitting on a park bench before realizing something was wrong. He'd been dead for some time, the ambulance attendant said.

For the last two years, since her enthusiasm for reality has developed, the basement is organized. Before, it was a towering mass of boxes randomly filled with objects. Now there are shelves and everything is labelled by category. Saucers. Chipped saucers. Coloured saucers. Good china saucers. Collectable saucers. There is a flock of ducks from Thailand or Burma or someplace where people smoke so much dope that they carve ducks with teeth and shoes. They are the most evil ducks in existence. There are pictures made from fish scales. Chamber pots in the shape of famous men. On the bottom of each one it says, according to the likeness, "Shit on Hitler. Shit on Churchill. Shit on Freud. Shit on Mozart." They have hundreds of moulds that include every important secular and religious man imaginable. She sells them on commission for a local feminist co-op. In an expensive red jewellery box there is a necklace made from gallstones.

She's taken over the two rooms in the basement plus the storage room and the garage. We have to park our truck in the driveway. Upstairs in the pantry, on the high shelves, a collection of stuffed birds glares down, and in the corner of the sunroom there is a six foot stuffed cobra with one glass eye. The cobra is six feet long, three feet of it curled in a basket and three feet of it raised up and swollen, its hood flared out. Its scales have faded to a dull grey and some previous owner, to make it more appealing, has painted its upper part pale purple.

I've been drawn into the business against my will. The marriage counselor said we should do more things together. I think he had other activities in mind, but of all the activities in which my wife is interested, buying and selling are the least unsettling. When she's hustling secondhand goods, she doesn't wear a nun's habit or insist upon my bringing her fanciful desserts.

I haven't seen the marriage counselor professionally for a year now. For a man steeped in people's problems, he seemed to have a lot of illusions. Compared to my wife, he's an irrepressible idealist. He said, for example, that most men were willing to pay a lot for a regular sexual relationship. Not the men I know. Three months to three years, maximum. After that sex is like cutting the lawn and shovelling snow. Something that has to be done because you own the house. He never could grasp that I was quite willing to skip the sex and keep the money. He used to get me to sit back and relax and then he'd turn his back to me and quietly, so I could just barely hear, ask me why I was so resistant to making love to my wife. Think of her, he used to say, as beautiful as she once was. The way she looked when you first met her. Remember the excitement of it all. All I could think of was the cobra looming among the plastic ferns.

The unwanted buying the unwanted. The rejects buying the rejected. That's why I fit right in. My captain's cap and pea jacket and a one-day growth of beard, my hands in my pockets. Listening to the auctioneer's patter and jokes, which I now know by heart.

My wife calls the regulars realists. The owners of small gift shops, antique stores, secondhand emporiums. They know the price of everything. I don't bother to argue with her any more but she's wrong. All of them, including her, are romantics. It's not the toaster bought for a dollar and sold for two that brings them here. It's the belief that one day they'll come across that spectacular find, that forgotten great master, that solid gold chandelier covered in enamel, the two-penny black. They whisper endlessly about what such a discovery would be worth but the money isn't what it's all about. Nearly all of them are poor. Barely hanging on, in spite of the brave front. At best they earn a living and pay their bills every second month. There are a thousand things they could do that would pay better. My wife once said to me, "Business must be good. They're open six days a week and evenings." I replied, "No one whose business is good stays open six days plus evenings."

They all tell stories of diamond rings found in button boxes, of gold jewellery tucked into cake pans. Strangely enough, now and again, it does happen. My wife bought a cracked plate for sixty dollars and sold it for six thousand. A porcelain stork so ugly you could frighten children with it, she bought for ninety and sold for nine hundred. But in between there have been thousands of colanders, kitchen chairs with loose legs, paintings on black velvet, bottles covered with macramé.

"Don't be absurd," I repeated but some time had elapsed since I first said it so she no longer was paying attention. I have lapses like that. A word or an image will pop up and my ferret-like mind will dash crazily after it, sometimes for minutes, sometimes for hours before I catch it or give up. The m.c. was concerned about that. When I did it in his office he always touched the back of my hand and said my name. If I didn't look at him and reply, he'd do it again. I always felt dazed. Sometimes, I'd slip away and start back after what I'd been pursuing, but he'd tap my hand again and repeat my name. Often, I'd give up the chase good-naturedly and we'd continue our conversation. Other times I'd come back sullenly, reluctantly, thinking of fields and underbrush and a darting, elusive figure.

It was like that now, hard to stay in the room. I was seeing the waitress standing outside the window with her foot on the bicycle pedal, then looking up and waving at me. As she disappeared from sight, I wanted to follow her, to dash after her, to stop her and say don't go, don't go wherever you are going, come with me, let's walk around the harbour, let's stop at the Empress for high tea, let's stand on this corner forever. I was seeing her hand as she waved, as if it was a close-up on a screen. I never realized how closely I'd observed her hands—they were broad and her nails, carefully filed, were unpolished. Her fourth finger on her right hand had a ring with the letter *f* on it.

My wife was busy polishing some silver plate. I finished taking the music box apart and reattached the spring.

5

"You don't look good," Evelyn said. I'd ordered a bran muffin with strawberry jam. The chef had sent me a watercress and cucumber sandwich. It cleaned the blood and reduced stress. I must have had more worry lines on my forehead than usual.

Evelyn looked as if she needed the sandwich more than me. Her eyes were bloodshot and she kept pulling her top lip between her teeth and biting it. She was anorexic and wore layered clothes to hide it. Her head was shaved except for the very top. Her red hair stood up like a bloom on a pale white stalk.

"I thought Sharon would be back by now."

"Nah," she said, trying to sound nonchalant but her eyes flicked to the left, away from mine, then down at her hands. "Everybody's making too much out of it. I once took off for a week. Nobody called the cops or nothing."

"Why'd you take off?"

She shrugged, then pulled up the green sweater that hung precariously from her shoulders. Underneath there was a red shirt and under that a white shirt. And under that were other layers. Inside this thick cocoon was eighty-five pounds of bone and skin. Without her clothes, I'd heard one of the waitresses say, she was just bones, no breasts, no hips, sticks for legs. Once, since I'd known her, she'd gone up to a hundred and five pounds, had started to nibble on date bars from the fridge, quit throwing up after a meal of yogurt and honey, then her mother had come to visit for the weekend and Evelyn had gone back to living on water and had ended up in the hospital. The other waitresses had taken turns going to the hospital, feeding her puréed vegetables and fruit, sitting beside her bed, reading to her.

"I don't know. This job gets boring. It's okay. But you know. It's not like movie stars are always dropping by. And sometimes the girls have a breakdown or something and have to stay in the hospital for a week. Sunbeam was gone when she had to have an abortion."

"You think Sharon's in the hospital?"

She looked startled, as if she'd forgotten the beginning of our conversation. Talking to her was always difficult. Sometimes she wouldn't even reply to direct questions. Other times, she'd stay to talk but her conversation was filled with pauses and disjointed statements. I was always scrambling to guess what she had thought between statements so I could follow what she was trying to tell me.

"Perhaps Sharon's gone away with the young man with the fingerless gloves," I suggested.

Evelyn looked more confused. She had told me once she never noticed what people wore. She also refused to have a mirror in her apartment. It was her protest against a world in which people put too much emphasis on looks. You should judge people by what they are like, not by how they look, she once said in reply to my comment that someone was looking nice that day.

Even if she wasn't anorexic, she wouldn't have been pretty. Filled out, her face would have been the shape of a lozenge. Her red hair, instead of being an asset, unkindly drew attention to her plainness. She was an only child and her mother was always angry with her for being plain. Her mother was a failed actress and she hungered for a daughter who would be another Shirley Temple. She'd paid for dance lessons, for singing lessons, for etiquette lessons, for acting lessons and constantly thrust her daughter at directors and producers and the friends of friends of directors and producers or even the friends of relatives of directors and producers. Once, when it was nearly closing time, I'd watched Evelyn perform a bitter parody of "The Good Ship Lollipop."

After she found out I was a poet and short story writer, she'd sometimes talk to me but even though I always asked her to sit down, she stood tensely, as if she might jump and flee if I made a sudden move. Most of the time, though, she spent her breaks reading romance novels. She decided I was all right after I recommended *Pride and Prejudice* to her. She liked that, she told me, because it had a happy ending without being fakey. And there was no sex. She didn't like the new romances with all the sex. She liked the older ones she found in secondhand bookstores, the kind in which, after many trials and tribulations, the story ended with the couple making up. If there was any physical contact, it was a lingering kiss in the final paragraph and the sense that once the kiss was over, neither person knew what to do next.

"He had long brown hair, wore a green jacket and runners without socks," I said but I realized I wasn't doing this right. "He always ordered café latte with a Nanaimo bar."

"Gerald," she said, looking relieved. "He's an actor. He does pantomime." She held her hands up, making her body stiff, then moving them with little jerks to illustrate. "He got a grant to do street theatre in Toronto."

"Maybe she was lonely," I said.

"Yes," she agreed but then had a thought. "Not for Gerald. He was just a friend. No hanky pank. They did stuff together."

"She was lonely?" I asked. "A beautiful girl like that?"

"She didn't want the bars," Evelyn explained. "Bar guys are runners. They don't even wait for breakfast."

"Is Gerald a good mime?"

"Yeah. I always go to watch him when he's working the street. He can stand there for hours. People come up, think he's not real. They move his arm, it stays that way, they move his leg, whatever. Just like he was a doll or something. Sometimes kids are real cruel. They'll try to grab money out of the top hat he sets on a stool. Can you believe that? This guy's performing for whatever people want to give and somebody'd steal his tips. Mostly, though, they do it to see if he'll break his pose. If I'm there, I tell them to bugger off."

"You like him?"

"He's got no time for girls. He's always practising. He wants to get a grant and go to Paris. That's his dream. When he goes, he's going to send me a beret. A real one like you see in the movies."

"You take good care of him. His Nanaimo bar is twice as big as everybody else's."

Evelyn blushed and hitched her clothes up. "He's a genius. You tell him how you feel and he can show you the feeling just by the way he moves his body. Watching him is like reading poetry."

"Are you still writing poetry?"

She shuffled and looked down at the order book. "Nah," she said. "I'm taking photographs. Maybe I'll do some more poetry later. I got nothin' against poetry, you know. It's great stuff. I read that book of yours, you know. I got it out of the library. But somebody told me nobody gets paid for poetry. Not even if you're really good."

"That's right," I said.

"Not even two dollars for a poem?"

"No."

"A poem's not even worth as much as a croissant? That's crazy. Like, if nobody wants them, why keep making them? One time we made pumpkin tomato soup. Nobody wanted it. We didn't make it again. Like what's the point?"

"I don't know," I admitted. She sounded like my wife. And the m.c. They both ganged up on me with that one. Quit farting around with something nobody needs or wants, she said. The m.c. hadn't put it quite that way. He said the way to success was to analyze the market and find a niche. Specialize in something that I could do better than anybody else. There was, he pointed out, a professor who started a newsletter on the weird things people do. The newspaper picked up on it and now it was syndicated to a hundred and fifty places. Even at ten bucks a publication, he was pulling down fifteen hundred a week plus speaking engagements. I tried to tell him about Dickinson and Stevens and Rimbaud but he didn't want to hear it. He wanted to know why I wasn't writing rock videos. You've got to go with the times, he said. Even the National Book Awards has dropped poetry as a category.

"The last time I saw Sharon, she told me she'd see me the next day."

"That's just her way of talking," Evelyn explained. "Maybe something changed her mind. You know, maybe she got a chance to try out. She gets more parts than anybody."

"In the movies?"

"Nah, not like that. She's not thin enough. The camera adds ten pounds. She gets stuff on the local scene. Once she got a part in a commercial in Vancouver. They paid her expenses and everything. She's always getting these parts where she has to go around in a slip. One guy wanted her to make a movie but it was all with her clothes off. She said if she wanted to do that, she'd work as a stripper."

"What about you? Do you want to be on TV?"

"I've been on channel ten. That's cable. I helped with a magic show." With that, she darted away, in that sudden, unpredictable movement of hers that reminded me of the Roadrunner.

Something at the Green Café had come apart, broken down. I'd heard more in the last few days than I had in two years. Most of the time the staff was polite but reserved, even secretive, keeping a wall of courtesy between themselves and the customers. Now they were talking, the way people do when there's a snowstorm or a disaster, when something happens to shake them out of their daily patterns.

An actress. I'd overheard that. But I'd taken it the way I took the other bits of information. The waitresses were all writing or painting or potting or weaving. I assumed it was therapy, not art, they were talking about. The local shrinks made a habit of sending the walking wounded to creative workshops. Sometimes a third of my evening students were writing poetry to discover themselves.

Usually, when I sat here, back to the wall, I noticed very little, letting my ferret hunt the rabbits that sprinted crazily through the brambles of my mind, old rabbits, young rabbits, following them through tunnels and underbrush. Sometimes I closed my eyes, leaned into the corner and discreetly dozed, safe under twenty feet of Pachelbel. Today, Pachelbel, the dark green walls, the light fixtures high above, like distant sunlight, weren't enough. Little things intruded. The fresh cut flowers in vinegar bottles. The antique dolls in the built-in cupboard. The cigarette burns on the thick slab tables. No one was allowed to smoke in the café. To light a cigarette was to be banished. I'd never noticed the anomaly before. I ran my finger over the long dark marks where someone had set a cigarette and forgotten it. Revenge, I wondered. Is that it? Rebellion against the lentils, the salads, the feta cheese. Late at night, after the shades were drawn, did someone secretly sit and smoke with satisfaction and spite to get even? And then I wondered why I wondered that and a rabbit scampered away through the brambles and my ferret lost him.

6

"Your wife didn't try to come with you this time?" the shrink asked.

This wasn't the m.c. I'd quit seeing the m.c. a year before. The final split had come when my wife had complained to the m.c. that we had no sex life. I'd tried to explain to the m.c. that it might have something to do with the fact that she said things like you stupid, moronic, goddamned fool, can't you get anything right. This was because I'd forgotten to put a tea bag in the teapot. Then she'd smile and grab me by the arm and try to drag me to the bedroom so that we could make love. The m.c. refused to believe that my reluctance in the bedroom might have something to do with what she'd said the moment before. After all, he explained, they were discrete events and as a mature individual I should keep them separate. My GP had been more sympathetic. He isn't one of these men who cries easily and feels guilty about being born with a cock and balls. He suggested dumping the m.c. and finding somebody else to talk to. When I did, my wife insisted that she come along. She was determined to tell the shrink what my problems were and give him suggestions about what he should do about them. The shrink left her cooling her heels in the waiting room. I was impressed.

"I'm the one with the problem," I said. "She's adjusted to reality. She's got her goals and her needs and abilities all worked out."

"Is that what you think?" he asked. He had, I noticed, a habit of rubbing his left thumbnail with his right thumb. I didn't wonder! If I had to deal all day every day with people like me, I'd have a few nervous habits myself.

"She's more practical than I am. She doesn't give money to panhandlers. The ugly things she buys at auction always outsell the beautiful pieces I buy. She says the world loves a bargain more than beauty. Last week she sold a stapler in the shape of a pair of false teeth." I hadn't told him about the flock of birds nesting above the dishes. Or the one-eyed cobra in the sunroom.

"Beauty is in the eye of the beholder."

I put my head in my hands and rested my elbows on my thighs. "Purple egg cups in the shape of shoes can't be kept in stock. Teapots in the shape of rose-covered cottages make people happy."

"You're more sensitive than most. It's difficult."

"There are beautiful things. Monarch butterflies in spring. Lily-of-the-valley growing out of sidewalk cracks. White patches of daisies. The early birds trample them underfoot hunting bargains."

"You didn't have a good experience with this marriage counselor? What did you want from him?"

"To get out of the trap without having to gnaw off my leg."

"You told him that?"

"He said he thought romantic love was responsible for more suffering than anything else in the world. I wondered if he thought Hitler started World War II for Eva Braun?"

The shrink tipped his head back, stared at the ceiling. His eyes crinkled with concentration. He sat forward again, pulling his knees together and looking directly at me. "He preferred?"

"Ethnic marriages. Arranged marriages. Marriages made by families for money and position. Marriages where divorce is not an option. But I laughed at him. I know those marriages. Their glue is fear and helplessness. The women can't speak English and are locked in the house all day long. After the children come, the men take mistresses and the women pray that they will live long enough to be widows living in Florida on life insurance."

"I ask questions," he declared. "I have no answers. If you continue to come, you may not like the questions."

"You may not like my answers," I said aggressively.

He shrugged, then pulled at his goatee. "They're not my answers. I don't have to live with them."

He was short, had white hair and wore a three-piece suit. I forgave him his shortness and white hair but the suit seemed unpardonable. Then I noticed he wore a pocket watch and a gold chain. He had the guts to go all the way, to take risks. That made the suit all right. He rubbed his left thumbnail as if polishing it. "We'll have to dig out the marriage counselor. It's like using a weed popper to get rid of dandelions. Get them out and the grass grows back. You never know they were there. You have a tic in your nose. Every so often you contract the left corner."

"I got that in grade three," I said, surprising myself by remembering. "They used to call me Rabbit. It started after the bitch hit Eddy in the face with a ruler. He got his two times table wrong."

"And what did she do to you?"

"Nothing," I said, but I was lying again. I could feel my bladder ready to burst and, involuntarily, I pulled my legs together, locking my ankles. Once again, I was waving my hand in the air, desperately trying to get permission to leave the room. "Put your hand down," she shouted, and when I waved it harder, she came up behind me and struck the back of my hand with her ruler so I yelled and loosened my legs. I couldn't hold it any longer and leaped from my seat and ran from the room. She was screaming behind, following me out into the hall, and before I could reach the stairs that led to the boy's washroom, the principal was in the hall, waving a strap, yelling stop. I bolted out the heavy doors but the cold made me piss myself. The principal was right behind and there, in front of the classroom windows, we ran round and round the slide, me soaking wet, scrambling desperately to stay ahead of the principal, him slipping on the hard-packed snow, cursing and screaming, swinging the strap, catching me on the head, the shoulder, the back, the leg.

"And then?" he said.

"Nothing, nothing, I just had to go home and change clothes. It didn't matter." But I began to squirm in the chair and I took out my glasses case and began to beat my open palm with it.

"They strapped you?" he said.

"No," I said, "I don't think so. I don't remember that."

"A memory," he said, "isn't just a thought. Memories can be feelings, bodily changes, smells. Look at your hand."

The palm of my left hand was, I realized, swollen and red. My hand was so stiff that when I tried, I couldn't close it.

"She strapped you," he said, leaning so close our knees nearly touched. "What else?"

"Ah," I said and my throat closed like I was going to choke and I pulled my shoulders together. "The robot. She said I was nothing and nobody and my father was nothing and nobody and my grandfather was nothing and nobody and I was never to forget it. We were all of no importance. I was nothing and nobody and I was never to forget it and I was to do what I was told and—" and I wasn't in the office any more. I was back in the classroom with my wet pants, my swollen hands, my tear-covered face, and she was giving me orders, sit, stand, lie down, get up, run, stop, kneel, turn right, turn left, holding the strap, ready to use it if I didn't immediately do as she ordered. Around me the class sat in petrified silence. *This is an idiot, class, this is what an idiot looks like. Say it after me. This is an idiot.* And they did, their faces white with fear. *This is an idiot.*

"Just you?" the shrink asked.

"No. I was the first. Later there were others. She said if we told anyone what went on in her classroom, we'd be punished worse. She said she could read our minds. She knew everything we were thinking."

"Nothing makes sense until you find the cause," he said, "and then it's perfectly logical. What's the first book you read by yourself?"

My mind came up blank. Not blank blank, but like when the TV gets screwed up and you get static. Then something flipped up, but it was so distorted I couldn't tell what it was. "*Billy Goat's Gruff*," I said because I wanted to please him but then I raised my hand, palm out, shook my head. "No, that's not right. I had that book. I remember looking at it. I don't know. Maybe my grandmother teaching me to read the coloured comics."

He made a note. "Lost treasure. We'll have to make a map and find it. Dig it up."

"No!" I said. I hadn't intended to say it. It shot out like a piece of food stuck in my windpipe.

"What?" he asked.

"Dig."

"Dig what?"

"Girl," I said. "I murdered her. I don't want to dig her up. I can't."

"Who?"

I'd lost the room. It had collapsed at the edges, was falling in on itself. The light at the centre was growing smaller and getting farther away. "They'll put me in prison," I said, but my voice seemed far away and small as if I was hearing it down a dark tunnel.

"Nobody'll put you in prison," he said. "You don't have to tell it to me. Just tell it to yourself."

"Yelling," I said. There were the dark, blurred images and noise, people yelling, and I was overwhelmed by the need to fall asleep.

"Bob," he said sharply, "look at me." I looked into his face. It blocked the end of the tunnel. The ferret scampered back and jumped into my eye and disappeared. "When?"

"I don't know."

"Yesterday? Last week?"

I felt confused. "I don't know. Nightmares. People outside my window digging up her grave. They're going to find her."

"We'll look for her together," he said. "You and me. You don't have to do it alone. You'd better see me tomorrow."

7

"You want me to change who I am," I said. "What's wrong with me being me? I'm working class. I'm ethnic. That's what you married."

"Everybody changes. You can change, become more middle class. Fit in. What's so wonderful about being different?"

She was fitting bits and pieces of a ceramic statue together. Once the glue was set she'd fill the cracks, then carefully match the paint. She was good at covering up damage. Only an expert would be able to see where the piece had been restored. She never claimed the pieces she offered for sale were perfect. She just set them out and left the buyer to discover what he could. I'd protested once and she'd said that reality was buyer beware. She was a believer in the greater fool theory. Her father had been a used car salesman for many years. When he died, as a joke, one of the other salesmen slipped a can of putty and a bottle of touch-up paint into his coffin. Like the Egyptians, he said. Can't go without your most precious possessions.

"Like the Rocket," I replied.

She nearly smeared the paint. The Rocket was her romantic interest. He's a member of the old-timer's hockey league. During his youth he played forward on his town's hockey team. The result was false front teeth, a number of scars and a nose that veered to the left. He also is a flea marketer. He specializes in hockey memorabilia. Uniforms, badges, cards, photographs. His proudest possession is a jockstrap worn by Wayne Gretzky. He also has a broken hockey stick supposedly used by Bobby Hull.

41

"At least he can get it up," she said.

She's like that. The life of the party. A quick wit. A magical creature of scales and fire, her claws clacking on the wood as she crosses the floor.

To be fair she's quite attractive. For a woman her age, that is. And she has developed certain skills. When I met her she looked, if not angelic, then innocent, with her smile and her bangs and glasses. I was in the library struggling with "The Miller's Tale" when she leaned over and quoted the first six lines in what sounded like impeccable Chaucer. I was so impressed that I sat and stared, open-mouthed. My description of her glasses and bangs probably makes her sound unattractive. Anything but. Bangs were the in thing and the glasses didn't hide the fact that she was a knockout. Put yourself in my shoes, a kid from the country who was still trying to figure out how to take notes and write essays, and this creature in a green angora sweater with a medallion set between her breasts, so there was no mistaking her assets, leans over and quotes Great Literature. Her eyes were the same colour as her sweater and had flecks of gold in them and her hair was the colour of pale wheat. She smelled of lavender. We went for coffee, and when she brushed against me getting in and out of the booth, my chest tightened and I wished I'd worn looser pants or tighter undershorts.

The Chaucer, of course, was a trick. It worked just as well on her male professors. She had memorized the first six lines from a tape and whipped them off in class. It created, as she said, a halo effect that lasted all year. She was clever, much cleverer than me, and all the time I thought I was courting her in my own indirect, insecure way, she was planning and organizing, finding out where I would be and then just happening to turn up. Each time I mentioned something I enjoyed she just happened to enjoy that, too. Finally, frustrated by my timidity, she suggested we go skating with another couple.

This was at a time when a fast girl was one who let you kiss her on a first date. In spite of her parka, sweater, blouse and bra, on the way home, sitting in the back seat, everything miraculously came undone and with fifteen miles still to go to her front door,

I was feeling a pair of breasts for the first time in my life, breasts that, although I couldn't see them, seemed as wonderful as the angora sweater had promised.

Afterwards, I felt guilty, as if I'd committed some terrible crime. If our Lutheran minister had appeared on the doorstep, Bible in hand, I would have instantly confessed my transgressions, begged forgiveness and prepared myself for some terrible, undefinable punishment. Now, as I look back, that seems preposterous, but then, at twenty, I was not long out of Sunday school. Sunday school was not about resurrection but about sin. When Pastor John visited our class, he never failed to bring paintings by Bosch or a green Christ being stuck full of spears or illustrations from the Inquisition. He believed the Catholic church was in league with the devil but he had no compunction about using it to keep us in line.

Rather than waiting for God's punishment, he encouraged us to administer our own. When we asked him what it should be, he always refused to tell us, saying he preferred to leave it to our own imagination. God would tell us, if we just prayed for enlightenment. He did, however, leave pictures of people flogging themselves, being locked in iron maidens, being branded. I knew what thumbscrews were before I knew what a baseball was. We had no thumbscrews, of course, but I distinctly remember, after having used the Lord's name in vain, putting one of my mother's quilting clamps on my thumb and tightening it until my thumb turned white.

I'd been brought up to believe that sex was something that men did to women and that women endured. Men were all lust and women all reluctance, without sexual needs or emotion, and men, when they lusted, were beasts.

My paroxysm of guilt for petting was all for nothing, my practised apology never given. When the object of my passion and guilt sat down beside me in the cafeteria, I had just taken a bite out of a hamburger. Instead of accusing me of violating her, she put her arm around my waist and said what a good time she had. Visions from Bosch didn't stop me from borrowing a friend's car so I could take her out again. We said we were going to a movie, but spent the evening parked on a side road.

When I drove her home, I parked in her parents' driveway. A good-night kiss turned into ten minutes more petting. It was forty below out. I had to keep the engine running because I'd never get the motor started if I stopped it. The windows had fogged over. Her mother had already clicked the porch light off and on as a signal for her to come in. Until then we'd been petting above the waist. As a grand finale for the evening, she undid my zipper, released my cock from my underwear. She leaned over and kissed it. I got so excited, I hit the horn. The noise startled her. She sat up and banged her head. Twenty-five years later when she took the blood oath and converted to feminism, she accused me of having taken advantage of her innocence, that she really hadn't wanted to undo my zipper, unbutton my long underwear, shift around until she could bend over, and that I was no better than any other man. We were all rapists.

If she was going to revise history, I thought, and turn ambivalence, if that is what it was, into forced participation, then I was more victimized than she. As I remember it, I was pulsatingly eager, in more ways than one, but at the same time, I was the one with the Lutheran minister in the white ruff and the black frock who mourned the passing of hair shirts. Once she'd gone inside the house—her mother had switched the light off and on twice in a row—I was overwhelmed by guilt and was certain that Pastor John, in spite of being a hundred miles away, would know, that my great-aunt would know and that I would arrive to a huge flashing neon light above the front door saying "Perverted Fornicator." Pastor John would be standing in the snow of the front yard. He'd be ten feet tall. He'd be reading from his Bible. My great-aunt would be in her black dress, kneeling at the feet of my great-uncle, her arms around his waist, weeping. When I got home my great-aunt was reading her favourite literature, a personal experience story in *Reader's Digest*, and Uncle Finni was sleeping in front of the TV. Pastor John was nowhere to be seen.

But this is water under the bridge. I'm resentful but no longer outraged by revisionist sexual history. It's a strange experience to have my wife join me on our living room couch, run her hand over my chest, slip her hand inside my shirt, unbutton my pants, slip her hand inside my shorts, take her clothes off and guide my hand between her legs, be sitting astride me, vigorously raising and lowering herself, exclaiming, no, oh no, every so often and the next time we have a fight, claiming that she has been raped because no means no.

Since the marriage counselor's advice that we add a little spice to our lives, that we include some variety, that we go on separate vacations and say yes to liaisons as long as they're discreet and don't threaten our marriage, she's been cooking with pepper, cinnamon, nutmeg, ginger. I've opted for plain boiled macaroni. It's not that I'm so pure. As my wife said after a couple of double whiskeys, the opportunities aren't there in the same way for a man. A woman opens her legs and fifteen hundred guys get hard dicks. A dog doesn't have to be a beauty to attract fleas.

I am, if the truth be told, not very attractive. I'm not deformed or anything. But in any shopping mall, I'm pretty well inter-changeable with any of the men you see sitting on those benches waiting obediently for their wives. You know what I mean. Forty-five and up. A fringe of grey hair. I haven't got a pot. That's in my favour, but I wear glasses, the kind that are so thick everyone knows that when I take them off, I can't see more than six inches. I look older than I am. I've got a long way to go to reach retirement but clerks keep giving me the seniors' discount. At first it hurt my feelings but after awhile I gave up being rude and took the money. A busy shopper could easily mistake me for her husband, hand me her packages, take me home and not notice the mistake for a day or two.

My wife really isn't a troglodyte. That's just how I feel about her. Since she's started taking aerobics and using deodorant and shaving her legs again, she's able to attract men who still have their teeth—except for the Rocket and that's different because he lost his when he was a kid—and don't have to wear a truss. For two weeks she was pursued by a younger man. He was nearly half her age. It made her all giddy. She started calling plastic surgeons in California to find out the cost of a face lift and a tummy tuck. Then her current interest hit her for a loan and, when she wouldn't give it to him, left her for someone who gave him a little red sports car. She got so depressed she didn't scream when I dropped a teapot worth sixty-five bucks.

It's easy for the m.c. to say get out and add some excitement to your marriage but this is a game for which I don't know the rules. You know by now that I wasn't any good at the boy-girl stuff when I was a teenager. My mother ran me around by the nose. Then she gave the ring to my wife. Some guys fool around when they're married and keep up to date. I'm still stuck at the "kiss on a first date fast girl" stuff. Do people still date? If the TV shows and videos are any indication, total strangers walk up to each other and say let's fuck and after it's over they may or may not exchange business cards. I asked one of my students about the rules and she said there are no rules. You do what you want. That scared me so much I even gave up asking anyone out for coffee.

Godzilla the Hen insists that my half of the housekeeping includes shopping—she hates shopping—so for awhile I tried talking to women in the grocery store but they all looked too tired for romance. Besides, I was sure only married women buy groceries. Single women eat out. Then I figured the ones in the nine items or less line-up were more likely to be on their own. Or the ones who bought no more than a hundred grams of ham or potato salad in the deli. I got good at reading groceries. Cat food, she's got a cat. Dog food, a dog. Tofu, she's a vegetarian. One per cent cottage cheese, sprouts, she's on a diet. A TV dinner, she can't cook. Sometimes I can't read them at all. Like the redhead with tofu, a pork chop, low-cal jam, a chocolate bar, a TV dinner and dried peas. I decided she was confused. Even worse was trying to think of something intelligent to say. "Those are great oranges you've got" sounded stupid. "I like your broccoli." I usually ended up being so embarrassed I'd grab something and buy it just to get out of the store. I ended up with six bottles of soy sauce that way.

If I was slow in adolescence, I'm motionless in a world that has been accelerating for twenty-five years. There was this student in one of my classes. She reminded me of my wife when she was the same age. Round everywhere. The kind that makes you dream of cantaloupes and honeydew. She wore see-through blouses, no bra and sat in the front row. When she turned up at my office, I jammed the door open with the wooden wedge the college provides to every male professor. I leaned back in my chair and talked for fifteen minutes without taking my eyes off the ceiling. I heard some weeks later that she'd tried to start an affair with one of my colleagues. It went on for two months. It never got past passionate petting, and either out of frustration or unrequited love, she tried to hang herself in the women's washroom. She used one of his ties. A couple of days after they carted her away to the hospital, he sent her flowers and a note asking for his tie back. It was pure silk. In similar circumstances, I'd have spent months eating light bulbs.

8

"WHAT BROUGHT ON THIS CRISIS?" the shrink asked. He was standing on the ball of his foot, as if he thought I was so dangerous he would have to flee for his life and wanted a head start. I wanted to reassure him that he was safe. I wasn't so confused that I mixed him up with the m.c. The m.c. didn't have a goatee.

"The café isn't safe anymore. Pachelbel isn't deep enough. It's like the tide's going out and there's no hole to crawl into, no crack in the rocks. I've seen what happens when the tide goes out. The sea gulls and the crows come and rip the crabs apart and tear their flesh out."

"There's no news of the dark-haired girl?" He waved me into his office. I went to the leather chair beside his desk but I couldn't sit in it. I grabbed the top and held on as if I was standing on a ship in a high sea, then I sat on the floor behind it, with my back pressed to the corner. He paid no attention and spoke to me just as he would have if I'd sat in the chair.

"They're coming to kill me," I said and pulled my knees up and my elbows in, making myself as small as possible.

"Who's coming to kill you?"

"They said." The edges of my vision were collapsing again, folding in upon themselves like dying flowers.

"They?" His voice was quiet, not a whisper, but soft, as if it might have been me thinking.

"At night. When I fall asleep. They'll kill my mommy and daddy and my little brother and me. It'll be my fault. They said."

"I want you to relax. Nobody's going to kill you now. You're safe here. Take a deep breath, that's it. Now, another one. Now, tell me, how big do you feel?"

I rested my head on my knees. I was so tired. I had to fight to keep from falling asleep. "Little," I answered and I did feel little, as if I were very small and very tired and desperately trying to stay awake.

"Going to school?"

"Not school. Not yet." I said and I thought how silly he was, thinking I could be going to school. I was too little to be going to school. That was for big kids. And I remembered swinging on the gate, watching the big kids going past. They had books and pencils and erasers and I wanted to be big like them. I wanted to go to the drugstore and have my mother buy me a pencil box and scribblers and all those things that smelled like school.

I wished I had a blanket. I felt cold. If I had a blanket, I could hide under it and no one would know I was there. And then no one could come and kill me. I would be invisible. That's what I wanted more than anything, to be invisible. When the violence started, when the drunkenness sprawled its way across the house, invading all the rooms, the violence, the shouting, the hitting, the crying, the screaming, glass breaking. People yelling they were going to kill someone. My mother throwing an iron at my father, making a hole in the living room wall. My father lunging after her. My uncle picking up his girlfriend and throwing her through the picture window. My father dancing around the room, smashing his fist through the small panes so his partner could flick her ashes outside instead of on the floor. A cousin poisoned on bad home-brew going berserk and being hunted through the back yards, fighting off his brothers and uncles and cousins until they dragged him down, tied him hand and foot and carted him to the hospital in the back of a truck. At the hospital he destroyed an operating room before they got him into a strait jacket. One of the women pissing her pants as she waltzed about the room.

"Frightening for a small child," he said.

I hadn't realized I was talking out loud. I thought I was only thinking it, remembering it, letting it ricochet inside my skull. I

49

began to hum, to stop the remembering, to drown it out.

"Stop humming," he ordered. "No humming." I stopped humming out loud. "Not inside your head, either. No singing. No humming. Just listening."

"I can't," I said. "It hurts too much. I'll get a migraine. I always get a migraine when I start to remember." And I started humming again, not a tune, just noise, drowning out my memories the way teenagers drown out thoughts with rock music.

"No," he said, "no humming. Quiet. Quiet. That's it. No humming. Just quiet." He was talking very softly. I could barely hear him. He'd left his chair and was sitting on the floor just to one side of me. "It's all right. You're safe now. Nobody is going to hurt you. You'll be fine. I won't let anybody hurt you. It all happened a long time ago. You're all grown up. It's just a memory."

I started to rock back and forth. Very gently. Back and forth. "No," he said. "No rocking. Let the anxiety surface."

I stopped rocking. The stillness, the silence were like a vacuum filling up with craziness, with images, with noise, as if a hundred or a thousand television sets, all tuned to different stations at once, were running simultaneously at full volume and I was sitting in the centre of them. I'm going to go insane, I thought but I didn't think it, this wasn't thought, I felt it, I felt the insanity and with it, panic.

"The dark-haired girl," he said. "What has she to do with this?"

"I killed her," I said and the words came out like they were squeezed from my lungs. "I murdered her. I murdered her."

"Why did you have to kill her?" he asked. "What had she done that was so terrible?"

"She was bad," I replied.

"But what had she done?"

"I don't know," I replied.

"How did you kill her?"

I tried to think how I'd done it. "I don't know."

"Did you shoot her? Did you stab her? Did you choke her?" Each time he asked, I shook my head. I didn't know what I'd done. I knew I hadn't done those things but I didn't know how I knew.

"Don't," I said and I started to rock again and this time, not even his whisper could stop me and I started to cry. He reached Kleenex to me but I couldn't take them, I couldn't let go of my knees. I made no sound, at least not that I was aware of. I cried until my pants were soaked where my face pressed against my knees. I couldn't stay awake then. The petals of the flower all collapsed inward and I felt as if I was falling helplessly down a long shaft and when I awoke it was dark and I remembered falling and I thought I must have survived the fall and be trapped deep underground, then I saw the light from his desk lamp. I felt confused, a jumble of memory and dream mixing together, stood up, saw him sitting at the desk filling out reports and was overcome with embarrassment.

"I'm sorry," I said. "I'm terribly sorry. I didn't mean to fall asleep." I fumbled apologetically with my watch, trying to see what time it was. "I'm sorry."

"You needed to sleep," he said. "It's been a long time since you've slept. Really slept. Sleep knits up the ravelled sleeve of care. You'll come again tomorrow at the same time?"

I let go of the back of the chair and staggered slightly. I felt weak and dizzy as if I'd been sick and was getting out of bed for the first time.

"What if I've killed someone?" I asked.

"Here," he said, "drink this." He handed me his cup of tea. Suddenly thirsty, I sat down and drank it all at once. "Now, go and have a double cappuccino. Maybe two. Lots of caffeine. It'll help stop the migraine."

"I'm afraid," I said.

"Yes," he agreed. "That's a start. Anger covers up fear and fear covers up pain."

"I want it to stop."

"Crises open doors. Doors that have been shut and barred for years. This is a chance to find the road back." He leaned close. "But you've got to promise you won't do any harm to anyone. Not yourself. Not anyone else. We're going to find an answer. After you've got it, then you can decide what to do. But not now. I'm not trying to blow you up."

"All right," I said but it felt vague. I felt vague. As if I was there and not there. In the room and not in the room. The way I felt when I'd been swung in a circle as a child, swung until I had completely lost my balance and couldn't stand, and the earth spun and every time I tried to get up, I fell over, and lying on the grass, felt everything turn as if I were caught up in the vortex of a whirlpool.

"No," he said, "really promise."

"I promise," I said, but I wasn't really sure what I was promising. Except as I said it, there was a dark image of a tree and me hanging from it and the fear and the beginning of a headache were instantly there.

"Get that coffee," he said, seeing me grimace. "Right away."

The corrugated circle was starting to flash. Still vague. I needed to get to the Green Café. To stop the headache but also to do other things. While I'd slept, I'd dreamed of the dark-haired girl. Not that I'd seen her. What I'd seen was a sarcophagus lying in a muddy river bed. The river bed had been drained. I was trying to lift the stone lid but it was too heavy. I was afraid and, at the same time, desperate to release her for I knew she was trapped inside. Somewhere, I thought, as I rushed out of the building, she's waiting for help and I've got to find her.

9

"SHE LIKES HAVING YOU for a customer," the waitress with the blue shark fin said. She was wearing a white hospital tag on her wrist. She had just brought my second cappuccino. The pain hadn't got any worse and the flashing of light in my left eye seemed to be fading. Thank God, I thought. I was trying to relax but it was impossible. Just the idea of a full-blown migraine made my body rigid. If the pain increased, I'd have to abandon everything, rush home and lie on my bed in the guest room, no light, no sound, fill myself with painkillers, and wait helplessly for a day, or two, or even three before I could move again, and then, for a day or more, ease gently back into life, feeling like an eggshell, so fragile the slightest touch might shatter it. The flashing light and my fear made it hard to concentrate.

"What?" I asked, staring at the large silver hoops in her ears, the star painted on her cheek, the fin of bright blue hair.

"There's my poet, she always says. When you're sitting in the corner with your little black book, she won't let anybody sit with you, not even if all the other tables are full. She doesn't want anybody disturbing your writing. I mean, don't you know that? Don't you get the vibes? Poets are ultrasensitive people. Why don't you want to get to know her better?" She stopped and looked serious. "Maybe it's because she's a waitress."

"It's not that." I replied. I didn't know how to explain that I came to the café to hide in a crevice, that knowing and caring and feeling were hooks that could be used to pull me into the open.

That on Wednesday I'd momentarily taken that chance. "What's your name?"

"Sunbeam," she answered, looking pleased at being asked. "That's not what I was born with. I chose it. I decided I didn't like being me so one morning just before dawn we had a ritual on the beach, like this special Greek dance where we all stood in line, and Sharon made me wear a white dress and put flowers in my hair." She leaned closer, looked to the side to see that no one was listening. "We stole the flowers out of Beacon Hill Park. Just when the sun came up they threw me in the water and when I surfaced they asked who I wanted to be and I yelled Sunbeam. That's the way it should be, don't you think? When we leave home we should be able to cast off our old name like snakes shed their skin."

"I hadn't thought of it like that," I said.

"And your name?"

"Bob. That's my birth name."

She shook her head at my lack of imagination or assertiveness, or my passivity, whatever kept me trapped inside such a mundane identity. "If I was a writer, I wouldn't call myself that. I'd call myself Shakespeare or something."

"Wouldn't that confuse people?" I asked. "If everybody went around calling themselves Hemingway or Stephen King."

"I'm seeing someone called Gandalf. Gandalf loves Sunbeam." She giggled. "If you saw that sprayed on a wall, wouldn't it make you think?"

"Do you like thinking?"

She was twisting one of the silver hoops back and forth. The lobe of her ear twisted with it. Watching gave me a queasy stomach. "Sometimes. When there's good things to think about. Good memories. Everybody being mellow." She put two fingers to her lips as if she was smoking a joint. "Like nude sun-bathing with your boyfriend and drinking wine."

"What about Sharon?" I asked. "Does she have another name?"

"It depends," she said. "On the day. And what she's wearing. I mean some days she's the gypsy. Some days the actress."

"Evelyn thinks she took off because she got a chance to act in a play."

"Not a chance," Sunbeam said. "We already had a date to see a movie Friday night. We . . ."

Demytro materialized behind her. For such a large man he was light on his feet. When he was young, he'd been a dancer. He put his arm around Sunbeam and gave her a reassuring hug. It was like watching a grizzly hug a fawn and not hurt it. She went off to serve some customers who were standing in the doorway. Demytro sat down.

"Too much talk," he said.

"I'm sorry if I kept her from her work."

"It's not that," he started, then stopped, searching for the words in English. I could see him thinking, sorting, finally settling for a simple précis. "Too fragile. Like a butterfly. Words hurt her. The music helps to keep her from thinking." He bobbed his head in time to Pachelbel. "You, me, all of us. So we can live here."

"Any news?"

His face grew heavy, the lines at the corner of his mouth deeper. "Nossing," he said. "What to do?" He lifted his shoulders and let them fall in a gesture of resignation.

"Maybe we're concerned for no reason."

"She always filled the salt shakers," he said. "I never had to ask her." I knew what he meant. She was dependable, reliable, predictable. "Sunbeam doesn't turn up, she's fallen in love again. For her, love lasts three days. If Evelyn disappears, her mother's called."

"The police," I suggested.

He looked at the ceiling and shook his head. "I called already. They said she's an adult. She can disappear if she wants. I'm not happy, fire her. Always missing persons. They've got better things to do. The girls look. They're calling their friends. Is she there? Did you see her? Did she say anything about going away? Every time they think of someone, they call." I raised myself slightly to look past him. Evelyn was talking on the phone. "I will put bars on the window. Make them all stay here," he said with a burst of energy but then his resolution passed. "But it is no good. Nobody can live in a cage."

"I'm worried," I admitted. "Something." I wanted to tell him about asking her to the ballet but I couldn't. In my heart of hearts, I kept thinking maybe she didn't come to work so as to avoid me. Maybe she'd agreed to go out of politeness and then didn't know how to tell me. "I don't know. Just . . ." I sat back and took a deep breath and let it out through pursed lips.

"You are a good customer." He patted my hand. "You come for a long time. Every week. The cappuccino is free." I could see his throat tighten. He wanted to be kind and it was the only way he knew how. I thought, he's a fine man, a good man. I hope he is strong enough to preserve the sanctuary no matter what happens. I thought about how I had fallen asleep in the safety of Shrinko's office. Sometimes, we all need someone to guard the door, to keep us safe.

Under the waves, on the ocean floor, everything was blurred and indistinct, beyond my touch. When people went out the door, they appeared briefly in the window, in that other world, then disappeared like brightly coloured fish seen through an underwater porthole. Each time I left the café, it was as if I was in a rowboat adrift on the ocean at night. No compass. Hunkered down, riding out an endless storm of rain and wind and waves.

For the past two years, since my wife's breakdown, I'd got through my days by habit. I slept in my office chair, woke to my watch alarm, stuck my head under the tap in the bathroom across the hall. Lectures on how to write a paragraph, how to develop a topic sentence, I knew by heart, reciting them woodenly, like a child does a memorized poem. In departmental meetings, I sat silent. Mail, I swept off my desk into the garbage can.

I can't, I thought, *I can't go looking for her. It's too much.* But I knew I had to do it, even if I had to crawl to the door. Behind the pain the sarcophagus loomed. White marble. Slightly tipped in the mud. Mud up to my knees. Me trying, with my bare hands, to lift the close-fitting lid.

Somewhere, away back, so I could barely hear the voice, someone was saying, "You care, what happened isn't right and you still care," and my chest tightened, like my heart was being squeezed so hard it could no longer beat. For a fraction of second I thought I saw something or someone and I felt so afraid I couldn't move but then it was gone.

No, I thought, then looked around, afraid I'd shouted it out loud but everyone was busy eating. No one was looking at me. I fumbled some money onto the table and walked out as if I had no knees. As I was going past the serving counter, I paused and pulled a picture of her off the wall and stuck it in my pocket. In it, she's standing, holding her bicycle, and in the carrier there's a baguette and a bouquet of flowers. And she's laughing, holding a wide-brimmed straw hat on with her other hand, her head tipped back.

10

AFTER I WAS ON THE SIDEWALK, Sunbeam leaned out the door and said, "She lived in that big apartment block just over there. The blue one with the balconies. I can't believe anything could have happened there. They've got security. A key to get in the front door. Another one to get off the elevator."

I knew the building. It was the one where the guy had been standing on the balcony in the rain. It was a subsidized rental. Single mothers and people on disability or old age pensions. They had a parking lot sale on Saturdays but I seldom went there. Good stuff isn't found in neighbourhoods like this. These people never owned anything with lasting value. Most of it is rental furniture or chipped Formica. A small push and they're sleeping on the street, all their worldly belongings in three or four shopping bags. The good stuff—the silver, the bone china, the crystal, the Persian rugs, the oak furniture—is found in neighbourhoods that had money but are on a slide. People used to the good life who want to keep up appearances but are stuck on pensions that don't quite cover their costs.

The first thing I did was look in the excavation next to the apartment block. I hoped they were still down there, the m.c. and his wife, hunting each other through the pilings and rods and concrete footings. But they weren't. Somebody had helped them out. The ladder was repaired. I could see the new wood.

I walked over to the parking lot. The rain had kept the sellers inside for a few weeks so there were more of them than usual.

Islands of trestle tables and card tables, umbrellas, people sitting on lawn chairs looking hopeful. There was a steady trickle of buyers but no dealers. A glance was enough to see that the goods weren't worth much. Mostly plastic toys and outgrown kids' clothes, fourth hand. I worked my way from table to table, picking up and putting down ceramic frogs and rude signs, curling irons and plastic bags of drapery hooks. One table had a large ashtray from Reno. It was a good size, unchipped. On the bottom there was a chorus girl with two feather fans strategically located. When I tipped the ashtray, the feathers disappeared and she was naked.

"Your friends will love it," the blonde sitting behind the table said.

I tipped the ashtray back so the feathers reappeared. "I don't think so."

"Be a sport," she said. "Give it to someone you don't like. Isn't that worth five dollars?"

I thought about the Rocket. The trouble was he'd love it. He'd put it out on his table and show it to every guy who passed. He'd tip it at the women and raise his eyebrows suggestively. He was the kind who thought whoopee cushions were a riot. There was something insulting about being replaced by someone like that. The only thing I could say in his favour was that he had hair. My better half was constantly contradicting herself. She said during sessions with the m.c. that she wanted romance. If she tried to have a candlelight dinner with the Rocket, he'd probably eat the candles.

There were six glasses with palm trees on them. They looked unused. The palm trees sat on a sand dune that said Las Vegas.

"Like to gamble?" I asked. "Big mover with the dice?"

"I can't even stand bingo," she replied. "My neighbour's stuff. Her last trip wasn't a winner. She needs some money to get to the end of the month."

She stood up and came to the table. She was cute. Maybe five feet, hair in a ponytail, western-style shirt, blue jeans.

"How much?" I held up the wire holder with the six glasses.

"Make me an offer," she countered. She was smarter than she looked. I remembered what the marriage counselor had said. He was thick as a brick but even bricks have their moments. He said everyone I'd meet would have a history. With eleven-year-olds having sex, someone sixteen had a trail of ex-lovers like the tail of a kite. There was no sign of five kids but a little girl with bright blue eyes was clinging to her leg and eyeing me suspiciously.

"Four dollars?"

She held out her hand. I gave her the four dollars. I hadn't done it right. To keep her talking I should have offered her less than she'd accept and then we could have haggled. I picked up and put down a number of items. She stayed at the table with her arms crossed in front of her. My wife would have known what to do. She would have asked the kid's name, maybe talked directly to her, taken a candy out of her pocket and held it out, complimented the blonde on something. I couldn't think of anything that wouldn't sound like a line. I wondered about just asking her for information.

"What about this waffle iron?"

"That's mine. It works. It's brand new."

I opened it up, dug into one of the little squares and scraped out some crumbs.

"Nearly brand new," she corrected herself. "I've used it five times. I'm selling it because I can't get it to work. The waffles stick. They pull apart and I end up having to scrape them out in pieces."

"You're washing it with soap," I said. She looked down. I assumed that meant yes. "Soak it in oil, top and bottom. Really soak it and let it sit. When you go to use it, cover it with oil again. These aren't supposed to be washed. Just wiped. If you've got to scrub it, use salt."

"You're a cook," she said.

"Stir fry," I replied. "Microwave magic."

Just then her little girl slapped her on the leg and I thought it was punishment for talking to me. "She's got to go," she said. She looked around. All the other sellers were busy. "Watch my table, will you?" She grabbed her cash box and her daughter and raced away. She wasn't gone long but by the time she came back, I'd sold ten dollars worth of knickknacks and the ashtray. I gave her the money and she handed me coffee in a real cup. I knew that meant she didn't expect me to leave right away.

I gave her back her kitchen chair and unfolded a lawn chair with a broken web.

"You married?" she asked.

"To the Freezer Queen. Why?"

"You moved in so nice and easy, I thought you might have had quite a bit of practice."

"I sell at the flea market all the time. That's the practice."

"Being married doesn't stop a lot of guys. I get an average of five propositions every Saturday."

"Better than a singles dance or putting an ad in the paper."

"Not the kind I meet. You should see them. Lie down, this'll take sixty seconds then I've got to catch up to my wife over there."

"What's your daughter's name?"

"Why do you want to know?" She half turned toward me and crossed her legs.

"I read somewhere that people like to be asked about themselves. If you want to be friendly you should ask people about something they care about. You obviously care about your daughter. Her hair's brushed, her clothes are clean, you took her to the bathroom right away, you didn't bitch at her because she needed to go, you didn't drag her along like a dog on a leash and you got her a cookie."

"Melissa," she said, looking pleased in spite of herself.

I'm glad I'm not courting her, I thought. It'd be like threading a room full of bear traps in the dark. So much for my idea that people just walked up to each other, said let's fuck and went at it.

"I'm Gloria," she said, "I'm twenty-eight, I'm a single mother, I'm on welfare and I'm not looking for a man. What about you?"

"I'm Bob. I'm forty-five. I teach at Cadboro College and I'm not looking for a man, either. That gives us something in common."

She looked as though she was going to take the coffee back. "My ex was a high school teacher. Biology. Couldn't resist the lab work. Said he was staying late dissecting frogs. Now he's married to her." Some of the other sellers were staring at us, then putting their heads together. "Ignore them. If they don't have something to talk about they feel deprived. There's no man in my life and they resent that. By tonight you'll be a seven foot stud with tattoos and a chain in your ear."

I had to rest my cup on the arm of the chair to keep the coffee from slopping over the edge.

"What's that?" she asked, looking at the waves.

"Nerves. I think I've had a breakdown."

"What's that like?"

Before I could answer, she got up to stand in front of a little old lady fingering a candy dish. It looked as if it might disappear up her coat sleeve at any moment. Gloria asked if she could help and she said no, she just was admiring it, she had had one like it in her china cabinet before she moved in with her daughter-in-law. Gloria came back and said, "Now I feel like shit. I thought she was going to steal it and she's thinking about what it was like when she was young. What's it like?"

"Feeling young?"

"A nervous breakdown. I sometimes feel like I'm having one but unless you've had one how do you know you're having one or not?"

"Wet cardboard," I replied. I was avoiding drinking the coffee and hoped she didn't notice. It was three-Divol coffee. I didn't think I had that many with me. I'd been feeling in my pocket and had only found two. "Everything just comes apart in slow motion. Picking up the milk and putting it away becomes a big decision. It can take all morning. You just sit there paralyzed. Answering the phone becomes a crisis."

"I feel like that sometimes," she admitted. "After the frog dissector ran off with his cute little student, I couldn't get it together. Like I'd sit around and wish somebody'd come in and feed me puréed apricots. No chewing. Then, one day when I took Melissa to day care, he snuck in and packed all his belongings. He left me a note that said, *Sorry, frog dissector.* I took out the photo album and dissected all his pictures. His ears, his eyes, everything."

She was busy watching a couple of kids trying on earrings. I tipped the coffee onto the ground on the far side of the chair.

"You're a bit of a mess, aren't you?"

"I guess," I said. "I don't think you're going to get any more business. End of the day for buyers. There'll be a few stragglers figuring they can grab leftovers for nothing. You don't want to do business with them. I'll help you pack and carry if you and Melissa will have a burger with me."

She let me carry the boxes back to the building. Underneath the building was a parking area and, at one end, there was a series of narrow closets with numbered metal doors. There was a bicycle rack next to the elevator. The blue bicycle was there. I hadn't expected to see it. My heart lurched. There was no mistaking it. It had a black metal basket. The kind paper boys used. For some reason I didn't think it would be there. It didn't seem right that it was sitting there as if it had just been put into the rack. In a movie there'd have been something abnormal, something significant about its being there and I'd have made a brilliant deduction.

When we were finished putting everything away, Melissa finally spoke.

"McDonald's," she said. It wasn't a question or an order. It was a statement of fact and didn't allow any argument so McDonald's it was.

Melissa didn't want a burger. She wanted fries and root beer. I bought her the mug. It was that or have her charged with theft. She fell asleep with a death grip on the handle.

Gloria was scraping ketchup off a package with the last fry when I finally worked up enough nerve to say, "A friend of mine's gone missing. She lives in your building. She's a waitress at the Green Café. Her name's Sharon. She rides a blue bicycle."

"Oh, yeah," Gloria said. "I've seen her. We've got a laundry room on the second floor. Sometimes she's in there. She's into theatre."

"We're worried about her. Her friends, I mean."

Gloria picked up her purse. "She's too heavy for me to carry." She pried Melissa's fingers off the mug.

I picked Melissa up. I'd forgotten how small children sleep totally. Melissa's arms hung limp. Her head rested on my shoulder. At the entrance to the apartment block, Gloria said, "All I heard from the janitor was somebody left a patio door open. Water got in and ran down the wall into the apartment below. He didn't say who, though. He was fit to be tied. He did say it was on the tenth floor. Oh, yeah, I remember. 'Young girls, young girls. They should stay home with mother until they get married.' He has a thing against unmarried women living on their own."

11

What can I tell you about this alley? It's narrow, not enough room for a car to get through. The brick paving has been shifted by endless small earthquakes. The city sits on a fault line. Although we hardly notice them, there are a hundred or more tremors recorded each month. Little by little they have shifted these bricks until they have formed this snake-like, waving line.

There are no lights. If one's put up, it's broken with a bit of brick. People like it dark here. In the spaces between the buildings there are people buying a baggie or shooting up. I can sense them more than see them. Darker spots in the darkness. There's a couple in one of the loading bays and from the sound of it he's having a good time and she's earning some money. I count the doors. The fourth door from the street is what I want. The building has tipped so the door and lintel don't meet. There is a pale triangle of light at the bottom.

I tapped on the door. There was no reply. I tapped again.

"Who is it?" he asked.

"Me," I replied. Not Bob. He'd know my voice but I doubted if he knew my name. He slid back the panel in the door and stared at me.

"What are you delivering at this time of night?"

All I could see was his eye and one rough eyebrow. I waited. His curiosity would get the better of him. He'd open the door just to find out why I'd come. When my wife sent him the items she thought would interest him, he was like an impatient child.

65

He'd rip off the paper and string and take the book or object in his hands and hold it up. If it was something he particularly coveted, he'd rub it with his hands, touch all of it, finger the pages if it was a book, pay me with a hastily scribbled cheque. He kept no money on the premises. It wasn't a neighbourhood where you wanted anyone to think there was cash about. Although of all the tenants he was the least likely to be robbed.

I'd met him delivering items for my wife. She had a number of regular customers, people who had particular interests. One was into erotic art work, mostly Oriental; another wanted nothing but jade jewellery; one bought any good-quality paste for export to Japan. There were a number of art-glass collectors. My wife's is a shotgun approach to life. Fill a warehouse from top to bottom and you'll have something for everyone. If she spotted an obvious object—a piece of glass signed Gallee—then she'd have me take it around. Collectables on the run. At first I was resentful of being an errand boy but then I decided to cut out a piece of the action for myself. I started reading up on what the specialists wanted.

Jerome bought and sold the occult. He was serious about it but he was also a businessman. He never missed a fad. Crystals, pyramids, match-your-colour kits were all in the front shop for the walk-in trade. The serious stuff was back here. I'd brought him a few interesting things. An African fetish, an Alrune, a skull lined with silver so it could be used as a cup. When I'd started, he used to keep me waiting while he served his customers. For a while now, he'd been making the customers wait.

I felt odd about coming here. It made me nervous and upset. My stomach got jumpy and sudden sounds startled me. I was afraid even though there was nothing to be afraid of. And yet I found myself searching for things I could bring. I'd pay a bit more for something, take a little less of a profit, just to be able to slip in the back door and be invited in.

I heard the bolt being pulled back. Then the door opened. Because the floor was two steps higher than the back lane, he stood staring down at me. I held up the little package. I'd put it in a box, wrapped it in brown paper, tied it with butcher's string. He snatched it from me. He snapped the string, pulled open the paper, ran his hand over the box. When he opened it, he took out the music box. I'd found it at a rummage sale, mixed in with kids' toys.

"Annwyn," he said as he took the music box. He released the catch and a Celtic tune began to play. "It even has the magic cauldron." Then he checked his enthusiasm and feigned indifference. "It's not bad," he said, "but not particularly rare. How much?"

"I'm looking for someone."

He jerked around to look at me. "There's no one here but me."

"I didn't expect to find her here. But she wears a silver ring with the letter *f* inscribed upon it."

"Her name?"

"Does not begin with F."

"A rune," he said. "The first letter of the *futharc*. That's the name of the runic alphabet. It pictures the head and horns of an ox and is called *feoh*."

He turned and went through the passageway, which was piled on either side right to the ceiling with secondhand books. The walls themselves seemed made of books. There were, in places, double piles, even one triple pile, so we had to turn sideways to pass. In his office the walls were jammed with books but these were on bookshelves because they were rare editions. This was the sanctum sanctorum where only serious collectors were allowed. Being able to pay for a book wasn't enough to get it out of this room. At the front of the store you might ask for a book and, even though he had six copies, if he thought you should not have the book, he would deny all knowledge of it and send you away on a fool's errand to some place filled with secondhand paperbacks. I'd been here more than a dozen times in the last year. Always through the back door because he did not want anyone to know where he got his stock.

The wall space not taken up with books was covered with prints. Spirit photos, psychographs, portraits of the Fox Sisters and magical diagrams. On his desk was a bronze of Mithra.

He sat down in the worn corduroy easy chair in the corner. There was a trilight beside it. I stared at it the way I'll stare at something that seems familiar but can't be placed. It had a salmon-coloured glass shade and I ducked my head to see the base but it was hidden by his chair. I thought I heard some noise, but far away, voices inside my head, maybe, or people in the lane, then they were gone. The shrink had said that I should listen carefully to the sounds and voices in my head, that they were memories locked away long ago, that my childhood was locked away behind many doors, the keys to which might be anything—a smell, a slant of light, a shadow on the wall, a tone of voice, an object. But now was not the time to listen. Jerome was sitting with his hands folded on his stomach and glaring at me. I didn't mind. He always glared when someone wanted something from him. He tipped his head forward and looked over the tops of his glasses.

I sneezed twice, violently. "I'm allergic to dust and mites," I explained.

"Be grateful to Jacob," he said and to avoid a lecture I didn't ask why. "Besides, you turned to the right. And it is well before midnight."

"I'm searching for a dark-haired woman."

"All of us are accounted for. But there are others." I knew he meant other covens. The city was alive with them. They met in rec rooms all over Oak Bay and Gordon Head, mixing ritual with smoked glass mirrors and food processors.

"But you'd have heard?"

"Probably."

Two years before, I wouldn't have taken him seriously but then there had been an incident I'll never forget. Twenty minutes out of the city there's a small mountain. During July, I had regularly hiked Mount Finlayson, going up the rough face rather than the public path. The mountainside is like a series of steps, with each riser a cliff and each step a meadow. The third time I made this trek, I climbed a crevice and entered a forest of broom that rose higher than my head. I followed a deer trail to an open meadow. There I stopped. Holding hands, dancing in a circle around a Garry oak, were a dozen naked women. Older women, young women, a girl barely adolescent. They had crowns of wildflowers. As I watched, they danced and sang, sometimes in English, sometimes not. I was trapped, unable to go back down the cliff, unable to cross the meadow because I'd be seen and unable to walk off in the opposite direction because cliffs formed a wall right to the meadow's edge.

When they finished, each hugged all the others. Then they dressed. In their hiking clothes, with their backpacks, their flower crowns cast aside, they might have been any group of women on an outing. If I'd met them on the path, I wouldn't have given them more than a glance. They filed away into the trees. They did it with the assurance of people who had been here before. I waited for half an hour after they'd gone before I left the broom. All there was to see were flowers scattered on the trampled grass. Dancing barefoot they had not broken the fragile alpine surface.

I stood there, looking at the flowers, listening to the faint hum of cars passing by on the highway below, suddenly thinking, "There are more things in heaven and earth, Horatio, than are dreamed of." I wasn't sure I had it right. I didn't care. I now knew what Hamlet meant.

Coming back to the room, I said, "You hear things. Things other people don't hear."

I knew that he, and others, had known of the desperate flight of a cult leader to escape being killed by a disillusioned acolyte. Knew of his death before the police were even aware a crime had been committed. Buying and selling took me to the edge of secret worlds. It was like touching the rims of numerous spinning circles. I heard about bankruptcies before the bankers. About fires to cover losses. Rumours that wouldn't hold up in court. The endless web of plans and deals. I tried to ignore it all. To sit at my table with my few beautiful objects, waiting for someone to come who valued them. My wife pushed into the circles themselves, let herself be caught up in the whirling current, let herself be dragged into the centre of one vortex after another.

"Give me her name," he said.

"I didn't come for magic," I replied. "I came to see if there'd been a hint, a nod, a word."

"There's no black chalice here. Only white." He waited, his hands on his knees, his eyes studying me from beneath his shaggy eyebrows.

I wrote her name on a scrap of paper and handed it to him. I wasn't sure I should do it. Even after the m.c. and his incessant talk about reality, I still believed in the power of names.

He sat still for a few minutes staring at the paper. It was as if he was sorting through a card file. "No one by that name here," he said.

"She's beautiful, with long dark hair that falls over one eye. She has a way of turning her head and looking from the side. She has about her an air of innocence."

"Innocence," he said sharply. "Are you sure?"

"As if something inside her was untouched. Not that she wasn't experienced. But you know what I mean. As if she carried a small child inside her."

"You want to possess her innocence?"

"No. I want her back. Inside the café. I want everything back in balance. In harmony. It's as if a piano has gone out of tune so no matter how well it's played, it's never right."

He sat for a long time, his mouth shaping the word *innocent*, his eyes far away, as if searching for someone or something lost long ago. He grasped his beard and squeezed it. Finally, he stood up, went to a door and unlocked it. Even though he didn't say come, he didn't say stay, either. I followed him down a rickety set of stairs into a low basement. He had to bend slightly to keep from hitting his head. I remained on the stairs.

I had heard all sorts of rumours about his basement. A blood-stained altar. Orgies of rape and perversion. Devil masks. Instead, there was an altar made from a piece of stone and a large hooked rug in the form of a pentagram. When I saw it I instinctively grabbed the balustrade. On the stone altar there was a white cloth and on the cloth a pottery statue of a naked woman, not the nubile love goddesses of today, but a heavy-set woman with pendulous breasts. He was stiff and got to his knees with some difficulty. He clapped his hands.

I sat on the stairs, trying to stay quiet, like a frightened child watching something he shouldn't be seeing and not wanting to be noticed. He looked up, held his right hand in a supplicating gesture. "I have a seeker. He searches for something missing. He searches for your child. Assist him, Mother." He bowed his head for a moment. Then he struggled to his feet, nearly hit his head, and waved me up the stairs.

"That's it?" I said.

"It's a nice music box," he replied, "but you couldn't have paid more than a dollar or two for it."

12

I LEANED AGAINST THE POST OFFICE WALL and watched the hookers. It was a miserable job, I thought, always trying to be desirable. They knew how to use make-up. You had to give them that. From across the street, through the drizzle, they looked attractive enough, but when I'd walked past them they were worn and ugly. Only someone drunk or drugged or lost in fantasy could make them beautiful.

The high heels, the mesh stockings, the tiny skirts and revealing tops. A hundred per cent. That's what they were offering. The traffic light normally stayed green at this time of night because it was for pedestrians to cross from the square to a side street. The hookers took turns punching the walk button so the light would turn red. When the traffic was forced to stop, they twirled their umbrellas and pranced up and down the curb. The boldest one, the one in pink, went up to the cars and tapped on the windows but no one was having any. The city was off sex for the night. The one in frilly white hung back, playing her role of innocent little girl to the hilt, but it was a parody of innocence. The cars whipped by. Rejected. Rejected. It was in the rhythm of the tires.

I found rejection bad enough when I had to suffer through bookstore autograph sessions. The patrons desperately trying to ignore me, afraid that if they met my eye they might have to buy a book they didn't want, some sonnets and a villenelle or two instead of monsters or science fiction or nurses or hot sex. At least, with me, it was just my books being rejected, not my body. Seeing my rejected books was hard enough. Remaindered books in a pile in some chain store. Remaindered women on the street. Going for ninety-nine cents. Still not wanted.

One of the hookers spotted me and waved. I turned up my jacket collar and walked away. The drizzle was turning to rain. There were more hookers on the next corner. All carrying umbrellas. One asked me if I wanted some loving. I waved her away, turning my jacket pocket inside out to let her know I had no money. I wondered for a moment if I should ask her if she'd heard about a missing waitress but decided against it. They always talked to the cops. There was a real relationship there, symbiotic. The cops used the best looking ones, the newest ones, for their annual convention. Anyone hassling the girls would get straightened out by the cops. At least that's what my wife heard from the ex-hooker who now sold religious medals and discount vitamins.

I wondered about the girl with the Botticelli face. About her life away from the café. Maybe she had a boyfriend who got fed up with living off tips and who said go make some real money, bitch. I wondered if real people talked like that. I once met a guy who never addressed his wife by name but as Woman. Come here, Woman, with a capital letter. "This here's my Woman." I'd never dare write a character like that. Nobody'd believe it. Too exaggerated. When he did it, I was always startled and looked to see if he was joking. She called him Man. "There's my Man," I heard her say to some students. "My Woman's knocked up," he told me proudly, like he was announcing the cure for cancer or the discovery of life on Mars. My dog's got fleas. My car's got a flat tire. My Woman's knocked up.

I was heading for the parking lot where I'd left my truck when I came upon a line-up. I stopped at the end to ask what was going on. A short man with dark hair was walking down the line saying sorry you've had to wait so long, sorry you've had to wait so long. A waiter was walking ahead of him, handing out wineglasses. The short guy had a bottle of wine in each hand. One red, one white. He was filling the glasses.

The waiter handed me a glass and the guy with the hair filled it and asked, "Supper or dessert?"

I suddenly realized I hadn't eaten since lunchtime. "Supper," I said.

"Just yourself? We can always find room for one. Follow me." And he led me through the crowd, shouting, "Coming through. Coming through," parting the bodies like the Red Sea.

There was a band getting its instruments ready. They were jammed into the window well. They all were wearing folk costumes but every costume was different. A black hat, a tasselled cap, a pillbox, two caps with peaks, a swirl of wide-sleeved shirts, some embroidered, some cut like lace, black pants, white pants, blue pants, boots and shoes with turned-up toes.

The restaurant was crazy. If the Green Café was twenty feet beneath the surface, this was a rocky shoreline in a storm. Tables were jammed together to make a place for the band and everyone was trying to talk over everyone else and the waitresses were yelling to be heard and customers were yelling back. There was no centre to the noise. The noise rose from clusters of customers, now one group, now another being the loudest.

"I'm Harry," the guy yelled. "I own this place." He stood on tiptoe to survey the room. "We'll squeeze you in. The prawns are very fresh tonight."

I followed him around the room. In places we had to force our way through, pushing against people on either side. No one moved. There was no place to move to. Here and there, patrons waved at Harry or yelled at him. He seemed to know everyone by name, yelling things like "Hiya, Helen, baby. Joe, how you doing?", reaching out and touching their hands or heads or shoulders. If he was close enough, he hugged them. All the time we forced ourselves around the elliptical island in the centre he kept trying to squeeze people closer together, measuring with his hands the space needed for a chair. Every so often, he'd glance back at me and yell, "It's all right. It's all right. We'll find something."

Someone yelled his name. In a momentary lull, it came through clearly. He looked up. There was a woman sitting at a table on a balcony.

"Karmen, baby," he yelled back, grabbed my sleeve and dragged me after him. We forced our way into the passageway to the kitchen, opened a door and climbed a set of stairs. It was obviously a storage area. There were coats and boxes of canned goods but there was a space at the front of the balcony and the balcony overlooked the entire room.

"What's your name?" Harry said.

I told him. The next moment we were at the table. He put his arm around my shoulders as if he'd known me all my life and said, "Bob, this is the beautiful Karmen. Karmen with a K. Karmen, Bob. He's shy but desperately hungry. He hasn't eaten all day. I don't want him dying on my doorstep. Take care of him for me."

I sat down. Harry leaned over the balustrade. He didn't just lean, he balanced on his stomach, with one hand gripping a post, while he waved frantically with the other.

"I was just standing in line and the next thing I knew, I was here."

Karmen laughed and clapped her hands delightedly. Her lipstick was dark red, her hair black and cut fashionably so it was longer on one side than the other. Her simple black dress was classy.

Harry's feet were off the floor. He tipped forward and I lunged and grabbed his foot. He looked back, yelled thanks and bent farther forward. A waitress held up a menu. He snatched it and I tipped him back. He stood up, straightened out his shirt and pants, then handed me the menu as if this was normal restaurant behaviour.

"Everything's good," he said, "especially the prawns."

"The fire marshal," I shouted. "How do you get away with this?"

"The fire marshal?" he yelled back. He leaned close to my ear. "Let me tell you about the difference between Canadians and Americans. Americans make fewer rules and enforce them. Canadians make lotsa rules and don't enforce them. There's one fire commissioner in town and he works nine to five. The same as the liquor inspector. What are you going to have?"

"The prawns," I yelled.

He nodded approvingly. "A good choice." He took the menu and left.

"Everyone shares tables here," Karmen said. She looked, I thought, like a flapper, a beautiful flapper right out of Fitzgerald. Fine bones, pale skin. A face that in the few minutes I'd been at the table had shifted through a visible range of emotions. "Everyone comes to hear the band." Over the noise, a bouzouki started, then stopped.

"That's my man," she cried excitedly, jumping up and looking into the corner of the room.

I leaned forward to see who she was pointing out. Handsome, with high cheekbones, hair past his collar, a beard, an open-necked white shirt, a black vest lined with gold braid. Loose white pants with a black sash. He was getting ready to play.

When Karmen sat down, she sighed and said, "I'm madly in love with him."

She said it with an intensity that brought back a memory. For a moment, I was in high school again and my chest ached and my throat felt it would close when I looked at Helen. Helen! I hadn't thought about Helen in thirty years. The moment was like a slide flashed on a screen except it wasn't just the picture but everything, the smell, the sounds, the entire experience. Then it was gone and I nearly said no out loud and wanted to grab for it and hold on to it.

"He's very good-looking," I said. I wasn't sure what to say when someone I had just met declared her love.

"Yes," she replied, smiling, looking into my eyes, "I'm waiting for him to leave his wife and come to me."

I was so disconcerted I didn't know how to reply so, instead, I said, "It was really starting to rain." I took off my jacket and hung it over the back of the chair.

"I believe in fate," she said. "In synchronicity, in serendipity, in coincidence. Like we're travelling through space and our trajectories are meant to cross and we think we willed it but it's all been decided long ago. That's why I can't be mad at him for marrying her before he met me. I must have been meant to suffer. If it's not meant to be, I'll fall in love with someone else."

Drugs, I thought, she's got to be taking something. Something that made her hyperactive.

"His wife's over there." She pointed indiscreetly. "The blonde in the green jump suit. I hate the way she follows him around. Wives should stay home and iron shirts and read their kids bedtime stories. Are you in love?"

"I'm not sure what love is," I said. The memory of Helen was nearly gone. I remembered what had happened but I didn't feel it, no longer experienced it. I wondered if that had been love, that exquisite pain that had lasted for a few weeks. I'd never told her. I doubted if she even knew my name. I'd followed her down the hall to classes, watched for her from the front steps of the school. Gradually, the magical glow around her had faded and she'd just become another pretty classmate. In grade twelve I'd even been in a play with her, but when I put my arm around her, my chest no longer ached, my stomach muscles stayed relaxed, my heart beat no faster than usual.

"If you fall in love, you'll know it," Karmen declared, absolutely certain. "You can't shake the person out of your mind. You want to hear every word they have to say. You want to be with them all the time. You think of things to make them happy. Just thinking of them makes you feel good. Everybody feels like that at some time. Don't you ever feel romantic?"

"Romantic love was supposed to last forever," I replied. "But no horniness. A knight swore eternal love for a lady's favour and she gave him a scarf to remember her by."

"I thought the favour was that he got to jump her."

"I'm afraid not," I said, wondering if the cook was down in the harbour catching the prawns.

"No sex?" she asked, astounded.

"No," I said, looking down the stairs, hoping I hadn't been forgotten.

"Oh, to hell with that," Karmen said. "Lazlo jumps me all the time."

"You said his wife follows him around."

"The washroom is commodious," she answered. "You just have to be creative."

I leaned over the rail to look at the bouzouki player's wife. I wondered if she suspected him of quickies. I had seen a lot of restaurant bathrooms. It probably would have a plunger, a pail, a

77

mop and paper towels stored in one corner, a stool and a sink. The entire staff was probably in on it. The band certainly was. A large and complex conspiracy. Everyone deceiving the wife to make possible fifteen minutes locked in a bathroom with brown paper towels and a sign saying *Turn Off The Lights When You're Finished.*

"You don't approve," Karmen said. She started to pout. "I can see it on your face."

"I don't approve of how long it's taking for those prawns. They could have swum here by now."

"Slut across the table. That's what you're thinking. I can see it in the way you tighten the corner of your lips."

"Gas," I said and took a strip of Divol out of my pocket. I held it up so she could see it. I didn't like the way the conversation was going. "Is that how you feel?" I asked, taking a leaf out of the shrink's book.

She slumped in her chair. "Sometimes," she admitted. "When I'm alone and I know he's home with her. Maybe I don't understand my fate. It's too bad you're not younger. The way you appeared just like that, out of the night."

As fate would have it, my prawns arrived at that moment, giving me an excuse not to comment. I dipped one in the creole sauce and put the entire thing in my mouth. After I'd swallowed, I said, "Food's more important to me than sex. That's how I know I'm over the hill."

"I don't wear underwear," she replied. "It's much more efficient." She had her self-confidence back.

"Do you always talk like this to strangers?" I asked, digging into the pasta. Now that the food had come, I realized how hungry I was. I hadn't been hungry like this for a long time. Usually I ordered a muffin or a salad and left most of it untouched. I mostly lived on cappuccinos. At the thought of another one, my stomach twisted.

Karmen shrugged and adjusted her top. "People put too much emphasis on privacy. I'd rather have communication."

"The pasta's al dente," I informed her approvingly. Harry was obviously a good man. The sauce was hot but not bitter. If I was still writing restaurant reviews, I would have given him eight out of ten.

"I've thought about it a lot. Like, is it his image? Maybe it's just the way he looks. What if that's all there is? Is that the way it's supposed to be? Everybody says looks don't count but they do for me. Look at you. You're bald. Don't get me wrong. There's nothing wrong with bald. My mother raves about Yul Brynner. *The King And I* comes on and she stops everything. He does nothing for me. Maybe when I'm older. One of the waitresses asked me what if Lazlo played the tuba. What kind of a question is that? I think she's got the hots for him. Every time she's serving in front of where he's playing, she does this little dance with her hips. Besides, he would never play the tuba. He's not the kind. Can you see him playing the tuba?"

I couldn't reply. I had a mouthful of pasta. I was eating too fast. I was trying to keep up with Karmen's talking. I was going to have to slow down. If I bolted my food, I'd be searching for an all-night drugstore so I could get another package of Divol. Me and Divol. It should be a title for a movie. I stopped to take a sip of water. I sat back and put my knife and fork down. It was a trick I'd learned to slow down my eating. When I was anxious, I ate so fast other people were still checking the cutlery for spots and I was finished.

The band was good. They were playing a little bit of everything. Each time they started a tune, Karmen would identify it, saying that's Croatian, that's Greek, that's Serbian, that's American rag. She pulsed to the music, bouncing slightly in her chair. If there was some part she particularly liked, she leaned over the balustrade and clapped. She was thin but thin like a cat. There was no awkwardness about her. Even her exuberance had an elegance about it.

"Where are these costumes from?" I asked.

"Nowhere. Everywhere," she shouted back. "The Goodwill mostly. I helped alter the pants and shirts. His sash is from a set of drapes."

She sang along until I'd finished eating, then pointed down.

Customers were dancing in a line, threading their way around the narrow elliptical pathway. I felt uncomfortable. I expected a teacher or a policeman to appear suddenly and tell everyone to sit down and behave themselves. Instead, more customers joined the line until there was a complete circle. They danced holding hands high, then shifted to hands on shoulders.

Karmen bounced out of her chair, grabbed my hand. "C'mon," she said and pulled me out of my chair. We ran down the stairs and joined the end of the line. "Step, step, hop," Karmen shouted into my ear, calling out the steps as I fumbled along. "Relax. You've got to learn to relax. Quit being so uptight."

"I am relaxed," I shouted back. We were passing in front of the band and they were playing flat out, something foreign and fast and very loud. She raised her hand. I had it gripped so tightly it was being crushed. I loosened my fingers and hopped when I should have stepped. "Sorry."

"Quit apologizing," she said. "Nobody else has got it right, either. Just enjoy yourself."

A failure, I thought, I'm always a failure. I can't get it right. The fucking bitch. Not Karmen, the voice in my head saying I was a stupid failure. The shrink had said to listen to the voices. When I criticized myself, I was to try to hear who was saying it. I'd thought it absurd but just in that moment I'd heard my grade three teacher. I was practising to be an elf for the class performance in the annual drama night. We were dancing in a circle at the front of the classroom and she was screaming, her face bright red with rage. She was slapping a ruler onto her desk to beat out the time. "You stupid idiot, Bobby. You bloody moron. You're absolutely useless. This is the third time you've got it wrong."

"What is it?" Karmen asked as we stopped and waited for another song to begin. "You went absolutely pale."

"A memory," I said. "Pavlov's dog."

"You remember Pavlov's dog? You're not that old."

"No, that's not what I mean," but my explanation was cut off as the band began again and Karmen started shouting instructions. Step, step, stamp, step, stamp. Pavlov's dog was salivating in the distance, off somewhere in a lab, and I was trembling with fear and shame in front of my classmates as the ruler smashed over and over onto the desk and the red face loomed over me, screaming. No wonder, I thought, my wife could never get me onto the dance floor. I was washed with the heat of humiliation. I would have fled, made some excuse to go back upstairs, cling to the table and chair like a drowning man to flotsam but there was no escape. Karmen held my right hand and another customer held my left. The path around the tables was filled with the line of dancers. Karmen kept calling the steps and I kept stepping sideways and stamping. Gradually, the shame faded and I became aware of the man holding my hand on my left. Normally, I don't like another male touching me, never mind holding my hand, but he wasn't interested in my hand. I was watching Karmen's feet and trying to imitate her and he was watching my feet and trying to imitate me. God help him, I thought.

We circled and recircled and raised our hands for waitresses to squeeze under, then someone shouted, "Outside, outside," and all the dancers rushed to the door, sweeping me with them, and Karmen and I formed part of a square in the middle of the road. The band came to the door and began to play a French-Canadian dance. Dancers pushed and pulled me along, turning me this way and that, and instead of fighting it, I let myself be guided. Harry, I realized, was on top of a parked Volvo. He was taking pictures. A patrol car pulled up at one end of the street and a cop got out to watch us. A paddy wagon blocked the other end of the street. The band ended with a flourish, everyone yelled and we all rushed back inside. When we were at our table, Karmen shouted down for two beers.

"You're okay," she said approvingly. "When you came in, I thought you had a poker up your ass. You could be a good time if you just let go. Just because you're bald doesn't mean you have to be dead."

Harry brought the beer. He put his hand on Karmen's shoulder. "I told you she's a great girl. Can I say that nowadays? A girl. Or have you got to be a great woman? A fox," he said suggestively, "like foxes should be. Ugly women hate her, you know what I mean? I love her. I love her so much my wife sees me talking to her more than twice an evening and I'm in deep shit."

She put her hand on his and squeezed it. "Girl is fine, Harry. You can still call me a girl when I'm eighty."

"You know how you've got to think of feminists? Revenge of the nerds." He beamed. "And not just a fox. A lawyer, too."

"A lawyer?" I asked after he had charged down the stairs to greet someone who had just come in.

"A law student." She laughed. "Corporate law. Just the place for a girl with no morals." She cocked her head to listen to the tune. "Got to go reserve the love room. They always end the set with this song. Stay till I come back. I don't want to lose my seat."

13

"WHERE HAVE YOU BEEN?" she demanded. My wife was ironing. Usually, her attitude was that if God had wanted clothes flat, he wouldn't have invented wrinkles. Ironing was a signal that something was wrong. Before I could reply, she put down the iron and slammed a cupboard door shut. That was another signal. One more signal and we'd be on the verge of a nuclear holocaust.

She was in a real cupboard-banging mood. I'd replaced the hinges a number of times. I thought of them as PMS hinges, if you know what I mean. I go down to the hardware store and I say to Herbert, I'll have another set of PMS hinges and he knows what I mean. With his wife, it's the fridge. He bought her a PMS fridge. They put it in the basement. He keeps his beer in it and she bangs the door. Glumdelclitch, my Glumdelclitch, with hair that looked like it'd been run through the blender, was wearing her red housecoat and blue moose slippers. Obviously, the Rocket hadn't shown her a good time. I imagined the headboard of his bed as a goalie net and every time she had a climax, a red light flashed on and a number flipped up on the board. Tonight obviously had been a shutout.

"Dancing," I said.

"Dancing," she repeated like an echo. "You dancing. What the hell were you doing dancing? You never dance with me."

"Do you know the Lesnoto?" I asked. "The czardash?" I did a few steps across the kitchen.

"You're cracking up," she said. "Who the hell would want to dance with an old fart like you?"

"Karmen," I said, "beautiful Karmen. She's an attorney," I explained, exaggerating a little and leaving out the bouzouki player. "She's twenty-eight."

She laughed. "You dirty old man! Some little bitch with a father fixation. What do you think she's turned on by? Your curly hair?"

I czardashed to the fridge for a glass of milk. Well, I shouldn't say I czardashed because I didn't really remember the steps. I gave my interpretation of a czardash.

"You've been drinking."

"A little," I admitted.

"You know what the marriage counselor said."

"One beer." I laughed. I was thinking of Harry in his sock feet, standing on top of the Volvo, popping flash bulbs and yelling this is great, this is fantastic. I had never guessed such things went on.

"Pick on someone your own age." She had her jaw clenched. When she did that, she looked like her grandmother, a small, pugnacious woman who never tired of telling stories about all the men who had tried to take advantage of her and whom she had decked with a sash weight she carried in her handkerchief.

"We danced in the streets. Just like in all those musicals you love so much."

"Get real," she said. "A bunch of old farts jumping up and down. Act your age."

"Like Michael," I countered. Michael was the two-week fling, which the m.c. explained would improve her self-esteem.

Her and her lousy marriage counselor. I curse the day I agreed to see him. I said I wouldn't talk to him but she never shut her mouth for three days. She's got perpetual-motion lips. Her lips move while her brain sleeps. I even locked myself in the bathroom. It did no good. She made a tape recording and turned it up full volume at the door.

So I agreed to go to the marriage counselor. I figured he'd be a referee, make both of us play by the rules, but it wasn't like that at all. We'd get into his office and they'd gang up on me. Everything I said and did was wrong.

"Cry," he was always saying. "If you just cry, you'll feel better."

I figured if I started crying about everything that's gone wrong in my life, I wouldn't have time for anything else. It's not that I'm against sensitivity, a little sensitivity never hurt anybody—you don't want people running over their grandmothers and spinning their wheels—but it was as if my wife had an idea of what she wanted to be married to and between them, they were going to turn me into whatever that was. I kept thinking about the people who don't fit into coffins so the undertakers break their legs to make them fit. What neither of them was telling me was that because she came to see him first, she was his primary patient. I had to read an article to find that out. That meant she was his flower and I was the manure he was going to use to help her grow. His job, as he saw it, was to get her whatever she wanted. If she wanted to drink my blood, he'd have brainwashed me into cutting a vein.

Sometimes he'd see me alone. One of these times he said I was a screwed-up mess, my compass was all wrong and he'd help me get it working right so I could sail straight. I told him the only place I wanted to sail was out of my marriage. He said I shouldn't consider other women because the only women who'd be interested in me would be as screwed up as I am. If they were not screwed up, they wouldn't hang around with me. So I'm in a funny position. The only women I can be interested in are women who aren't interested in me. For giving out advice like that, he gets to drive a green Jag and take cruises to Hawaii.

One time he gave me this song and dance about how important marriage is and how he came to town to save marriages and found a hell of a mess because the m.c. ahead of him was banging his clients. Of the twelve couples, all of them got divorced. He wasn't going to let that happen. He was going to keep people together. That's when it clicked. Everybody's supposed to stay chained in hell to keep his self-image as the great marriage saver intact. It doesn't matter if you hang yourself, just so long as you're still married when you do it.

Every time I'd try to get out of the ring, he'd grab me and drag me back. He'd nail me with a hammer lock or bang my head into the ring buckle until I was staggering. All the time he was beating the shit out of me, he was saying stay married, stay married, then I'd crawl home and my wife would hit me with a body slam. I wouldn't have my shoes off before she'd be wailing. One day it was that I was lousy in bed. The next day it was I was always trying to paw her. Sometimes it was my fault she didn't have a career because I'd exploited her for my success. Another time I was a monster because I'd not let her have more than two kids. When I told her to get it straight, she'd yell back, "Today's today. You can't live in the past. Only the present. What I said yesterday doesn't matter." The m.c. was having a great effect on her.

I'd still be staggering around the ring or lying on the mat begging for mercy if it wasn't for my dentist. I tried to see him a couple of times to get my teeth cleaned but he was away. When I finally got an appointment, I asked him where he'd been and he said in an ashram. "What the hell's an ashram?" I asked him, and he says, it's like a monastery, except there's women, but nobody hassles you, there's veggy food and you just lie around and think all day. He's the only dentist I know who wears sandals and prayer beads. He ties his hair back in a ponytail and has a beard. He's got a painting nailed to the ceiling over the dentist's chair so patients have something to look at while he's mucking around in their mouths. If you take the last appointment of the evening, he breaks open a bottle of wine after you pay your bill.

"I'd been working six days a week," he says, "eight hours a day, sometimes ten. My wife spends the same amount of time shopping. It comes in here, it goes out there. Drapes, chesterfields, dining room suites, interior decorators, new cars, shoes second only to Imelda. She's in this competition with her friends. I can spend more than you can. Most of the time I'm too busy to think about it but then I started having trouble with my legs from standing all the time. She wanted me to go to the Mayo Clinic. Instead, I took a month to meditate and eat brown rice and smoke a little home grown. Three weeks after I get there I'm sitting in front of a bowl with a single flower floating in it, thinking of nothing at all, and this image of my wife riding a mule walks across my head. Left to right. My wife's beating the mule with a stick to make it go faster. That's it. Enter left, exit right. Then I went to work in the garden pulling weeds. The longer I worked, the madder I got, until I was pulling weeds like a maniac. I was ripping them out of the ground and yelling, 'I'm nobody's goddamned mule.' One of the women came and took my hand and led me away and gave me a massage and told me I had to quit eating meat. I was experiencing aggressive withdrawal symptoms. I promised not to eat meat ever again and we made love in a field full of flowers. I slept for twenty-four hours and when I woke up I'd dreamed I was kicking the mule in the ass."

"And that's it?" I asked. He didn't say this all at once, like I've written it down. It took the whole tooth-cleaning appointment, with him stopping to X-ray and scrape and suction and polish.

He smiled. "I came home and I told her, calm, no anger. I just said, I'm nobody's mule. She asked what that meant and I said I was working three days a week from now on. That would bring in forty thousand a year. She wanted more she could get her lazy ass out of the beauty parlour and the bridge club and make more."

Nobody's mule. I liked that. That's what I said at the next therapy session. I'm going half-time. One semester on. One off. You want more, you earn more. They both nearly shit. My wife cried and the m.c. gave me a lecture on responsibility but I hung onto the image of my dentist kicking the mule's ass. They were like a couple of Pekingese barking. Lots of noise but not much threat. I'll always be grateful to my dentist. He spent a month choking down brown rice to get the answer and gave it to me in half an hour.

What I learned from this is you gotta listen. Like I said, you never know where the message is going to come from. There are more places to hear the word than the road to Damascus.

My wife was back at the ironing board punishing another pillowcase. I'd been furious about Michael but now, seeing her standing there, dishevelled, bent over the iron, I felt sorry for her and with that it was like someone had flipped a switch, disconnected a circuit, and the anger went out. I realized I didn't care, that it didn't matter and under the furious jerking of the iron back and forth I saw desperation. It was like watching someone drowning in slow motion, drowning in the same river in which I was drowning—in time and fear and disappointment. Or maybe I was only projecting, maybe that wasn't what she felt at all. I wished I'd used my life better, had learned more, understood more, was smart and tough and capable, was really Superman under my Clark Kent exterior, instead of just being Clark Kent in a silly costume. When I was a kid, I believed in magic solutions, reading the Hardy Boys endlessly because they always figured out the answers. But that was all fantasy.

The Girl with the Botticelli Face. That's how I thought of her. With capital letters. She brought me a cup of coffee without being asked, she touched my shoulder, she was silent when she realized that words hurt, she wouldn't let anyone sit at my table when I was writing. She had, I realized, made a space around me and I'd never known it. I had no skin, the shrink said. He was going to try to graft skin onto me so everything didn't hurt. But she'd known that, had felt that.

I went out on the patio then, to stand under the lilac, now bare and twisted against the moon. Someone once told me that you can tell how deprived someone is by how little it takes of what is lacking to make them react. A drop of water for a man dying of thirst. A speck of food for someone who is starving. Kindness, I thought, and I couldn't stop tears from trickling out of my left eye. I wiped them away with my hand.

I'll find you, I whispered. Wherever you are. I'll bring you back. Except for the occasional car passing by, the city was silent. From where I stood, I could see across the shallow valley in which the city sat. Somewhere out there the sarcophagus of my dream loomed. All I had to do was find it and have the strength to pry it open.

14

LIPOSUCTION, LARD, LARDIEST, the way to happiness. Three Danishes, eaten slowly while masturbating, guarantees an orgasm. When she dreamed, she said, she dreamed of Danish, lemon, raspberry, blueberry, all colours, all sizes, big Danishes, small Danishes, nobody got AIDS from Danishes, they were cooked too well. Even if the baker was promiscuous, it would not matter, the bugs would be baked out. Dear God, she prayed, let me live next to a bakery. Croissants, muffins, carrot cake, rum balls, long johns dripping with cream.

I may not be able to tell you this in the first person, not if I'm to keep from ranting and raving. That's one thing I learned in therapy. When it's too emotional, distance it, put it over there and think about it objectively, as if I was thinking about someone else. Objectify it. That way it's easier to see if I'm being reasonable. Like sometimes the shrink has me sit and scream at an empty chair while I am imagining my wife sitting in it. Sometimes he tells me to talk about her without ever referring to myself. That way I won't feel as if the things she is doing are being done to me. No judging, he says, just understanding. You mustn't judge. Leave that to God.

I'm lying on the couch, wrapped in a comforter, watching the TV screen with the sound off. Nobody needs the sound. Cowboys chasing Indians, Indians chasing cowboys, people in funny costumes hacking at each other with swords, cars chasing each other down empty streets. An endless cycle of violence. Someone's beating someone else to death with a fence post. Someone else is being garroted. I wonder if insomniacs who watch this night in and night out become afraid to leave their homes? I wonder if aliens, flying by, picking up TV signals, wonder if we're all insane?

"It doesn't affect anyone," my son insists when we argue about TV. "Does it turn you into a demented, violent crazy?" he demands of me. If not you, then why somebody else? But there's a fallacy, I think, I just don't know the name for it. A fallacy of sameness and there are, as we hear on the news every night, people who get pushed over the edge. Not the copycat killings, not the I-saw-it-on-TV killings. Something more pervasive, the endless message that it's normal to settle conflict with violence.

As if, at this moment, wrapped in this comforter, lying on the couch, flicking from channel to channel, wondering how the hell it all ended up like this, it would be all right to take an ax or a gun or a plastic bag into the bedroom where she sleeps and kill her, kill her for a lifetime's insults, hurts, disappointments, and I wonder if she's lying there awake wondering if it would be all right to come into the living room and kill me, let out all her fear and rage as she swung a knife or a hammer. I want to let it go, to fall into a deep sleep but I can't, like a TV with the off control broken, I can only switch channels.

Wanderlust, she said, she wanted to wander, over the face of the earth, and the thought of pastry shops in exotic locales with bakers sweating night and day to please her every wish filled her with joy.

She'd been a beauty once, with her slightly full face, her large breasts, her round hips, but it had started before that, before she had hips and breasts, when she was still a scrawny little kid, although she'd never really been scrawny. Even in her childhood photographs you could see she was a woman in miniature. The craving for baked goods started when she was nine. Before that there'd just been the excitement of doing something forbidden. In neighbourhood garages with other children. All of them taking turns undressing and looking at each other. The secrecy gave her a feeling of power. She knew something her mother didn't and she hated anyone who said they'd tell, not because of fear of being punished but of no longer having control.

She was very curious about the boys. She wondered where hers was and when she was alone, tried to squeeze it out and had even put her fingers inside and tried to find it and pull it out. One time she squeezed so hard she wet her pants.

When there were no adults around, she and her little friends would take their clothes off, and following the instructions of one of the older children, they'd lie on top of one another, except no one knew why. Someone had seen adults lie on top of each other and go up and down but when they tried it, it didn't seem like much fun. Then she played the game with her brother and his best friend. The boys were older, around thirteen, and when her brother's friend lay on top of her, he shoved it in and she said stop and he said, "I'll give you a Danish"—his father owned the bakery—and she let him keep doing it. After he was finished they went to the back door of the bakery and he stole her a raspberry Danish. After that when she wanted something sweet, she would go and hang around the back of the bakery until he saw her and he'd bring a pastry and do it to her on top of a pile of flour bags.

She had been popular in school. Moody, but willing to do anything if there was something especially sweet at the end of it. Then rumours, not rumours exactly, but hints of rumours, reached her parents and they put her in a convent boarding school. Nuns who looked like birds of prey made her walk the Stations of the Cross on her knees, made her scrub floors with a toothbrush, determined to punish her flesh back to innocence. Even in the convent, she had found someone to smuggle in pastries. She and her friend ate them hidden in the closet where the nuns' habits were stored.

By the time they let her out, her reputation was only a faint memory. Her father got a new job and they moved to a new city. She went to college unblemished as any virgin. She had gone determined to be normal, not to give in to her fantasies, and she searched for the most normal individual she could find. Normal height, normal weight, normal colouring, normal intelligence. Joe Average. She studied all the males in the college for several weeks before quoting Chaucer to me.

It only had taken her five minutes to memorize the Chaucer. She knew it would impress me no end. It had taken her longer than that to pick out the sweater and pendant. She hinted and suggested and played coy, plied me with compliments. Any of the pack that followed female students up and down the halls making lewd comments and suggestions would have figured they had permission to rip her clothes off. She brushed her breasts against me. She asked for help with math problems that she had solved as soon as she saw them. In desperation she arranged a double date. On the way home, she did everything she could to encourage me. I was defeated by her bra clasp so she undid it herself.

Because she thought she was abnormal, she assumed I was normal. That my behaviour was average. She helped me get my hand inside her sweater, wanting all the while for me to hurry up so we could get married and move into an apartment and have two children and a mortgage. I could teach school and wear white shirts and ties and she could go to PTA meetings and bake cookies and our kids could have measles. That way she'd know she was normal. That was my job, to help her be normal. To stop her fantasies about pastries, to stop her from wanting to have sex with every man buying lemon tarts or petit fours, fantasies that made her lock the doors when she was alone, set up plaster statues of Christ in the basement, on the main floor, on the second floor and then walk on her knees from plaster Christ to plaster Christ. She'd bought the plaster Christs at a bankruptcy auction. There were a dozen of them in a box, two feet tall, unpainted. Normal, that was my job, to make her normal, and I'd do it by reading newspapers at the kitchen table, by washing my car in the driveway, by watching sports on TV. I hate sports. I haven't watched a hockey game or football game in thirty years. I have lousy eye-hand coordination and high school sports were an exercise in humiliation. She was certain, she told the m.c., I'd do things like that because I had thick glasses and wore pants that were too short.

The first time we made love was when her parents were at a movie. She was used to secrecy. It made her excited. She knew her parents wouldn't be home early. Once her father paid for something, he got his money's worth. But they might, and that excited her. She couldn't understand my reluctance, why I was always going to check when I thought I heard a car door slam. She thought it was her fault, that she wasn't doing something right. She talked to the girls in the common room and borrowed a copy of the Kama Sutra. She memorized the positions and possibilities until she read an article that said the missionary position was normal. Luckily, she then found a book that suggested whatever felt good was all right.

Even after we were married and she was lying on our apartment roll-away with her legs spread, she felt disappointment. There was going to be no jam buster, no cream puff. She tried to liven things up by taking an old bra and cutting the centre out of each cup and cutting the crotch out of a pair of panties, but I still made love as if I was listening for someone to thunder up the stairs and strike me with lightning. She didn't know that Pastor John sometimes rose from floor to ceiling, one arm raised, like a slide projected on the bedroom wall.

She tried to compromise, buying strawberry flan and peanut butter cookies for after we made love. She got me to make tea and bring it in on a tray with the sweets but it did no good. In desperation, she asked me to offer her a slice of Nanaimo bar in return for whatever I wanted her to do but not to give it to her until afterwards and I looked at her, she told the marriage counselor, as if she'd gone stark raving mad. "You don't extort sex," I'd said stiffly, and she locked herself in the bathroom to cry. She hoped I'd offer her something sweet to come out. Instead, in awhile, she heard the typewriter and knew I was working on my suite of love sonnets.

She never, never, even after all these years, she told the marriage counselor, had forgiven me for that.

The sonnets were written for her, or maybe not, maybe they were to who I wanted her to be. I don't like that idea. It makes me agitated. The shrink is always saying, "Sit still, don't distract yourself with movement, let your mind empty, and the answers will come," and I feel someone or something close by and I begin to shake until I have to get up and go to the window.

Outside, the city sparkles in its hollow bowl. Peaceful, innocent, like a city under snow, but inside the darkened houses, in the lanes and alleyways there are things going on that aren't innocent. The night is full of smells and sounds. The thick, decaying smell of rotting oak leaves, the sharper smell of wood smoke, the bitter smell of exhaust that never completely dissipates. A cat screams, and someone's yelling, then two or three but the words are indistinct, only the angry tone is clear. Sharon's out there somewhere. I shut my eyes and think that if I just started walking, my instinct would lead me to her.

When I turn back the cavalry is riding over the crest of a hill, their colours flying, a bugler playing. If it's Custer you've come to rescue, it's too late, I think. Even the magic of Hollywood can't change that.

15

"LET ME OUT," the marriage counselor whined. He was imprisoned in an iron cage that hung from the ceiling. He was filthy and his hair was matted. The guards came and unlocked the door and pulled him out as he begged for mercy. They dragged him along the floor by the feet. In the torture chamber, they clubbed him until he quit struggling, then they laid him in an iron maiden, slammed the door shut, put a pin through the lock and tipped it onto its feet. His screaming was muffled. One of the guards took a hammer and beat on the head of the iron maiden until the m.c. quit screaming.

Maybe not the iron maiden, I said, maybe the grill. He could be tied on that and suspended over a fire sprinkled with hot peppers.

"You didn't like him," Gloria said.

I stretched. The rain had quit for awhile and the sun felt good. We were at Fisherman's Wharf. It was one of those clear, warm winter days that mimicked summer. The kind of day that convinced you there was no frost, no snow, that tempted you to start clearing the flower beds of mulch and setting out young plants.

"Count Dracula impaled whole goddamned villages. If I get the chance, I'll impale the whole tribe of shrinks. A sharp stake up the asshole and then I'll roast them over an open fire," I said. "Psychobob."

"You're the unhappiest person I know," she said. "Why don't you go back and have it out with this guy. You'd probably feel better."

I'd called Gloria, apologizing for bothering her. She sounded surprised but she said yes, yes, sure, when I suggested breakfast and taking Melissa down to the dock to look at the boats. We were sharing a large fries. Melissa had her own package and was sharing it with the gulls. One for her, one for them. She threw them ineptly into the water so that the bullies at the front got everything.

"If I let go, I'd probably kill him. I used to want to smash everything in his office. Him included. He's not worth going to prison for."

"Nobody has to stay married. I got out. You at least have a job."

"Family, I guess. There's never been a divorce. One of my cousins separated for a couple of weeks and there was this incredible uproar. Yelling and screaming and threats and tears. They had a prayer meeting every night. They tracked him down at the motel and prayed in his room, on their knees."

"I understand that," she said. She was shaking malt vinegar onto the chips. She sprinkled on salt aggressively, as if she hoped some health nut was watching and would have a heart attack and die on the spot. "The first time I was married, I was seventeen. My high school sweetheart. Except after a year he couldn't have a good time unless he was drunk and when he got drunk I was to blame for everything wrong with his life. I went to our minister and said I was being abused and he said to submit to God's will. I see he's been charged with molesting little boys and has got the best lawyer he can afford. I sent him a card reminding him to submit to God's will. My mother thinks I'm a loser. I should have stayed married. It's a woman's job to keep the marriage together. Every time I try to tell her my ex can't keep his hands off anything female, she says he has a good job and a nice car. My mother can't tell the difference between a man and his car. If Jack the Ripper drove a Mercedes he'd be a good catch."

The fries were the way I liked them, soft with the skin on them. I kept eating them, refusing to think about how I was going to feel in awhile.

"I'm sorry if I interrupted anything," I said.

"I wasn't entertaining the queen," she said. "I was staring at the black and white and Melissa was colouring pictures in yesterday's newspaper. My neighbour gives me her paper after she's finished with it. I just wasn't expecting to hear from you."

"I'm sorry if I surprised you."

"What's wrong with surprises?"

"I don't know. It's just me, I guess. I hate surprises. I hate it when I don't know what's going to happen. My wife had a surprise party for me once. I went completely berserk. I told her if she ever did that again, I'd never speak to her." The memory gripped me and for a moment I felt the rage, the sense of being tricked, but then it flipped away. "You hear any gossip in the laundry room?" I asked, changing the subject.

"You in love with her?"

"I don't know what love is any more. I used to think it was caring. You know, you're sick and I care enough to be quiet, to bring you hot soup, to get aspirin, to wipe your ass if you can't do it for yourself. I guess I got it wrong."

"I thought it was candy and flowers."

"The m.c. said romantic love causes nothing but suffering. According to him a marriage licence isn't a love licence. It's a business licence. The guy gets sex. The woman gets board and room. He was real hot about it for awhile."

"How's that different from being a whore?" she asked.

"I don't know," I said. We were sitting at a picnic table. There was a take-out restaurant on a float. It served oyster burgers and fries and fish and hamburgers for those who wanted the ambience but not the seafood. The tables were clustered at one end of the dock. Off to one side there were houseboats. We finished the fries and took Melissa for a walk, inspecting the pots of thyme and marjoram and marigolds and chives. There were baskets of flowers and pots of flowers. The colour helped disguise the drabness. A German shepherd with a grizzled muzzle raised his head to see if we had any food. When he saw we didn't, he put his head back down. There was a catamaran being rebuilt. It was a hodgepodge of old blue sheeting and new plywood.

"That's how I feel," I said. "Bits and pieces."

Some of the houseboats were little more than plywood boxes

set on a boat hull. They looked as if the slightest chop would sink them. Others were quite elaborate, with sun decks, real kitchens and bedrooms. One boat had a sign saying *Fortunes Read*. A woman with hennaed hair was sitting with her feet up. I recognized her. She read palms and tarot cards at the flea market.

"If she can see the future," I said derisively, "she should have anticipated how much oak was going to go up. Anybody bought oak furniture and stored it wouldn't be living on a houseboat."

"She can't see her own fate," Gloria explained. "And she can't control or change the future."

A young woman in shorts and a halter top was fishing. Melissa went to where she was, then leaned over the edge to see the shiners swimming close to the surface.

"Get away from there," Gloria snapped. She grabbed Melissa's arm and jerked her away. Melissa started to cry. "She was too close to the edge. She could have fallen in. We've got to go back." Her voice was shrill with panic. She started to hurry. I locked my arm through hers and held her back. The dock was covered with equipment and hoses. The surface was slippery with water and oil. It was no place to start running.

On the parking lot, she gave a shiver. "I'm sorry. I can't help it. Every time I go out on the water, I feel like there's something underneath me. A shark or something. Swimming around, following us. Just waiting for one false step."

"It's okay," I replied, making light of it. "There are no sharks at the duck pond. We can go there." And we did. We sat on the grass and Melissa courted the ducks.

"Sometimes," she said, "I lose it. I just can't believe this is happening to me. Married twice. I was thinking university and my mother was saying in the old country you'd be an old maid. The first time same ethnic group, same church, same social class. A match made in heaven. My mother was happy. He had a wonderful car. Then we split. One day about a year later, George drove by and saw me cutting grass in my short shorts and for the next six months it was roses and chocolates and candlelight dinners. He'd been married twice before. He was fifteen years older than me and knew all the moves. He drove a Lincoln. My mother prostrated herself every time she saw him. It was great for awhile, then I had Melissa and it wasn't great any more. Everything, I discovered, was on credit. The car, the chocolates, the roses, the dinners. Everything. We lost the house, the car. And here I am." She kicked the ground with her heel, then kicked it again.

We were sitting beside some giant salvia. There were water lilies and a sculpture of a frog. Melissa was playing along the edge, squatting and splashing her hands in the water.

"Me," Gloria burst out. "Me," she repeated bitterly, "I can't believe it. Divorced twice. I wake up at night and I think this has to be a nightmare. I'm not like this. I'm just the high school girl who wanted to get married and have some kids."

I was sitting beside her with my legs pulled up and my chin resting on my knees. I was staring at the sculpture wondering how many girls went around kissing frogs, believing that the frogs were really going to turn into a prince. One of my classmates had married a guy who hadn't been sober for three years. She firmly believed that marriage would miraculously change him. Now she drinks more than he does and has four kids who have the haunted look of refugees.

"The m.c. said there was no point in trying to get out. Half his patients were unhappy because they were married and half were unhappy because they weren't married. It's not the marriage. It's the people."

Gloria rubbed at her cheek. She wasn't crying but a couple of tears had seeped out of her eyes.

"I had all these plans. Now I'm living in a subsidized apartment, barely getting by on welfare. You're going to think I'm crazy. You know how I feel right now? I feel like if I don't rush over and grab Melissa and drag her away from that pool, something's going to jump out and grab her."

"No, I don't think you're crazy," I reassured her. I knew how she felt. That's just the anxiety, I wanted to say. You've got lots to be anxious about. But I didn't. It would have been too bloody patronizing. "Could you ask some questions for me? About Sharon? If anybody's seen her around."

"Maybe," Gloria said, "she wouldn't appreciate that. What if you took off for a few days and one of your students had a crush on you and started fantasizing about all the terrible things that might have happened? Would you really want someone checking into your private life?"

"We had a date for the next day. She was supposed to work. She's never missed before. She never told anyone she was planning on leaving," I said stubbornly.

"You want to come and check yourself? We can knock on a couple of doors."

"Can't," I replied, "at least not right away. Shrinko time in forty-five. That'll be an hour. Sometimes we go over."

"What are you seeing a shrink for? You've got a job, you've got a house, you can pay your bills. You can dress yourself."

"Yeah," I said. But everything was out of sync, like being inside a kaleidoscope that kept turning. Every time I thought I had the pattern worked out, it changed and I couldn't escape. "It's like I can't behave normally. Something happens that's not important. Nobody else reacts. I go right off the deep end. Like the way you felt on the dock. Except with me it's nearly everything. I want to quit running away. Somebody starts getting drunk, I want to leave right away. Somebody gets angry, I want to run. Somebody touches me and I want to punch them. Before we moved here we were always on the move. I always told people it was because I wanted to see the country but it really was because I couldn't stand anybody telling me what to do."

"Sorry," she said. "Sorry. It's just next to me you look like you've got everything."

"The closest I've got to friends are the people in the café," I said.

"Shit," she said, "I hate this. Not you. Life. Why the hell has it got to be like this? Come on, we'd better get back if you've got an appointment. Afterwards, come over. Ring apartment six four two. You'll have to get past Mrs. Joe. She'll do everything but take your picture. She's the super's wife."

"Can I talk to her?"

She shook her head and called to Melissa. "Not unless you speak Portuguese."

16

"DOES YOUR CHARACTER NEED rebuilding?" Shrinko asked. All the time I'd been ranting, he was sitting with his back to me. He'd explained that it wasn't to ignore me. It's just that if he wasn't watching he was better able to hear what I was saying. I'd suggested I just send in tapes but he said, no, that most of the time he wanted to have more than the words, that he wanted me there and I'd admitted that I really hadn't meant it, that it was the bitterness spilling out like pollution from a pulp mill, contaminating everything. He made it hard for me to sustain the anger, hard to be unfair and not feel like a shit.

"No," I said. And I waited for him to say it did, but instead he waited, not like a boxer looking for an opening but somebody who refused to fight. I clenched my fist.

"Hit this," he said and picked up a pillow. He held it with both hands.

I felt stupid, embarrassed. He kept holding the pillow. To humour him, I tapped it, as if it was a joke between us, but as my fist touched it, anger, like bile, rushed hotly up my throat and everything became unfocussed. I hit the pillow so hard it pulled loose from one of his hands. I lost him, the office, could have leaped at him and killed him if he'd moved. Instead, he sat perfectly still and my body jerked as it had once when I'd grabbed an electric fence.

When I was sitting limply in my chair, he said, "Do you see it isn't me? I didn't do it. You hate it when other people treat you unfairly. You told me that. Do you remember? You told me you hate it when people don't treat you as you. I hate it when people don't treat me as me. I'm not the marriage counselor, I'm not your wife, or your parents or anybody else. You don't need a baseball bat to make me listen."

"It was the m.c. I needed it for," I said. I'd told Shrinko about bringing a baseball bat to a session with the marriage counselor. Every week when I went to see the m.c., he had kept insisting that what had happened the week before didn't matter, that I was to forget about whatever my wife had done and focus on the future. When I couldn't stand it anymore, I'd bought this foam bat that looked real and told him I was going to smash his kneecap but that I didn't want him calling the cops when it was over, because over was over, after all, and if I could forgive, then surely he could also.

"Someone not listening is frustrating. But not to the point of murderous rage. For you to be so angry about it, it's got to have been done to you before. In some important way." He rubbed his thumbnail for a minute. I'd learned to be quiet while he was doing that. It meant he was thinking. "Did you ever try to tell someone something important and they wouldn't listen?"

"I don't know," I said.

"Tuck the question away. Let it work its way inside. Then when you get something, write it down. Don't analyze. Just free associate. Just remember, no settling scores. You don't do anything without our talking about it first. No getting a plane ticket and beating somebody to death with a bat."

"Okay," I said. It was easier to agree now that I'd felt the rage. I could imagine myself going berserk and not remembering anything I'd done afterwards. I wondered if that was what happened. When quiet neighbours suddenly went crazy, then shot themselves when they realized what they'd done.

"Has your friend come back yet?" he asked.

"I'm still looking." I held out the photograph.

He took it and studied it. "She's very pretty. A nice smile."

"Everybody likes her."

"Being beautiful," he said, "provokes jealousy. Pretty and popular. I doubt if everyone likes her."

"I hadn't thought of it like that."

"What about your wife? Are things any better between you?"

I shook my head.

"Are you going to leave her?"

"I don't know. I can't make up my mind what to do. The m.c. said there wasn't any point. Nothing would get better."

"He was trying to keep the marriage together. I'm not. But you've got to think about the cost. You could lose your kids."

"My daughter's gone already," I answered and I felt empty and yet full of pain. "She's seventeen and she's living with two of her girlfriends."

"And your son?"

"He drifts in and out like a shadow, slipping in through the basement door, getting clean clothes, making himself a meal. At least he still comes home some of the time. I don't know," I said, and I didn't know. I rubbed my face with the palms of my hands. "I talk to him but mostly he just stares at me. I keep trying. I keep telling myself that it's like I'm in a canoe and if I can just keep it upright until the storm is over, we'll be all right. But I've found kitchen knives with blue tips."

"And his mother? Mothers and sons often have special relationships."

"They don't speak."

"And the dark-haired girl you talk about? Do you still think you killed her?"

"I've made a chart of how I spent my time since I saw her last. There isn't any time missing. I can account for where I was."

"Your friend? The waitress, you mean. But you said you'd had this fear for a long time."

"It just comes and goes. Sometimes it just seems absurd. I know I couldn't have killed anyone. And then there's times I'm positive I have. You must think I'm crazy."

"No," he said. "But something crazy has happened to you. The question is what? All we've go to work with are symptoms. If you were in physical distress, I'd ask you for the symptoms. Does it hurt when I press here? Does it hurt when you cough? Have you a fever? Do you feel dizzy? Then I'd try to figure out what was wrong from the symptoms. Sometimes it's easy. Sometimes it hard. You're bringing me symptoms. I want you to write down symptoms. Sometimes, if somebody's been sick a long time, they forget what it was like to be well. Then they think the symptoms are just part of normal life. They don't even know they're symptoms. That's why we've got to watch together."

I stared past him, out the window at the horse chestnut trees. They made an interesting pattern. Each pane could be a painting.

"What are you doing?" he asked.

"Thinking about the horse chestnuts and the pattern they make."

"But we were talking about your not being well, not about art."

"What'd you write down?" I asked.

"Distracts himself when subject matter becomes painful. Fair?"

"Yeah," I agreed. I didn't like it but he was right. I daydreamed my way through high school. If I get bored or someone is making me pissed off, I wander away into fantasy. I hadn't thought about why.

"Like the humming," he said. "The singing. Jiggling your foot up and down. You've needed to learn all the tricks. Most people don't need them. Did you know that?"

"I don't do drugs," I said rather defensively. "And I don't drink."

"Thank God for that," he said. "If you did, you wouldn't be here. You'd be dead or panhandling downtown. I'll see you tomorrow over lunch hour."

17

GLORIA WAS RIGHT ABOUT Mrs. Joe. I buzzed Gloria's number and before Gloria could say who's there and buzz the door open, Mrs. Joe was in the doorway. Mrs. Joe must have had all the buzzers in the building wired into her apartment. Maybe even an implant. And I knew it was Mrs. Joe right away. She was short and dark with crimped hair and a squint. She had a wooden spoon in her hand. It was covered in tomato sauce or blood. If someone asked me to guess, I'd say blood.

One look and all my assertiveness drained away. I was ready to say I promise to be good and then I remembered it wouldn't help. She couldn't speak English. Body language might do it. I could fall to my knees and clasp my hands. Just then Gloria buzzed me in and I was saved from some act of hysterical idiocy. Mrs. Joe came and looked to see what floor I punched. I was surprised she didn't take my picture and fingerprints. Gloria had coffee ready. "I've no cream," she said. I put the paper bag on the table, took out cream and three doughnuts. I even had some packets of sugar.

"Can't handle it black," I explained. "My nerves are bad today."

"You've got circles under your eyes," she agreed. "And if you're not jiggling your thumb, it's your foot."

I stopped the jiggling but my stomach cramped so I went back to jiggling my foot.

"That must drive your wife crazy," she said.

"We all have our habits," I replied defensively.

I wasn't sure why I'd come. I found Gloria's apartment

depressing. I don't want to know people live like this. Hardly any furniture. Less food. When I put the cream in the fridge, there was a loaf of bread, an onion, some carrots and empty shelves. I felt like I should have brought a bag of groceries. But I don't want to start anything. She's cute, I like her, I like Melissa, but I don't want to rip Gloria's clothes off, wrap my arms around her and drag her to bed. I want to be close to someone, I want to hold someone, I want to lie in bed naked and feel someone's breath against my cheek but when it's over I want to feel good about it, not guilty. Bar guys are runners, Sunbeam said. I don't want to be a runner.

"What do you want?" Gloria asked.

"I don't know," I admitted.

And I don't. Right at this moment what do I want? To go to the tenth floor and knock on Sharon's door and have her open it. And then what? Say, "We had a date. You didn't turn up. I was worried something had happened to you."

"You've got it bad," Gloria said. "You barely know her and you've got the look of someone who's lost their best friend. What are you like when you know somebody?"

"Poets," I replied, making light of it. "We're overly emotional. It's nothing."

"Sure," she said, giving Melissa one of the doughnuts and some cream mixed with water and a taste of coffee. I took a colouring book and a box of crayons out of the bag and put them on the table beside her. She looked at her mom and Gloria said it was okay. She gulped down her drink, grabbed the crayons and book and ran off to the bedroom.

"You don't think I should be doing this?"

"I'd be pissed off if I went away for a few days and some guy I hardly knew starts snooping into my life. I'd figure he had a problem. Like back off, buddy. Don't get hysterical."

"Mrs. Joe doesn't miss much. Would she have known if Sharon came home on Wednesday? If anybody came to visit her?"

"You really can't leave it alone."

"Obsessive compulsive. That's what the m.c. said. When I was a kid I sometimes never made it home for lunch. I had to step on every crack. If I missed one, I had to keep going back to the beginning and starting over again."

"You shouldn't have brought that stuff for Melissa. You do that a couple of times and then you quit coming around and she's going to feel bad. Like maybe she did something wrong. That's the way she feels about her dad. She told one of my friends that she doesn't have a dad because she did something bad."

"Sorry," I said. "Got it wrong again, I guess. I should have given it to you and you could have given it to her."

"My ex never said he was sorry in his life. For anything. I'll go ask Mrs. Joe."

What the hell was that all about? I'll never figure out women. There are buttons you don't even know exist. They won't and then they will. They don't and then they do. You try to do something nice like bring the kid something to play with and you screw up. You say you're sorry and you can have any favour you want. No wonder some people lavish their affection on dogs or cars. Dogs and cars are more predictable.

Gloria came back and announced, "She came home. Mrs. Joe saw her come in. She didn't have any visitors."

"Did she see her go out?" I asked.

"She doesn't look to see who's going out. Just coming in. If they're in, they're supposed to be in. And she doesn't watch all the time, anyway. Sometimes, she's busy with the kids. Sometimes, she's cleaning the hallways. That sort of thing."

"This is nuts," I said.

"You said it, not me."

"That's why I'm going to a shrink. Like I know I'm being crazy but I can't help it."

"Like the farmer and Anne Murray?"

"I never followed Sharon around or anything. I don't think she's secretly in love with me. I don't think she's sending me messages."

"But she likes you?"

"Sunbeam says she does. Evelyn says she's just friendly with everybody. They're waitresses at the café."

"You've got to get some friends. At least I've got the girls for coffee klatches. You got a hobby?"

"Writing. At least my wife thinks it's a hobby. I told her it's my profession. And collecting Popsicle sticks is mine, she said."

"Your wife is your hobby," Gloria said. She didn't look amused. I had the feeling she wasn't as understanding and empathetic as the shrink. "Some of the girls have hobby husbands. They've been split for five years and their husband is still their hobby. They can do an hour on them without stopping except to light up another cigarette. Keep it up and you'll be giving them competition."

"Hiking," I said desperately. I didn't like the way the conversation was going. I didn't realize I talked so much about my wife. Most of the time I never talked to anybody but the shrink. Maybe that was it. Certainly, there was no one at work to talk to. I wouldn't have told them if I was bleeding to death. The gossip was so bad that if I wore new socks, it was all over the college by noon. The dean, bless his pointed little head, loved gossip. Except he didn't call it that. He called it perception. "It is the perception that . . ." was his favourite expression. He ran everything on gossip. His model was Saddam Hussein. It was rumoured that if you got down on the prayer rug in front of his desk and touched your head to the floor, you could get an extra hundred dollars duplicating money. If you kissed his feet, you got travel money to Vancouver. "Gardening. I love chrysanthemums. I've got twenty varieties. And lilies. I'm no good with vegetables. My green peppers turn yellow, my dill dies and my cucumbers wilt. But I still enjoy it."

"You're weird," she said. "You never talk about hockey or baseball or rugby. You don't drink. You like the ballet. You sure you're not gay?"

I quit tapping my thumb on the table. I sat there not moving, not looking at her. I looked at my watch. "I think I'd better be going." I said. "There's lots to do."

"Like what?" she asked.

"Papers to grade. Lessons to prepare. Shirts to iron. That sort of thing."

"I hurt your feelings," she said. "I'm sorry."

"Okay."

"Not okay. I said I was sorry. I mean it. It was a dumb joke. You said you were sorry. I forgave you. Now, it's your turn."

"Okay," I said, but I said it with some feeling, and the numbness in my face eased. "I'm really uptight about some things. I'm not used to anybody saying they're sorry."

"There's a key to her apartment."

"Where?"

"At the café where she works. I heard that having coffee. Lona from nine eleven once heard your friend say that she'd forgot her key but that was okay because she always left a duplicate at work."

That's when my imagination started working overtime. A key at work. Anybody might have access to it. They could borrow it, lend it, make a duplicate. Even a customer. After all, I'd lifted the Polaroid of her and no one had noticed. You do that sort of thing casual like, as if it's your right, and no one notices.

I took out the picture of Sharon and put it on the table so Gloria could see it.

"I've seen her around," Gloria said. "Long skirts. Folksy tops. I thought she might be sort of hippy dippy."

"What you guys looking at?" Melissa asked. She'd come out with crayons in one hand and the colouring book in the other. There was a bright purple giraffe and two green zebras in her picture. She climbed up on her mother's lap to look.

"That's my teacher," she said.

"That's not Mrs. Sanders," Gloria replied.

"One of her helpers. She comes and helps us pretend. She makes plays and costumes and stuff. I'll show you." She climbed down and ran out of the room.

"She doesn't go to school yet?"

Gloria shook her head. "Wednesdays she goes to a free school in the morning. It's to keep single mothers from going stark raving mad. It's in an empty building down on Wharf."

"Here it is," Melissa shouted happily. "She helped us make masks." It was a mask cut from red cardboard, with brightly dyed feathers and sequins glued to it and then the whole thing glued to a stick.

"Do you like her?" I asked.

Melissa waved her mask happily. "She's neat," she said. "We play dress up. I was a princess saving the forest. Next time we're going to be refugees with camels and things."

"Socially conscious," Gloria said. "They've even learned to compost."

18

I WENT LOOKING FOR THE KEY THEN. It was as if I couldn't help myself. There was a kind of ferocious madness about it. As if everything that I had ever dreamed of, everything that I thought life had promised me, was being taken away again. As if I was fighting an unfinished battle somewhere on the edge of memory. I felt pushed towards that edge. So close that I could look down. Not again, I thought. Never again.

I'd told Shrinko that I didn't care enough about anything to hang on to it. If someone wanted it more than I did, let it go. Let them have it. That there was nothing worth fighting about. And my wife was the opposite. She wanted to hang on to everything, never let anything go, pile up belongings, used clothes, magazines, old newspapers, everything, even the garbage if I'd let her. Be like me, I'd said, be free, they're just objects and objects don't matter. But she wanted to cling to her friends. You'll make new ones, I said, every time we moved. That's what our life was like. We were always loading and unloading U-Haul trailers. I could discuss the virtues of trailers the way some people discuss wine. Advantages, disadvantages, load size, brakes, bumper hitches. Until, finally, I'd come to Cadboro College. And then it was the sudden lack of jobs for teachers that trapped me like an insect in amber and all my plans for moving endlessly across North America came to a halt. I'd never thought of spending a lifetime teaching in a girl's college. A lifetime of having to deal with twenty-year-olds. Fat ones, thin ones, short ones, tall ones. Smart ones, dumb ones. All learning to write paragraphs and essays, to identify participal phrases. Never getting to deal with women who were twenty-five, or thirty, or forty. Stuck in a world that never grew up.

That's when the flotsam and jetsam began to accumulate. I knew how the Indians must have felt when they no longer could pack up their tents and move on and leave behind their midden. There's no horizon in Victoria. And I can't afford to live close to the ocean. Sometimes, when the essays are very bad and the endless arguing over grades is too much, I go down to the beach and sit on the sand and watch the freighters and wonder what it would be like to get on one and sail away. Except *there* is probably no better than *here*. Worse, I expect. *This is all there is* is the lousiest thought in the world.

There isn't anything worth fighting over. There isn't anything worth hanging on to. If someone else wants what you have, give it to him. Or her. It was an attitude that had let me weave my way through life, avoiding contact, living from day to day, slipping away like a boat into fog. Not caring enough to actually do something.

That's why it felt strange to be looking for Sharon. As if some other mind was making my body move. I thought I should be at home, digging over the compost, trimming the cedar hedge, cutting back the blackberry canes. The oak leaves needed raking in the lane. But I was determined to find out about the key.

The café was nearly empty. I paused at the counter, watching the cook make a strawberry fan to go with a piece of cheesecake. There were no keys on hooks on the wall. It might, of course, be in the cash register.

I slipped into my corner and Evelyn appeared. Twenty-five per cent of anorexics die, I thought. Her layers of clothes probably weighed more than she did. I ordered coffee and a chocolate croissant.

When she brought them, I said, "Who's taking care of Sharon's goldfish?"

"Sharon hasn't got goldfish."

"She told me she had goldfish and guppies."

"Sharon?" She looked confused. "When did she get pets?"

"That's what she told me," I said. "They'll need to be fed. You can't let them all go belly up."

"I can't do anything about it."

"She's got a key here. Somebody can go over and feed the fish."

She started to pull at her sweater, ripping little bits of wool off and letting them drift away. The fate of guppies would worry her. I'd watched her herd flies out the door rather than kill them.

"Demytro's got the key. Anyway—" She paused conspiratorially and leaned forward so that her mouth was right against my ear. "Don't say anything to anybody? Okay?" When I nodded, she said, "Promise?" and I held up my first two fingers in what I thought was the Boy Scout sign. "I think she's gone off with a very special friend for a real romantic time. If you know what I mean."

Everything stopped. My heart, my head. Suspended animation.

"You're sure?" I asked. I barely choked out the words.

"Nobody's supposed to know, okay. Like when she gets back, there's going to be a big surprise."

Let it go, I said to myself. Let it go. There's nothing worth hanging on to. Not a thing, not a fantasy, not a person, nothing. Nothing. Nothing. And I remembered the glass car my grandfather gave me before he died, a glass car filled with brightly coloured candies. Magical. Filled with light. Rainbows in the glass when the angle was right. Mine. Mine. No one else's. He gave it to me. He was all bone, like Evelyn, but his skin was yellow. We thought it was the carrot juice he drank to combat his cancer but it was jaundice from his cancerous liver. Tall and dark and handsome, he eroded to a yellow bag of bones my father could carry from kitchen to bedroom. He lay helpless like a yellow stain while everyone wandered about the house in sock feet, not speaking unless the kitchen door was shut and then only in whispers. Nothing must disturb his sleep because only then was he not in pain. And then the undertakers came with a long wicker basket and laid him in it and carried him away. And I thought about how cancer must be like a ball of tangled string, snarled and knotted, and how one day I'd be a doctor and in my mind, I practised untangling the string. And I cherished the glass car, not letting anyone else touch it. Mine. No one else's. Just mine. And as long as I had it, he really hadn't been carried away in a black hearse and buried deep in the earth. And one day on the front porch my mother said, let your cousin play with it, and I said no, it was mine, as precious as if carved from diamond, and she said, don't be selfish and she'd taken it from me and given it to him and when, in a few minutes, he tired of running it back and forth along a stair, I picked it up and smashed it on the sidewalk.

Let her go, I said to myself. There's no one, there's nothing worth keeping. Let her go.

"She called?" I said as I paid my bill. Evelyn gave me my change. I put fifty cents on the counter for her.

She had another romance novel in her hand. A man in a frock coat was standing facing a woman in an elegant pink dress. "You should write like this," she said. "You'd be a millionaire."

"You've got to believe in it," I replied.

Stupid, I thought, when I was out on the street. The day was colder. There was a damp wind. An old fart with fantasies, I thought. The m.c. had been right. I needed to get in touch with reality. People your age have a hard time accepting that they're not sexually attractive anymore, he said. Women even more than men. You got to learn to look in the mirror and see what's really there. More wrinkles, less hair.

Let it go, I thought. Nothing's worth fighting over. Nothing's worth killing for. Jealousy is an act of insecurity and flatters no one. One woman is good as any other. They've got all the same parts. Make love to the qualities you admire, not to their physical looks. Let it go and try not to be a fool.

And I did. I let her go. I don't know how you do that. I just did it. I stood there on the street corner, staring at the travel poster, and I let the wind blow through me, until it blew her right out of me. Until I began to shiver. And then I got into my truck and drove away.

19

THE M.C. SAID HE MUST have been doing something right, otherwise why did I keep coming back? I said when my aunt had cancer, she used her savings, borrowed money, sold her house, so she could go to Mexico for injections. She kept going back until a month before she died. Her going back didn't say anything about the effectiveness of the treatment, only how desperate she was.

It's amazing how angry bad advice can make you. Bad legal advice, bad financial advice, bad medical advice. The only question is who do you end up angriest with? The lawyer, the stockbroker, the doctor, or yourself for being stupid enough to follow their advice. This is what I was thinking about while I was sitting in my truck at the breakwater. I dug into my pocket for another Divol and felt a piece of paper. When I took it out, it said, *Passport to the Republic of Godvinia*. I'd forgotten about it. The night before, Karmen had shoved it into my pocket. The band, she said, was playing at a private party and they had free tickets for some of the dancers. The dancers were to supply atmosphere. In return, they got free food and booze and a good time.

Normally, I wouldn't go to something like this but the wind had blown Sharon out of me and, with it, the last of my warmth. I was so cold that I sat there with the heater turned on full and still shivered. I hadn't been cold like this since I'd been a child and I'd stayed too long skating on the local pond. My fingers were so cold that I couldn't undo my skates and had to wear them all the way home, stumbling through the snow with them, twisting my ankles, falling down, until at the back door of our house, I had to bang with my forearm until my mother rescued me. I felt this way now. Numb and cold but there was no mother to untie the knots, to feed me warm soup, to put my feet into a basin of warm water.

Beyond the breakwater, the sky and sea were empty. Grey skies and grey waves. Behind me the graveyard was heavy with rain. As each wave broke, the truck trembled and spray rattled on the windshield. I could feel the dead shifting in their coffins. An armada of coffins, their tombstones like white sails. When I began to think like this, in desperate images, it was time to walk the malls or sit in a doughnut shop, washed in light, surrounded by other people.

I didn't feel like a party. I'd be like Banquo's ghost. The lights of a freighter appeared and they made me feel more isolated. I threw the ticket on the floor. I'd always despised people who felt sorry for themselves, people who sold their agony instead of their art, people who, for the slightest attention, would be endlessly grateful, but more and more that was the way I felt. If anyone did me a favour, no matter how slight, I clung to them. Like I'd clung to Demytro, to the brightly coloured waitresses of the Green Café, to Sharon.

I rested my head on the steering wheel and let the vibrations from the waves make me tremble. Somehow, the pounding of the waves was right, as if I were being attacked by a great, avenging hand, but vengeance for what? What sin? I'll have to hose off the salt, I thought, before I fell asleep. As I slept, I felt the dead shift in their coffins, and coffins rising from the earth like a great armada, rocking with the motion of the waves.

I woke up afraid, but the graveyard, when I turned to look, was still just a graveyard. I switched on the light and picked the ticket off the floor. The address was in Oak Bay. Oak Bay is one of those neighbourhoods where everyone wears English tweed, listens to subliminal tapes of upper-class English accents, invents relatives who might be related to some minor royal, but all of it, including the carefully tended gardens and the picture of the queen over the kitchen sink, is an act. Behind the drawn curtains the women wear black nylons while riding naked on their husbands' backs, whipping them through the halls. At least that's what they'd like you to think. The truth is most of them come from Saskatchewan, drink beer and watch reruns of *Dallas*.

Twelve sixty-four was an old mansion. Brown shingle and stone behind a black iron fence. At the gate there was a young man in a World War II army jacket, blue jeans and puttees. He was carrying a plastic rifle with a rubber bayonet and was drinking beer from a bottle. He put the beer down and tore the ticket in half.

"If you leave, you can't get back in," he said, before putting the bottle back in his mouth. "Keeps gatecrashers from Gordon Head out."

There was a long driveway. At the end of it there were a dozen hibachis and the ground was littered with charred bamboo skewers. There was no one outside but I could hear a lot of noise inside. I peered through the screen door. The kitchen was crowded with people eating ice cream. Someone yelled for me to come in. There was hardly room to move. Help yourself, a young man with three earrings in his left ear said, waving his pale hand grandly towards pails of ice cream and dishes of topping. The air was blue with marijuana smoke.

The women were all dressed in brightly coloured wraparounds. The dresses were obviously supposed to be some ethnic costume—Polynesian, African, Chinese, Hawaiian—but they mostly looked like what they were, brightly coloured sheets with two holes cut for the arms. I was surprised. Godvinia had sounded positively European. Wraparounds weren't European. I knew about wraparounds. My wife made one once. After a hard day teaching subjects and predicates, I'd come home thinking of supper and lying on the couch watching the news. She met me at the door in a wraparound, whipping it open to reveal that she had nothing on underneath. The idea that the evening might be filled with horsy women whipping open their dresses nearly made me head back to the truck.

But then, I thought, this is what I need. Lots of noise, the mindlessness of people jammed together determined to have a good time. Someone would have a joint, there'd be beer, and in a crowd this size, there'd be the wounded, the lonely, someone who could be cut out of the crowd with a little attention, a few words of flattery, who would repay me with some groping and sex. I'd watched my colleagues do that. Like wolves hunting a herd, picking out the women who were the most desperate, the most needy, the most damaged. I knew about that now, knew how much someone would pay for the loneliness to stop, even if only for an hour or two.

I avoided the ice cream and wandered into an adjoining room, which had been decorated to resemble a Bohemian cafe. Toulouse-Lautrec posters on the wall. Tables covered with checkered tablecloths. Wine bottles with carefully dripped candles. There was a couple with matching purple hair and pink sunglasses in an embrace. I backed out into what was normally the living room. All the furniture had been taken away and the band was setting up.

"You decided to come," Karmen squealed, grasping my sleeve. She pulled me into a corner and leaned close. "I asked the staff at the restaurant about your true love. Waitresses usually move in the same circles. They remember her. She used to come to hear the band. She was one of the dancers."

"I don't see the wife," I said, changing the topic.

Karmen smiled. "She had to baby-sit. Break time, we've been promised the use of an upstairs bedroom. That's if his kid doesn't get an asthma attack. I swear she stuffs his head in a feather pillow. When the kid's with a baby sitter it doesn't happen."

"Why are you in love with him?"

"It has nothing to do with me," she said. "I'm a hostage to fate."

People were crowded together in a horseshoe shape around three walls of the room. Against the fourth wall, the band was organizing itself. A video camera fixed to a television set had been put up to record the band. Even though the band was doing nothing more interesting than plugging instruments into outlets and untangling cords, the crowd was watching the monitors. All the time they watched, they also talked so there was a steady rise and fall of voices. A space had been left in the centre of the floor and I thought someone might have entered it, done something, stood on his hands, performed back flips, or a couple might have danced without music but, instead, they contented themselves with putting their hands or faces close to the video camera so everyone else could see them on the screen.

When, at last, the band began playing, the crowd continued to watch the monitor. A thin man with dark hair and a mustache walked onto the floor and began to dance to "Never On Sunday." Two women joined him and waved for others to join the line. Everyone pulled back, flowing away like mercury that has been touched. Four more people joined the line but it was obvious that they, too, belonged to the dance group that had come with the band.

"C'mon," Karmen said, "let's do it," and she led me across the floor, past the curious eyes. I stumbled along, watching Karmen's feet, listening to her voice as she described what I was to do— "Walk, walk, turn, walk"—interspersing the instructions with, "Relax, relax, nobody's going to dump on you for getting it wrong. It's not a performance." But I, too, was conscious of the video camera and all the faces turned towards the TV set.

"Good for you," she said as the dance ended. "You're improving. There's still some circulation in my hand."

I danced nearly all of the dances. When I stopped, the armada of graves appeared, sailing towards me, their white sails vague in the driving rain. On the floor, trying to follow Karmen's lead, listening to her call, "Step, stamp, step, step, stamp, walk, walk," the steps changing at what seemed an impossible speed, I danced away from the armada. Holding her hand and the hand of the person on the other side, the warmth of it, the intimacy of a basket hold as we danced in a circle, carried me farther from the dead in their disintegrating boats.

Gradually, some of the crowd joined in but the rest, intimidated by the idea that the dances actually had steps, that there was a right way and a wrong way, and that it was not a matter of simply doing what felt right at the moment, clung to the walls and each other. The band finished its first set and, in an instant, Karmen vanished. I caught sight of the bouzouki player taking the stairs two at a time.

I leaned against the wall and thought about Karmen. So

fashionable, so chic, like someone plucked from a Paris salon, and already, if what she said about how rushed their lovemaking was, the bouzouki player was on top of her, inside her, and her arms and legs were wrapped around him, while the rest of the band was still putting their instruments away before going for a beer.

This is how betrayal happens, not in distant romantic settings but grabbed in the midst of ordinariness. I wondered about the pale blonde wife. If she really was home, baby-sitting, or if she, too, was making love to someone else who was betraying some other woman who was making love to someone else. Like a long chain of unhappiness and infidelity. Forever and ever, snaking down through the ages in an unbroken line. Betrayal and deceit justified by the right to momentary joy. And I felt Pastor John beside me. Faded a little, because I liked Karmen, silenced a little because his wrath seemed so unreasonable and had nothing to do with people, only with some abstract set of rules. Thinking of him, his right arm upraised, Bible in his hand, I willed him a stroke, so that his arm fell, his face was momentarily surprised and when he went to speak, he'd been struck dumb. He stood there, staring at me, a ghost in the crowd of beer-drinking dancers, for now that a tape of rock music was playing, the crowd was hopping up and down. He turned and walked away, through the wall. He'd be back. He wasn't so easily defeated. He had a storehouse of suffering built up over the years to sustain him.

I wondered, though, what would happen if Karmen got her wish, if the bouzouki player left his wife for her. Would she go everywhere with the band? Would she become the clinging wife, resented by someone like herself but a bit younger, a bit more attractive, someone reckless with her own life and the lives of others, someone satisfied with fifteen minutes in a bedroom in some stranger's house, satisfied to be a quick lay in place of a quick beer?

I was pressed into a corner, sucking on a beer, when the dance leader came up.

"Karmen says you're looking for someone," he said.

"Was," I replied. "She's fine. She forgot to tell people she'd be away for awhile."

"The little Croat," he said, "is that the one?"

"I don't know. She's an actress."

"Aren't they all? Or singers in a rock band. It's her dancing that impressed me. She danced with her eyes closed. No looking at anyone's feet. Sometimes, I did the czardash with her, very fast. She never missed a step. But she hasn't come for awhile. I thought maybe she'd moved away."

"She's working as a waitress," I said.

"Sharon," he said and I nodded. "Her husband used to hang around Harry's. He never danced. Sometimes, she would try to get him to join us for the simple dances. He wasn't interested. A stupid man. With a wife like that who likes to dance, it is good to at least attempt it. A night of dancing together makes for good sex. Don't you think so?"

"I don't know," I said. "I'm not much of a dancer."

"But you try," he said, tapping me on the chest with his finger. "Women like that. It makes them feel you care." He shook his head. "She would put her arms around him from behind, whisper in his ear, sometimes pull his hand but he would shake her away the way an impatient adult shakes off a child. All he was interested in was talking with the American with one arm. They would huddle at the back, beside the kitchen door, maybe four or five of them. They were always talking politics."

"What was her husband like?" I asked. I didn't want to ask it. It was as if my mouth was operating on its own. I just wanted the music to start, for Karmen to come back, for the armada to quit sailing so close.

"Charming," he said, "when he knew someone was watching. A big spender. He was always flashing his credit card. But after a few drinks, no sense of humour. If a dancer bumped his chair, it was a personal offense."

"He still around?" I asked.

He shook his head. "Not for quite awhile. His business went under."

Karmen appeared and the dancer left. Karmen's cheeks were flushed and the skin above the top of her dress was red. "Musicians," she said, "do it with rhythm."

The bouzouki player had materialized beside his stool.

"Is there a man with one arm who comes to the restaurant?" I asked.

"The Survivalist," she answered. She gave an exaggerated shudder. "The white race must prepare for the final battle against the inferior races of the world. I don't like him. Some men undress you with their eyes because they want to have fun. I don't think I'd like his idea of fun."

"Does he have a name?"

"I don't know," she said. "I told Harry I don't want him upstairs with me on the balcony."

20

TWO SKINHEADS CAUGHT UP TO ME on the parking lot the next morning. I'd just finished a class on how to organize the argumentative essay. My head was throbbing because I'd stayed up late, drank beer and shared a marijuana cigarette with Karmen. She'd shrieked with laughter when I'd called it that. A reefer, I'd corrected myself, remembering that from some movie. She was laughing so hard, she had to hold on to me to keep from falling down. The two skinheads were big and wore big boots and pants with suspenders. One of them had a swastika tattooed on his head. At least, I thought, when he grows up and changes his mind, he can let his hair grow and cover it up.

"Did you want something?" I asked. One of them had his knee against my truck door and the other was standing so close behind me I could feel his breath on my neck.

"We got a friend wants to talk to you," Swastika Head informed me. It wasn't a question or a request.

"I teach composition," was all that I could think to say. "I don't tutor."

They both thought that was funny. A white van pulled up and the driver opened the sliding door. There are times to protest and there are times to keep your mouth shut and do what you're told. They took my arms just above the elbow and popped me into a back seat.

"Do up your belt," the driver said. "I don't want the cops hassling us."

"What's going on?" I asked.

"Delivery service," Swastika Head replied. "That's us. Pizza, people, it's all the same. Relax. Nobody's going to break your head. He just wants to talk."

We drove out of the city, followed the road north, then turned off onto a dirt road. They hadn't blindfolded me so they obviously didn't care if I knew where we were going. The road was one lane wide with car-size pull offs between the trees. It wound through outcrops and along sudden slopes. Occasionally, we passed a driveway with a quick glimpse of a house. I'd always wondered how the kidnappers in Lebanon had managed to pick people up and carry them away. Now I knew. Broad daylight, in a parking lot, and nobody noticed anything wrong. The few people getting into their cars were busy with their own problems. Like Sharon, I thought. Here and then not here. They could have picked her up like that. It would have been over in an instant.

We pulled up to a cattle gate. There were two men with rifles waiting.

"Is he a Jew?" one of them asked. "Black? Indian? Chinese?"

"He wants to see him. He didn't ask for his pedigree."

"Nowadays, you're never sure," the talker at the gate said. "There's so much mixing of the races. I know niggers whiter than him."

The member of the master race who was giving me the third degree was short, shaped like a watermelon gone soft in the middle. He wore a belt so tight it caused him to bulge below and above. He was wearing a brown, western-style shirt with rearing horses embroidered on it, brown flared polyester pants, cowboy boots and was carrying his rifle slung over his shoulder. His sidekick was dressed identically except he wore a Stetson. He was shaped like a tube. He carried his rifle in one hand.

"He said he wanted to see him," Swastika Head grumbled.

"So you said." The Watermelon took a cellular phone off his belt and made a call. "Show me some ID."

Swastika Head plucked my wallet out of my shirt pocket and showed him my birth certificate, my driver's licence and my library card.

"You're a professor," he said. It wasn't a compliment. I thought he was going to add *a pointy-headed intellectual.* "What kind of name is that?"

"Scandinavian," I replied.

The Tube was thumbing through a booklet filled with drawings. He'd look at a drawing, then study one of my physical characteristics. One page was noses, another was eyes, another was lips. I passed all those. When he got to ears, he held the book out so his partner could see it. I resisted the impulse to reach up and try to feel what was non-Aryan about my ears. They studied the page, my ears, the page again, then decided in my favour and unchained the gate. I got out of the van and went through the gate. They chained it behind me. There was an eight-foot wire fence leading away from both sides of the gate. Swastika Head leaned out of the van. "That's to keep the deer out." They all thought it was a great joke.

We started down the path, one in front, the other behind me.

"The sign on the gate says Survival School," I said.

"That's right," the Watermelon said. He was the talker. The Tube was the looker.

The dirt road ran into a grove of alder. Light was streaming through the branches. The air was heavy and damp. In spite of the light, it felt like rain.

"What do you teach?" I asked. I was asking questions to keep busy. If I quit asking questions, I was going to start shaking with nerves. James Bond was always so cool. In charge. Everything under control. I needed to go to the can. I felt like I was going to have diarrhea.

"Survival," he said. He was breathing noisily from the strain of the slope but his need to talk overcame the whistling of his lungs. "When Armageddon comes, we'll be ready. The Bible tells it all. The dark races will rise up against the white race."

The loony bin, I thought. The patients have taken over and are picking up sane people and taking them to the loony bin. This is nuts. I thought I should just turn around and start back but when I looked over my shoulder and saw Mr. Tube's eyes, it didn't seem like such a good idea. What the fuck have I done? I wondered.

They've got the wrong person. I'd been going home to get some aspirin before my next class. My head was beginning to pound. My doctor had warned me not to drink. According to him I was allergic to alcohol. Having a beer was like someone allergic to mold eating blue cheese. I'd had three beer to drown my sorrow. It had just made me sick and dreadfully sad.

"Africa's a long ways away," I said to keep the conversation going.

The Watermelon glanced back with undisguised contempt. "Immigration is making a third world here. They'll rise up. We'll be ready for them. We have weapons training, living off the land, military tactics, food preservation. I can go into the bush with nothing but a knife and a piece of wire and live for a week. Longer if I have to. We've got supplies here to last more than a year. Food. Medicine. You liberals will be begging to get in here but it won't do you any good. Mexicans coming from the south. Turbans flying in."

"Don't waste your breath," the Tube said. His voice was thin and reedy. "He's too educated to understand."

We came around a small outcrop into a space in front of some log buildings dug into the ground. They looked like bunkers. A dozen or so people in camouflage outfits were practising a martial art. An instructor was standing in front. He would make a move and they'd imitate him. Most of them looked as if they probably were wearing pacemakers under their outfits. A couple of the women had wrinkles deeper than the Grand Canyon. At the end of each move, they all yelled together. Unless Armageddon hurried up, they'd all be dead of natural causes.

My two companions led me to a building with a screen door. They stopped there and a voice shouted come in. The Watermelon opened the door for me and motioned me forward.

There was a man sitting in front of a computer. He glanced my way. "Thank you for coming. My name's Daniel." I stayed where I was and didn't say anything. The two goons had left. "Sit down. There's no need to look so resentful. You were asking about me. I don't like people asking anybody else about me. It gets people talking. I'd rather you came to see me directly." He turned to face me. He had one arm and, I realized, an American accent, although I couldn't place it. A touch of the Midwest maybe.

Behind him was a large painting of Christ, a cross and an American flag. Pastor John wouldn't have recognized this Christ. There was no suffering in his face or posture. No crown of thorns. This was Christ as Rambo. A Christ who lifted weights, a Christ you could follow over the top into machine-gun fire.

"I wasn't really looking," I said. "I started to look but then I gave it up. People didn't understand that I'd quit looking."

"Momentum," he said. "A basic law of physics. That's the way things are. You push a stone down a mountainside. You didn't expect to start an avalanche."

"What avalanche?"

"There isn't one yet. That's why I wanted to have this little talk. Just you and me. So you didn't need to ask questions." He thought for a moment. Behind him there were rows of rifles on the wall.

"Looks like you're going to start a war."

He laughed. Handsome, I thought. A Kennedy kind of face, the kind that would show up well on television. A kind of confidence that would reassure. If he lost the arm in Vietnam, he had it all. Except for the eyes. It was as if the irises were frozen in place. I had the feeling he could laugh like that and put his arm around your shoulders at the same time as he was sending you to your death. What the hell have I gotten into? I wondered. I didn't bargain on this. This was the kind of thing my wife, with her lack of limits, with her plunging into whatever came her way, stumbled into. She knew things about the city I had never dreamed of. Late at night, when we still slept together, still spoke, we'd lie in bed and she'd tell me dark gossip, of the candy men delivering coke and hash to parties, of group rape in private jets, of innocent-looking homes where ritual sacrifice was practised, of terrorists on the run living country lives, of marijuana plantations wired with booby traps.

"Not us," he said. "We don't start anything. But we're prepared to finish it."

"A friend of mine's gone missing," I risked saying.

127

"So I've heard."

"But she's okay. Everything's fine. End of story. It was all a misunderstanding."

Our conversation was punctuated by the cries of the people practising martial arts. There was a steady rhythm to it, a coordinated anger. They had obviously been in training for awhile. No stragglers hi-ing when they should have been ho-ing.

He saw me listening. "They're going to be ready."

"No one survives Armageddon. The world ends in flames," I said.

"Out of the ashes, the phoenix rises," he replied.

This wasn't a conversation I wanted to have. I couldn't win it. And baiting a bear in his own den was stupid beyond measure.

"We have a lot of work to do," he said. "We don't want anyone paying attention to us. Nobody coming snooping around. We practise discipline here. No posturing for the media." I waited, not moving, feeling once again like I was back in grade school, terrified of moving even enough to make the chair squeak for fear of the consequences. "Your friend's not here. We've had nothing to do with her leaving."

"I didn't think you did," I replied. "I'd just heard that you used to spend time with her husband."

"No discipline," he said and his face shifted, became narrower, harder, matching his eyes. "A loose cannon. We don't need people like that. They cause trouble. He isn't welcome here and he knows that. That's what I want to tell you. He's out. There's no use looking here for him."

"I wasn't looking for him," I said. "It's Sharon who's missing."

"What's she to you?"

"A friend," I said.

"But you hope for more? A bit young, isn't she?" He took some sheets of paper off his desk. "College professor. Married man. Does your wife approve?" He put the papers down. "That's the way it is, isn't it? None of us want to get older. A last fling."

"She's not here?" I said, feeling affronted.

"No," he replied. "We haven't got her locked away somewhere. Would you like to search?"

"Are you saying she's never been here?" It was a shot in the dark. Most of the time when I shoot my mouth off, I never even come close to the target. But his eyes jerked to the left, then back, and his smile was forced. Oh, Christ, what have I done now, I thought, but the anger was making me reckless. In spite of his sheets of paper he couldn't know much. Whatever he had must have been gathered quickly, with a phone call or two. "Why was she here?"

"She wanted to buy a pistol."

"And?"

"We don't sell weapons. That would be illegal. Besides, we don't want to be drawn into anyone's personal problems."

"Maybe she wanted to take up target shooting?"

He looked at me with contempt. "No," he said. "She wanted a little gun for her handbag or her pocket. Something she could carry around. Guns like that are no good for hitting anything over six feet away. After that you could miss an elephant. They need to be used up close. Shove it in somebody's face, up against their chest. Little pieces like that are for friends and acquaintances. Or people who were."

"Like?"

"That would be speculation," he said. "We deal in facts."

Like the book of non-Aryan noses and ears, I thought, but the anger was folding back on itself. "You brought me up here to tell me this?"

He shrugged. "Better to get it from the horse's mouth. Now you know. If everything doesn't work out, there's no need to mention us."

"And if I don't believe you?"

"There were other ways of handling this," he said. "Those fellows who brought you here. They could have robbed you. It happens all the time. A robbery that gets out of hand. A month or two in the hospital."

They dropped me off at the parking lot gate. I walked over to my truck. My briefcase was gone but there was a note under the windshield wiper saying that I could pick it up from security. The guard gave it to me after I signed a receipt.

"Victoria's a great place to live," he said. "That wouldn't happen anywhere else. Leave your briefcase beside your vehicle and someone turns it in."

"Thanks," I said and, as I was walking away, I could hear him thinking *absent-minded professors* and see him shaking his head.

21

"WHAT ABOUT THE DARK-HAIRED GIRL? Have you found her yet?" Shrinko asked.

"I'm not looking," I said. "I gave up."

"No more dreams of the sarcophagus? No more nightmares of people digging in the garden late at night burying something?"

"No," I said but I was lying again. I was always lying. Big lies, little lies. A crooked path. Zigzagging my way through life. I felt sick again. "Yes," I admitted. I wanted to throw up. From somewhere deep inside, as if I was full of poison. The helplessness and the rage towards the skinheads was part of it, my sense of being unable to defend myself. The screaming was starting again inside my head. It was never more than that. Just screaming. Like someone screaming and screaming and unable to stop.

"Tell me about your wife."

"My wife," I replied, "I don't want to talk about my wife. I should have put her on a cruise ship, given the captain a thousand dollars and told him to drop her off when the money ran out. My saying no to a cruise of the Baltic was what set her off. I'd been trying to get the mortgage paid, save enough for a new car and put something into an RRSP so we wouldn't end up eating cat food and pickle sandwiches after I retired."

"What have you got against cruises?"

"I've got nothing against cruises. Don't you start. I'm not here to discuss cruises."

"How do you feel about holidays? Do you think people have the right to go on holidays?"

"It has nothing to do with how I feel. It has to do with paying the bills. No money, no holiday." I could feel the irritation starting. He was pushing my buttons and I knew he was pushing my buttons but there seemed to be no way to stop it. The anger was too close to the surface, too intense. I wasn't at the shouting stage but the anger was there and the sense of injustice. You would think that after two years, I'd have quit being upset about it. "We never have any money. The college doesn't pay all that well. I've always tried to make more by giving speeches and readings and workshops. I told her no cruise. Then I went up-island to give a speech. Do you think I want to spend Saturday afternoon making speeches and eating rubber chicken? I do it because it pays five hundred plus expenses. It's called being able to pay for the plastic. I made a two-hour drive, I ate the chicken, I made the speech, I shook hands and smiled like hell, grabbed the cheque and drove two hours back."

I got back about seven. All the blinds were down. That's a bad sign. When all the blinds are down and there are no lights on, she's usually into her Holy Mary, Mother of God routine. I could hear the Gregorian chants before I reached the back door. Inside, every light was off and there were more candles than you'd find in a Russian cathedral at Easter. Every dish in the house had a candle and every candle was lit. Jesus was in all his regular places. My wife was on her knees in the kitchen, in front of one of the statues. She was wrapped in a white sheet and running a rosary through her hands. I'd never seen her in a white sheet before.

I turned off the Gregorian chants, then came into the kitchen and tried to be casual. I said, "Hi, how's your day been?"

"Mother Teresa is saying penance," she said.

"Any chance of getting some supper?" When you step through the front door into cuckoo land, the best thing you can do is act normal. Maybe, I told myself, she's got a part in a play or something. I started blowing out candles. Our insurance policy doesn't even allow smoking and every surface in the house looked like it was on fire. If I just stay cool and act as if everything's copesetic maybe she'll click into scrambled eggs, toast and coffee. "A virgin," she said. "Tempted but pure."

"Good for Mother T," I said. "Does she know that the poor have to eat? Did she remember to buy groceries for the starving? Some canned sardines, perhaps."

"She suffers," she said. Her voice was so full of pain that I snapped on the light. The rosary was a piece of barbed wire she'd braided into a circle. There was blood running through her fingers and down her arms. I'll never forget that. The white sheet and the bright red blood and the look on her face that told me she wasn't going to snap back to having dinner while we watched *Wheel of Fortune*.

The only person I could think of to call was our GP, who called a psychologist he knew. I even drove her to the private hospital. That, it turned out, was like driving myself to meet Godzilla the Hun. I had a premonition, though. All the way there, I kept easing back on the gas pedal and thinking about turning around but then I'd look at the bloody J-cloths I'd wrapped around her hands and taped in place with masking tape. I'd step on the pedal again. She wasn't drooling but her eyes looked like broken yolks and she kept rocking back and forth. Every so often she'd yell no. I'm not talking whisper, I'm not talking normal, I'm talking about screaming it. The first time she did it, I slammed on the brakes and nearly got rear ended. Then she undid the seat belt and started to bang her head on the dash. There I was trying to drive with one hand, trying to hold her in her seat with my other hand. Her bandages were coming unwound and she was getting blood all over herself, on me, on the truck. Sit still and shut up, I was yelling. She tried to jump out of the truck. I had to stop and do her seat belt up again. By the time we got to the hospital, I wished I'd let her jump.

She's conveniently forgotten about that, about my calling the GP and driving her to the hospital. After they taped up her hands properly, a shrink talked to her. He wanted me to stay but I wasn't having any. I went to the washroom and got some of the blood off, then went out to the truck. I didn't want anyone seeing me there and thinking it was me who'd gone round the bend. Everybody's suspicious of writers, anyway. Where I come from, everyone knows that if a shrink touches you, you start to drool and shuffle.

I read my insurance policy while I waited. I figured that after they had their talk, she'd come back and we'd go home. Instead, a shrink nurse rapped on the window and I rolled it down a crack.

"You're wanted inside," she said and waited to be sure I came.

My wife had agreed to stay, the psychologist announced.

If she needs a holiday, I said, we can go stay at the Flamingo Motel for a few days. They've got a weekend special. That should perk her up.

The psychologist sat and stared at me. Well, maybe that's not such a hot idea, I admitted. He wanted to know how things had been. I told him about her trying to smother me one night with a pillow after she thought I was asleep. Since then I'd been sleeping in the spare room and locking the door. Bad PMS, I thought. Like slamming the cupboard doors and breaking the good china. Four Petit Point cups and saucers we'd been given when we got married. Not like it was every minute of every day. It was more like when the TV starts to go and you don't want to admit you're going to have to buy a new one. The picture's fine, except once in a while it scrambles and you curse it and say you'll trade it in but then it's fine for a day, maybe a week before it does it again and then the edges give a little but not much so you can't watch and you get so used to watching it, it's not until someone comes over and says something about it that you realize how bad it is.

I'm not the most secure person in the world so all the time this conversation was going on, I was worrying somebody might see me. This hospital is an old green mansion on three or four lots. There's a high fence and lots of flowers. It's the kind of place Cabinet ministers or their wives go. Discreet's the operative word. Anybody sees you here and they're not supposed notice so I know I shouldn't feel like I want to put a paper bag over my head. But it's like when I go bowling and the people from the retarded school are there playing five pin. I've played five pin ever since I was a kid. But they take up three lanes and there are only four. The clerk offers me lane four and I think about it but I always say no, no thanks, I'll try tenpin today. I'm over that now, not the retarded thing, but worrying about people knowing I've been to see an m.c. and am seeing a shrink.

My wife being in the hospital made me nervous but I visited her every evening. I didn't want to go but then I thought if it was me, I'd want somebody to come and visit. I'd microwave supper and then I'd drive over and park three blocks away so nobody'd notice my truck. At first, I was really uptight but then I relaxed and talked to some of the other patients. I thought it'd be like something out of *The Snake Pit*. But they all just seemed like ordinary people who couldn't take any more. Somebody had piled on the last straw. There was the kid who'd fried himself on LSD and kept dumping his meals on his head. And the guy who kept appearing in the hallway naked. There was the attractive chick who seemed perfectly normal except she kept whipping off her top in public places. The one I felt sorriest for was the kid who was always on the phone crying and saying, "Daddy, Daddy, why don't you love me anymore?" It took me awhile to clue into the fact that no one was on the other end.

Nobody was chained to the wall. You might think that's funny but when you first have to deal with something, you don't even know what you think. When I was a kid, that's the way everybody talked about being crazy. People in strait jackets and chains screaming and yelling and after that it just never came up. So it sits there like a file that's been put away and then something happens and you bring it out and all this stuff is in it that's thirty, forty years old and you have to update it. But it's not that easy. It's not just scraps of paper, it's the truth as you've learned it. Unlearning is hard. I see that with my students. They've got bad habits somebody's taught them. Even when I tell them to change how they do something, it's not that easy. They've got to work at it.

Nearly everybody was stoned. They all had the stoned shuffle. Most of them sat around staring at nothing in particular. When I talked to them, I kept thinking they were like people who'd got badly sunburned. Everything that touched them hurt and they needed dope to stop the pain.

At the end of the third week, when my wife was feeling better, not laughing better, but she knew who she was and was starting to comb her hair and put on some make-up, we went into the lounge to watch TV. All the seats were taken so we went to a room with big bow windows that had a pool table. There was a ping-pong table fitted over the pool table. If we'd wanted, we could have had an attendant take the ping-pong table off but ping-pong seemed a better choice so we got the paddles and a ball out of the cupboard.

It felt like when we first met and I'd go over to visit her. We'd be in her basement rec room and her parents would be upstairs but you could hear them listening. There wasn't really anything to do in her rec room except play ping-pong. We batted a ball back and forth. The ball quit bouncing for too long and her mother came looking for pickles or something.

The wife-to-be was a serious competitor. The whole family was like that. None of them could stand losing. We'd start out batting the ball around, as I said, but then she'd start flipping the ball into corners and I'd give it a little backhand and she'd say let's have a real game. We were pretty evenly matched. She'd win one. I'd win one. No lopsided scores. She kept track of them, too. I never could remember who was up on games. She knew exactly. About a month after our first date, she said, let's make it interesting, let's play for supper out. I said sure, why not, and we settled on a restaurant both of us could afford. All she had to do was ask me to take her to the restaurant but that wasn't what it was all about. It had something to do with winning and losing. I already knew that when her family played Monopoly, her father wouldn't let her or her kid brother go to bed until he had all the money. Sometimes, he made them stay up all night.

I'm not competitive, not like that. But I don't like to lose. We were playing two games out of three. She won the first. Twenty-one, nineteen. I won the second. Twenty, twenty-one. She was better on control. I had a better serve. We played the third game to eighteen all. Then she put down her paddle and pulled her sweater over her head and undid her bra and took it off. I missed the first two serves completely and lost the last point on the first return.

Anyway, this night there were no games like that being played. At least, not by us. She was doing great just to hit the ball when I tapped it over to her. We'd been there for ten minutes when two men came in with one of the women patients. The guys looked as if they were born to be hanged. Their faces were battered and scarred but it wasn't that, it was their shifty eyes. The one had a red, drinker's face, with veins spreading out from his nose. The other's face was the colour of old piano keys.

The two of them seemed taken aback at seeing us there. I thought they were going to leave but there really was no place to go except the lounge and that was full. The one with the accordion set it down and took it out of its case. He sat on a chair, pulled the straps over his shoulders and began to play. All the time he was getting ready, they were looking at the woman, then at us, then at each other. When they looked at each other, it was as if there was an understanding between them, if you know what I mean. They didn't need to say anything. A jerk of the head, the nudge of a shoulder, the tap of a toe was enough. The accordion player wiggled his thumb at the woman and his partner put his arms around her and began to dance.

He wasn't a dancer. I'm no dancer but I'm better than that. He stepped to the right, then back, pulling her after him. She wasn't dressed in a hospital dressing gown but in a Japanese kimono. I couldn't have guessed her age. Not young, not old. Somewhere between thirty and fifty. If thirty, she looked old. If fifty, she looked young. The kimono was quite elegant. I'd never seen anything like it. It was gold with a peacock's open tail reaching all the way around. She might have been a dancer but you couldn't tell. She was so drugged, she just followed her partner's steps, dragging her feet in that loose, disconnected way. None of them said a word. All the time she was dancing, she was smiling at something.

It's hard to get it exactly right. The feeling that I was watching two cunning animals hunting. If you were someplace, downtown late or at a fair, and you caught them looking at you, you'd check your wallet. They weren't the kind to jump you. They'd wait for somebody who was drunk and stumbling, or lying on the ground, and then they'd rifle his pockets and if he didn't have any money on him, kick him in the ribs.

The kimono was expensive, elegant, but the red-faced man was dressed in a suit that looked as if it had come off the rack at Goodwill. It was too large and too long. He had the cuffs of the jacket and the pants rolled back. The dancer was wearing mismatched pants and jacket, both checks. The jacket was too tight and when he raised his arms, the whole jacket rose.

All the time they danced, the woman never looked at him. She held her head to the left, staring at the floor. She moved slowly, one step for two beats. Gradually, her partner steered her behind my wife and then, as if he assumed I was part of the same conspiracy, he let go with one hand, pulled her kimono apart and put his hand inside so he could grasp her breast. As they shuffled about, I could see his hand moving like a rat inside the material. I wondered if perhaps he was her husband or her boyfriend, but the accordion player stopped after awhile and they changed places. He, too, once he had danced to the blind spot behind my wife, slipped his hand inside the housecoat and then, when he'd had enough of that, put his hand between her legs.

"Maybe we should go," my wife said. Her face was white and strained.

I made a small motion with my head towards the dancers, then looked at her and served. We played for another twenty minutes. The dancers finally left. Once they were gone, we stopped playing. I took my wife's arm. The drugs and her illness had made her unsteady.

"We should have stopped playing long ago," I said. "But I didn't want to leave her alone with them."

"Why not?" Shrinko said, bringing me back to the room. I'd lost him, drifted away into the memory, could hear the ping-pong ball, see the shifty eyes and the cunning faces. Feel my wife's weight on my arm and feeling sorry for her, for how things had gone wrong.

"I don't know," I said. "It just didn't seem right. Two of them and her."

22

THE CAFÉ HAD SUNK DEEPER, slipped off the shelf where it usually sat and drifted farther into the abyss. It was darker, colder. Staff moved about by touch and habit, like blind fish, their yellow and green faces appearing and disappearing. Evelyn brought me muffins and orange juice and heavy silence. At this deeper level, it was harder to breathe, harder to sit up straight, to reach out.

Demytro materialized from the darkness, sat down heavily on the chair opposite me. Evelyn brought him weak tea with milk and two teaspoons of sugar.

"I sell the best coffee," he complained, "but I can't drink it. I'm spitting blood some more. You want to teach your kids something? Teach them not to worry. It does no good." He took four large pills from a bottle and washed them down. "I hate it."

"I always thought of you as solid as a rock. You've got loyal customers, efficient staff, an excellent chef."

"I worry. About everything. At night I worry about not enough customers. Then I worry about too many customers. I worry about the rent going up. About the owner selling the building. About the girls taking another job. Maybe my chef wants to have his own restaurant again. I want everybody to get well but not too fast. When they get well, they leave." As he listed his worries, he counted on his fingers. He looked terribly sad, and it was the inconsolable sadness of a good man caught in a dilemma, like a cancer specialist who both hoped for a miracle cure and feared it.

"I live upstairs," he said, pointing to the ceiling, "like a bear in a cave. Here all day. There all night."

"You could rent a bigger place," I suggested. "Hire a manager."

"Moving." He shook his head as if he was seeing something in the middle distance. "It's not good. The staff get ideas. Even one block and there are customers who won't come anymore. Every day they come, like sheep. You change and they are confused. You would come." The thought seemed to make him happy. "You always come."

"It's good here," I told him. "I can sit as long as I need."

"My regulars," he said with a touch of pride, "they are like family. But they don't like surprises. Once, I changed the soup of the day. People were offended. I learned my lesson. Let people have their habits. Break one habit and you break everything." He breathed deeply and sipped his tea. "Most of all, I worry about the banker. Last year I told him, give me your jacket. I work most of the time for the bank."

I had not thought of him capable of such passion, of such resentment. "Christ," I said to console him, "drove the moneychangers out of the temple."

He shook his massive head. "The next day they came back. The Bible says usury is evil. The Koran says no interest. The bankers make their own laws. We should give all parents tests. If they might create a banker, we sterilize them."

I was used to seeing him organizing the staff, helping when the café was busy, chopping fruit and vegetables for the chef, taking cash. He was always friendly, making a point of saying hello to customers as he passed a table. He seemed placid, unflappable, ballast keeping everything in place. Seeing him like this created in me a feeling of panic, as if the café would rise to the surface and tear apart, leaving nothing but bits of debris floating on the water.

"Sometimes, I have nightmares about the ferries not running. No strawberries, no grapes, no pineapple. I have to go to the door and say there is nothing to eat. I cannot multiply loaves and fishes."

"But you could call someone for help. Ask them to bring what you need." I was thinking about my wife saying that nowadays anyone can be Christ, all it takes is a telephone and twenty-four-hour delivery service. Instead of loaves and fishes it's pizza, double cheese, with a Coke.

"Never. I say I can't perform miracles. They will have to find food for themselves."

"But you hire these young women. You give them jobs. You make a place for them."

"Yes, yes," he said impatiently, "but what am I able to give them? Minimum wage. I should have led a better life. I should be more successful so I can pay twenty dollars an hour. Then they could live in nice houses instead of run-down apartments. When we are young, we only think of ourselves. We should think of what we can do for others."

"You have a good heart," I said.

He smiled at that and sighed. "And you, do you worry?"

"All the time."

"You see. How little someone like me knows. You come here all the time. Someone tells me you are a professor, a writer. You are a great success. What have you to worry about except how to spend your money? Except," he paused, remembering, "the girls all agreed you were very unhappy."

"I'm surprised they noticed me."

"Oh, the girls notice everyone. After we lock the door and pull down the blinds, they discuss everything."

"You're not supposed to call them girls anymore. They will have you thrown in jail for sexually harassing them."

He raised his eyebrows and rolled his eyes. "When I was eighteen, they would have been women. But then I also thought I was a man. Now, if they are under forty, they are girls. I will trade them places and they can call me a boy all they want. Except Sharon. She wasn't a girl. She was a woman. Probably since she was twelve. You should have asked her out."

I picked up my orange juice and sipped it and avoided his eyes.

"You always left her a bigger tip than any of the others. They even arranged for her to serve you when you sat in someone else's section."

"She was too young," I protested. "If I was younger . . ." I waved my hand to indicate how hopeless such an idea was.

"She'd have gone out with you if you'd asked. They all discussed it. I heard her tell Evelyn you were very sad but very nice. She thought you might take her to the theatre. You don't drink. She liked that. And you don't smoke. You read a lot. She even read some of the books you told her about. Once, you said you were going to the opera. She thought you were going to ask her to go with you."

"Yes," I said, "it's true. I had two tickets in my pocket. But then I thought why should she go out with me and I couldn't think of a single good reason." That had been nearly a year ago. When I hadn't had enough nerve to ask her, I gave away the opera tickets to two of my students. But the ballet tickets, which had been for Thursday night, were still in my pocket, like good-luck tokens. "A father fixation," I said, repeating what the m.c. had told me when I'd mentioned Sharon. This was after he'd said that my wife had the right to satisfy her emotional needs, that I had no right to stand in the way of her sexual satisfaction but when I mentioned that I found Sharon attractive, he said that I shouldn't have anything to do with her.

Demytro gave a grunt of exasperation. "Too much brains," he said. "If a woman finds you attractive, don't look a gift horse in the mouth. I once had a beautiful woman fall in love with me because she thought I looked like a big, clumsy bear. Who am I to argue? She was a channeler and thought she'd been a bear in another life. Should I have said to her this isn't a good enough reason? Look here, beautiful woman, you've got to have a better reason for wanting to go to bed with me?"

Me, I was thinking, the whole time, she would have gone out with me long ago if only I had asked her. All the times I'd come for a cappuccino and she'd make it as soon as I came in the door and put chocolate on it and set it down in front of me without a word. And me feeling so bad after an hour in the ring with the tag team, an hour of hearing how everything about me was no good and had to be changed until I felt there was no me left. And after awhile, when being submerged in Pachelbel made me feel a little better, she'd come back and ask if she could get me something and would wait as I struggled with a decision. And when I couldn't make it, when even deciding on a sandwich seemed like a crisis, she'd say that was okay, she'd get the chef to make something nice. Thinking about it, my eyes stung with tears.

She'd been right, of course. For a long time, I had wanted to say something to her, to ask her to go to the art gallery or the theatre, instead of always going by myself, but not knowing how to ask because the tag team made me feel no decent human being would want anything to do with me. And that, I realized now, wasn't an accident, that was a therapeutic strategy to keep me a mule.

I wanted to ask him about what Evelyn had said, about Sharon going off with someone, but then I remembered my promise to say nothing, that Sharon didn't want anyone to know. She'd call when she was ready. Also, there was this men's thing, I'd asked her out and she'd said yes, then stood me up. I didn't want him to know about that. It was a bit as if I'd failed some test of manhood.

"A younger woman," the m.c. had said, "won't solve anything. All that will happen is that you'll get old and she'll still be young. She'll be at her peak of sexuality and you'll be finished. She'll want to go out and you'll want to stay home and sleep. All you need is one woman. You've got one." And when he said that I thought of that one woman, coiled in a corner of the house, waiting to strike.

Demytro had gone to see about fresh strawberries. Evelyn appeared to ask if I wanted anything else. While she waited, she pulled absent-mindedly at a thread. It came loose, opening up the seam. She gasped and stared open-mouthed at the havoc she'd created.

23

"HI, JOE," GLORIA SAID to the janitor. He was short, dark, Portuguese and suspicious.

We were standing at the front of her apartment building. Joe was picking up glass and putting it into a plastic bucket. Someone had broken a six pack of beer bottles at the entrance. He looked at us as if it was our fault.

"Have you heard anything about that girl on the tenth floor?"

Joe barely glanced at her. He'd cut his thumb and was sucking on it. He spit out the blood.

"Maybe it's not a good time to ask him," I suggested quietly. Gloria had called me and said Joe had reappeared. He had two or three extra jobs the owner of the building didn't know about and he was gone more than he was around. I tried to tell her I wasn't looking any more but since I'd talked to Demytro I didn't feel so rejected and I wasn't so sure of Evelyn's information. Maybe, I thought, I just didn't fit her image of someone who could be romantically involved. All her novels had tall dark men dressed in open-necked shirts or fancy suits.

Gloria laughed. "It's never a good time for Joe. Ask him to change a light bulb in the hallway and he stomps away like you've insulted his grandmother." She pointed to me. "He's a friend of hers."

Joe jumped up, jabbed his finger at me. "You sent flowers," he said accusingly. "She no like that."

"What flowers?" I asked.

"You sent." He said it like he was confirming his first statement. In Portuguese it was, I suspected, more grammatically complex, something like, *You probably were the one who sent them* and then, *yes, you did send them, you're the type.*

"What flowers, Joe?" Gloria was being sweet, helpless. Twelve and trusting.

"You no have nothing to do with him." He made a horizontal cutting motion with the flat of his hand.

Sending flowers was now a crime, I thought. Even the Portuguese are into feminism. Flowers were a sign of subjugation. Tomorrow we'll have feminists fire bombing flower stores and cutting the heads off daffodils in Beacon Hill Park.

There are times it doesn't pay to deny guilt. "Did she like the flowers?" I asked.

"She gave me for wife. Makes trouble."

God, even Portuguese women don't want flowers. Buying chocolates will be good for six to twelve months at hard labour. Opening doors for a woman on campus was enough to get you spit on. The last time I'd held a door open for a young thing in black lipstick and not much else, she said, "I can open my own fucking door, Gramps. Don't patronize me."

"Your wife doesn't like flowers?"

"She said, 'Joe, what you up to? You keep broom to yourself.' She think I do something. Too many women by self in apartment. Cause trouble. Joe no bring more flowers. Throw in garbage."

"I paid for a dozen roses," I said, guessing that clichés were still rampant.

"Ha," Joe exclaimed, delighted, "you get cheated. Six."

"How often did he send flowers, Joe?" Gloria sounded angry, as though she believed him and I was in big trouble. Ask my wife, I thought, she'll tell you. Not a chance, not even if you hit him with a hammer, she'd say and laugh all day at the idea. He hasn't got a romantic bone in his body.

"Some peoples have no money, no money for bread, no money for kids, no money for anything."

"Men in love do stupid things," Gloria explained.

"Not me," Joe said. "I took wife olives, cheese. Gave her parents goat."

"Too much education," Gloria said. She tapped the side of her head and they both looked at me.

"All that money," Joe said. He let his breath out in a hiss of disapproval. "Every Wednesday."

"This week?"

"No. Stopped. Two weeks." He turned his attention to me. "Why no come and knock on door, say I . . ." He stopped.

"Bob," Gloria coached. She obviously had had discussions with him before.

"Bob," Joe repeated. "I, Bob, love. I want . . ." He stopped and struggled with the word and finally settled for a shrug neither of us understood. "Why you with him?"

"Cousin," Gloria said, shocking me. Joe nodded but didn't look convinced. He obviously had some experience with cousins. "We need to get his money back for the roses. They only sent half. What was the name of the florist?"

"I no know," he said. Then he snapped his fingers. "I keep boxes."

And he did. We went to the underground garage where I'd helped Gloria store her flea-market stock. Joe unlocked a storage room full of boxes. Boxes of every kind piled to the ceiling. As we waited at the door, there was a sudden bang that startled me.

"What's that?" I said.

Gloria pointed to one side. There was a hole in the ceiling. Below it was a metal dumpster. As I watched, a full garbage bag came hurtling out.

"Renters never know when need boxes," Joe called. "Fifty cents each. People move. They come to Joe, say where I get boxes, Joe? Joe got boxes."

Gloria nudged me. "Give him fifty cents," she whispered.

I dug around in my pocket and found two quarters and some lint. I kept the lint and gave him the quarters. He stuffed them into his pocket. He might be ethnic but the NDP would never get him to vote Socialist, no matter what happened. Free enterprise

146

all the way. He reached into a pile and came back with a florist's box. "You want all of them?" he asked hopefully. I suddenly doubted he'd thrown away the flowers.

"No, that's fine." Outside, I said, "I'm your cousin?"

"He doesn't understand friend. The idea doesn't exist. Man, woman, fucky, fucky, or whatever he says."

Gloria agreed to phone the florist and pretend that the flowers had been sent to her. The clerk said the flowers had been paid for in Regina, that payment was in cash and he'd explained this before. If she felt she was being harassed, she should call the police.

"If you got anonymous roses once a week, how'd you feel?" I asked.

"Paranoid," she replied. "I'd feel someone was watching me. Stalking me."

"Enough to want a gun?"

"Maybe," she said. "I wouldn't take any lonely walks and I'd be watching over my shoulder to see if anyone was behind me. You said you sent them. Did you?"

"Too cheap," I said. "I'm with Joe. Olives, cheese. If she's really hot stuff, maybe a goat."

"She had two secret admirers. You and the rose man. She seems to have been popular."

Not so secret, I thought. I wondered if anyone at the café thought I might be responsible for Sharon's disappearance. That's all I'd need. Half an hour of digging and they'd have my medical records. Medical records are about as confidential as house taxes. I could see the headline now. "Drooling professor abducts bicyclist for love slave."

"A lot of money," I said, thinking of what I had left after my wife went shopping every month. To her a credit card that wasn't over its limit was a crime against humanity. "Roses used to be a dollar apiece. What are they now?"

Gloria grimaced. "They're not on my shopping list."

"I may be an old fart," I said, "but I'm not a rich old fart."

"You've got to quit doing that," she said. "Negative self talk. Quit putting yourself down all the time. It's neurotic."

"My wife says someday, if the world's lucky, I'll be a DWEM."

"Dead white European male," Gloria said. "It's not particularly original. It goes with dinks and yuppies."

"Does your family kiss snakes?" I asked.

"No," she said, treating it like any other normal question, "but my former in-laws do. They're southern Baptists in Louisiana and they kiss snakes for the Lord. They stand up on stage and hang them around their necks. Why?"

"I don't know," I said. "It just occurred to me."

Half the house, the m.c. said. Half of everything. Stay married or you'll lose half of it all. Maybe more. You'll have to sell your house. Those gardens you've worked so hard on. All those plants you've nurtured. The California poppy, the daylilies, the bleeding heart, your two hundred tulips. Somebody else will get them. He sounded like a snake kisser himself. When he was making this speech, he got out of his chair and raised his right arm towards the ceiling. I kept looking behind me for the multitude he was addressing but the multitude was me. Marriage is a business, he said, a legal contract. You've got to think of your profit and loss. Think of the bottom line. I'd seen his wife's bottom line. It was pretty hefty. A private-school girl in love with chocolate. Mater and pater, I'd heard, were worth a bundle. When they went to that big condominium in the sky, she'd get it all as an only child. Victoria's a small city. You eventually hear everything. Which of us, I wondered, was he lecturing?

I knew, though, what he was talking about. One time, I bought a pile of top-quality silver plate at an auction. Bowls, candy dishes, serving dishes. Not the thin stuff but solid, heavy triple plate, decorated with birds and flowers and grapevines. The kind of stuff you pay for with a credit card because you don't carry around enough cash, at least not if you've got a brain in your head. I polished them, set them out at an antique show. I hoped to sell a piece at a time over a period of months. A few people thumbed them so I had to keep a cloth handy and give them a wipe. Then this guy, about ten years younger than me, comes along and stops cold, goes white and stands like a deadhead in the middle of the crowd swarming by. I thought he was having a heart attack or something and then he swallows two or three times so I can hear it and finally breaks his feet loose from the floor and comes over. He picks up the big bowl.

"These belong to me," he says and his voice isn't right. It's high and sounds like it's going to break. Right away I'm thinking his house has been robbed and I'm trying to remember where I put the receipts.

"I got them at an auction," I protested.

"Yeah," he says and that's all he can manage. It's the same sound as a hook makes when you're prying it out of a fish's jaw.

A nut, I think. At antique sales there are lots of nuts. They want to tell you their life stories. They're usually an antique themselves and they start off with when I was a girl. It's nearly always widows who've worked their husbands to death and are living off the avails. They say, "I had one just like that," and then they start to drag me through their childhood when they walked to school uphill both ways. This guy was too young for a life story. From the strained look on his face, he was still carrying someone around on his back.

He put the bowl down. "She wouldn't let me have them. She insisted she get them. If she didn't get them, she'd keep me from seeing the kids on weekends. I told her if she changed her mind, I'd buy them back."

"You want them?" I asked. I was already lowering the price.

"Yeah."

"Should I wrap them up?"

"I can't pay that for them. I haven't got it. The bloodsucker gets most of it."

"You'll take them all?" He agreed and I took a cheque.

"It's no good right now," he said, "but it'll be good at the end of the month. I swear to God. Here's my card."

After he left, my wife sidled over. "He took it all. What a hit."

"It was his," I said, "I took ten per cent over what I paid."

She went hysterical. "You had him by the balls," she said loud enough to make people turn and look. "You could have made him pay anything you wanted. You should have jacked the price."

I couldn't have done it. I'd seen him when he froze and how he looked when he picked up the bowl. I knew it wasn't what it cost but that they were his. I was thinking about the prize irises in my garden. If I lost the house, I already had a plan for liberating the flowers. If I couldn't get them out, I'd fertilize the beds with Weed and Feed.

His wife was into revenge. I'd already seen revenge at the flea market. There's no logic to what people do when they want to get even. One day after I'd got my display set up, I was cruising the other tables before the public got in. We always did that, buying and selling from each other, looking for pieces for our own collections or for bargains in our specialties. Suddenly there was a rush. The dealers converged on a table like piranha on bloody beef. A one-timer in green polyester pants was selling jewellery. Mounds of it. The dealers were grabbing whatever they could hold. I did the same. Afterwards, I felt guilty, but when a feeding frenzy starts, it's contagious. Mob greed.

This was real jewellery. Not the nickel-and-dime shit the stores gyp kids with at Christmas or Valentine's Day. Real jewellery, real stones, antique pieces. Eighteen and twenty-one k. gold. English silver. The highest price I paid was two-fifty for a pendant. That's two dollars and fifty cents. The table was cleared in three minutes. All that was left was the white tablecloth and that was on the floor.

As she was leaving, I said, "Why'd you give it away?"

"It's my mother-in-law's. She's gone into an old folk's home. She collected it all her life and I hate her guts."

"What about you?" I asked Gloria. All the time I'd been thinking, we were walking. Melissa was staying with a neighbour who had a kid the same age. "Do you hate your ex?"

"Which one?" she said. She took a deep breath and pulled her arms against her sides. "Eenie, meenie, minie, mo."

"Seriously," I said.

"Not the first one," she replied. "He's too far in the past. I just feel sad when I think about him. The second one." She stopped and turned away and I could see how painful it was for her. She didn't look angry, just confused, the way a child might who was being punished and didn't know for what. "When Melissa can't have things that other kids have and when I have to call people and make excuses about why I can't pay the bills. Mostly I hate me."

Are we all crazy? I wondered. She's young, attractive, seems sensible, has a sense of humour, is intelligent but she twice married men who weren't right for her, or her for them. She even married someone whose relatives kiss snakes to prove their faith. What, I wondered, remembering what the m.c. had said about any woman who would have anything to do with me, was wrong with her? If his family is crazy, then he was probably crazy in the same way, and if she found him attractive, then what did that say about her? Or me? If you don't change yourself, you'll just keep making the same mistake, the m.c. said. One of his patients married three alcoholics who beat her up and she put it down to bad luck. The m.c. said it took her three years of frantic searching between marriages to find three men who were emotional clones. Keep it in your pants, he said to me, until you've changed enough to attract someone else. You don't want to change, then stay with your wife because you'll just end up with her twin sister. This was when he knew I finally was ripping the hook loose no matter how cleverly he played his line.

I kept it in my pants. It wasn't hard. While the flying nun was going crazy, I spent a lot of time holed up in my office. There was no room to sleep, what with a computer and typewriter and filing cabinet and too many books for the shelves. I got a light blanket, which I kept in the bottom drawer, and I'd lock the door and sleep tipped back in the chair with my feet on the desk. I'd set my watch alarm for five minutes before class, wash my face with cold water and then spew out fifty minutes on how to develop a topic sentence.

On the nights the Wicked Witch of the East got onto the thighbone of a horse, flew into the darkness and didn't come back, I unplugged the phone. If she collided with a 747, I didn't want to know about it. Then I turned on the tv, the radio and the hi-fi and lay in the middle of the floor and listened to the windows vibrate. On my days off, if the wind and surf were up, I bought a can of beans and some wieners and buns and drove up-island. I'd build a fire on the beach and listen to the waves. The surf was like thunder. I couldn't even hear the cedar bark crack. I'd make coffee in an old metal pot I got out of a box of kitchen goods. I said to hell with cholesterol and drank the coffee with cream and lots of sugar. Even after three cups, I was so tired, when I lay down in the shelter of a log, I'd drift off to sleep for hours at a time. When it rained, I still made my fire but I slept in the back of the truck. Just me and the ocean. Not having to argue, or negotiate, or be responsible for somebody else's unhappiness.

A couple of times the retired couples lined up along the berm in their Airstreams and Winnebagoes, seeing me alone, would call me over for coffee. I appreciated the thought, but after a cup, I'd go back to the truck and move farther north until I found a beach with nobody on it, and start another fire and make another pot of coffee. Then I'd just sit there, not thinking, not feeling, just me and the waves and the fire and the stones.

24

"WHAT A LAY," Ben said, his fingers excitedly tapping his cane. He was holding up a picture of one of his former neighbours. "Hot stuff. I felt like I was on fire when I made love to her." He said it with conviction but there were sixty portraits of other women pinned to the wall behind him. I'd counted them. He referred to it as his Rogue's Gallery. He'd been a detective for a good part of his life and he collected pictures and licence plate numbers, bits of information, more by habit than desire.

I'd stopped for tea. It was my first visit in over a year and he was so pleased he turned off the television. He got settled in his overstuffed chair and asked me if I remembered how to make tea. There were a dozen dead tea bags lined up on the window sill. He lived alone and made his tea one cup at a time and a tea bag would make six reasonable cups. He would use one, turn a cup over on the window sill, put the tea bag on top of the cup to use later. The next time he was making tea he'd forget and use a new tea bag and rather than waste it, put it on an upturned cup. He had an excuse for forgetting. He always lied about his age, shading it this way or that, depending on the advantage, such as getting an extra birthday cake, but he was at least ninety.

His body had failed a bit since I'd last seen him. He leaned more heavily upon his cane but you'd have to know him to notice. As I was filling the teapot, he called for me to get the Fig Newtons. He kept a package of Fig Newtons to serve to company. I took them down, knocked the dust off them and brought the package out with the tea.

I'd met him on the breakwater years before. He was between girlfriends and he wanted someone to argue politics with, so he invited me over. After that, I'd made a habit of dropping by. I stopped visiting when my marriage, like a satellite with a decaying orbit, began to disintegrate. I dropped all my friends just when I needed them most and now I felt apologetic.

He liked me all the better for not having come by. It proved to him that I didn't want to get my hands on his waterfront property. It was an old house, older than him and in worse repair. The building had settled and tilted at various times so that none of the joints quite met. He hadn't done any upkeep in years. The outside, which was covered with fireproof tiles, was battered and chipped. The paint had faded until it was difficult to tell what the original colours had been. None of this mattered to the real estate agents who pushed so many free evaluation offers through his front mail slot that he had a garbage bag permanently clipped behind it. The mailman left his real mail under the mat.

"If you want to be loved when you haven't got any teeth and need two hearing aids, own waterfront," he said. "They started courting me before I retired. That was twenty-five years ago and they're all dead and I'm still here. The apartment promoters. The condo promoters. At last year's convention the real estate agents put up a big photograph of me and hired a witch to lead them in a chant. Lord let his liver fail. Let his kidneys collapse."

"C'mon," I said. "Don't exaggerate."

"The horse's mouth," he said. "Straight from." He waved a Fig Newton at me. "I had a kid here the other day telling me what I could do with all the money he could get me for this property. I said, Sonny, I've outlived one hundred and two developers and four hundred real estate agents. They all were going to sell this property. And he didn't believe me so I showed him the book."

I'd seen the book. It was a big, old-fashioned scrapbook. Actually, it was three scrapbooks. In them, he'd pasted the business cards with the obituaries of all the developers and real estate agents who'd tried to get his property away from him. On the front of each one, he'd written in black crayon in large block letters, *The Book of the Dead*. He never passed up an opportunity to show it to some fresh-faced, eager real estate agent.

"Scared the bejesus out of him," he said.

His battles with developers were legendary. One time, he was being harassed so much he broke out in a rash and his skin started to flake. He told everyone who came to the door that he had leprosy. He hung onto his property like a barnacle to a rock. His property was his life's career. He read all the real estate papers, watched the real estate TV channel, borrowed real estate books from the library and hustled agents for so many free dinners that he'd lost track of them.

"I'm still an old bugger," he announced proudly. "The only thing I miss is Mary. Forty-five years married to the same good woman. It's hard to get used to an empty bed."

I didn't shed any tears for him. Mary had died when he was sixty-five. That was the same year an American company built a fancy retirement home on four lots next to him. As everyone knows, there are a lot of blue-haired widows living in Victoria. The retirement home filled up with women and the very occasional couple. The women who had men guarded them like pit bulls, their false teeth snapping viciously when any of their less fortunate sisters tried claim jumping. Ben, being the generous, thoughtful, considerate soul he was, did everything possible to remedy the situation. He had two strategies. To troll along the breakwater in his Sunday best, with his black cane and his felt hat and a flower in his lapel. Or to work in his yard, fiddling with his few bedraggled geraniums. He never went into the retirement home itself. When I asked him why, he said he wasn't interested in anyone unless she was able to get out and about.

The relationships didn't last long. Not that he was particularly fickle. It was just under the circumstances, his girlfriends were inclined to appear and disappear pretty quickly. In his bed today, out the back door of the retirement home on a stretcher tomorrow. Many were so grateful for this last fling that they remembered him in their wills. His *amorati* were all recorded in Polaroids on the wall. The last picture had been added five years ago.

Although, as he said, he was now fishing without a hook, he still liked to get dressed up and walk the breakwater on a sunny day. He was a leg man and appreciated the stiff ocean breeze. "Sex objects," he said, "that's the way I like them. None of this appreciate-their-souls shit. When they're dead and in heaven they can get their souls appreciated."

The house was piled high with objects. His wife had left behind enough antimacassars for a hotel. In all colours. He grew plants in pots but was inclined to believe plants did best if left to their own devices, forgetting that it didn't rain inside. He hated to throw anything out so there were dead plants located in corners and lined up on the porch. Once when I mentioned he might safely toss out some mums that were positively mummified, he said it was never too late to give up hope. He had more plates and cups and saucers than the Empress Hotel. None of them were in the cupboards. He had a wood cook stove in the kitchen and considered himself incredibly clever because he'd seen wood heaters being advertized in the local hardware store. "Stoves," he announced to me after seeing the ad, "are like ties. What goes around comes around." He used the top of his stove to store pots and pans and cooked in a microwave one of his dollies had left him.

"You're unfaithful," he said suddenly, as if just thinking of it. "You've not come around for over a year. You were probably surprised when I answered the door."

"I wondered if you hadn't kicked the bucket," I admitted. "But I hadn't read anything about the devil being evicted so I figured you were still here."

"You've got a long face," he said. "It doesn't become you. Where's that slick chick of yours?" He often picked up bits of slang from the television but never dropped any. The result was that a single sentence might include "twenty-three skidoo" and "awesome."

"We're not getting along," I said.

"A sailor!" he exclaimed. "It's always a sailor. Mary left me for a sailor once. Did I ever tell you that?" I told him he had but never stopped him when he wanted to tell a story. "For two weeks. She met him at the naval base. Every time she saw him her pants fell down. She couldn't do anything about it. Coming around a corner and there he was and her pants would fall down. Saw him in the PX and her pants would fall down. Packed her bag and went off with him for two weeks and one morning her pants didn't fall down. She turned up at the front door wanting to be let in and I said, 'Do you promise you'll never do it again?' and she cried and said she couldn't promise. Of course, she couldn't. Nobody knows when that sort of thing is going to happen."

"I go to a different church," I said.

"That so?" he said. "Pour the tea." He tapped his Fig Newton on the table. "They're hard enough to be worth eating."

I went to get milk out of the fridge and he yelled after me, "You've been moping. I can tell. You're in there moping now. Quit moping. I can't stand people who mope. If you want her, haul her in. If you don't want her, cut the line." I brought the milk carton and put it on the table. I knew he hated that. He'd been brought up to put milk into a jug. "You want a new woman? You come back tomorrow. We'll go for a stroll on the breakwater. I've got twenty women who stop to talk to me. Not from next door, either. Joggers. Strollers. Dog walkers. I'll introduce you."

"I'm not as eligible as you are. I haven't got a house on the waterfront." He laughed. "Woman problems," I explained. I showed him the picture. "One moment she was here and then she was gone."

"A sailor," he said.

"I don't think so."

"I knew a woman who was trimming roses in her front yard and a salesman came by selling magazines. She left her gloves and clippers on the sidewalk and followed him out the gate. Women can be like that." He was trying to be encouraging.

"I've been watching her for the past two years. I finally asked her out for a date."

"Disappointed? Wasn't what you expected? They never are," he added, taking on his sage's tone.

"Stood up," I said. "On Wednesday I asked her to the ballet for Thursday and she said yes."

"No manners," he pronounced. "That's the problem with

today's generation. Latchkey kids. No one to teach them to say please and thank you. No one to teach them etiquette."

"She's not like that," I said. "Lots of manners. She's a waitress at that café I told you about. She's also an actress."

"Fickle," he said, shaking his head. "I never thought of you as a stage-door Johnny."

"No, not fickle. She hasn't missed a day of work for two years."

He sat up straighter and his face took on a look I'd seldom seen. A watchful, concentrated look. I wondered if this was the way he'd looked when he'd been on the police force. Sometimes when I came over, instead of talking about women or real estate, we talked about cases he'd worked on. I'd asked about him and he'd been a good detective. He was famous among his colleagues for never letting go, keeping files open in his head long after the department considered them closed. He was legendary for remembering faces. Many of his arrests were made when he was off-duty at a movie or the race course, anywhere a crowd collected. He'd spot a face and instantly he'd know who it was and what he was wanted for.

"Did she call in sick?" he said.

I shook my head.

"Did she tell anyone she was going away?"

"No, not even the owner. You're going to think I'm an idiot but I started to play detective. I even went to her apartment block to see what I could find out. I mean," I said, making excuses for my juvenile behaviour, "everybody was worried. It wasn't just me. Everybody else in the café. Anyway, it doesn't matter, one of the waitresses says she's gone off with some guy for a holiday."

"Fickle," he said.

"No, she's not fickle," I said.

He sat there soaking his Fig Newton. He was good at waiting. That must have been an asset when he was on the police force. You knew he was waiting and he knew you knew.

"She's not fickle," I insisted. "She's more responsible than anyone there. When the other girls gather at the back when things are slow, she fills salt and peppers shakers, cleans the fridge."

"Bad-mannered," he said.

I could feel myself becoming annoyed. "What are you getting at?"

"You're telling me two different things. She's not fickle but she suddenly acts in a fickle manner. She's not bad-mannered but she acts out of character by being bad-mannered. Love is blind. Maybe that's it. A guy's got the hots and all he can see is tits and ass."

"People are terribly inconsistent. Do you always do things exactly the same?"

"Habits are hard to break," he said. "Inconsistencies only look like inconsistencies because you haven't got a long enough stretch of time. Otherwise something new's been added in. Or something's not known. Is there any money missing?"

"No. Not that I know of. Anyway, Evelyn said . . ."

"Evelyn said what?"

"I told you," I said. "She's off banging some guy and she's having such a good time she forgot to come to work."

He sat back and whistled the first few bars of "Jealousy." I wanted to throw his tea at him. I wished I'd never come. I got so angry that I said, "Somebody was sending her roses and she tried to buy a gun." That stopped his whistling. I wondered how often he'd done that to someone, goading them into shouting out bits of incriminating evidence.

"That's what's brought you over. You want an old man's advice." He tried to sound affronted but I could see that he was pleased. "Ninety per cent of people who disappear want to disappear. They don't want to be found. TV's making that harder." He never missed programs on real criminals. "If she's running, she'll turn up."

"The other stuff. If she didn't want to disappear."

"Nine per cent of what's left is somebody close. A neighbour, a co-worker, a relative. The one per cent's random. Getting them's just luck. Their bad luck. Picked up on a coincidence. Get drunk and talk too much."

We both soaked our Fig Newtons. I scraped a bit off with my teeth and dipped the cookie back in the tea.

"What can I do?"

159

"Nothing. One civilian doing something is fantasy. Even with all the department's resources there's not much chance of finding someone. We had a case with a kid who disappeared. He was locked in a room three houses away from his parents. Two years. Then something went wrong with the waterline. A city worker thought something was funny and called us and we went to take a look. There he was. Pale as paper because he hadn't been outside in all that time. We'd built up a file six feet long. Thousands of tips. None of them was even close."

"I didn't ask for this," I said.

"Most of us don't," he replied. "Life gives us lots of things we don't want."

"I'm nuts," I said. "I'm seeing a shrink. My marriage is falling apart. I can barely keep my job together."

"I trusted my hunches for years. Everything looked fine on the surface. It was the little things that didn't match. The gaps. It's like a bit of flaking paint. You pull off one piece, then another."

"You think I should keep looking? You said one person looking wouldn't do any good."

"What harm will it do? You might end up embarrassed. Or you might not like what you find."

I shook my head. I was staring at the blank screen of the TV. I thought what a liar it was, the house liar. Week in and week out people committed crimes on TV shows and someone knew just where to look and what to look for and drew brilliant deductions. Or the guilty party, on the verge of exposure, confessed. I was smart as most and I didn't know shit. That's not the way it was supposed to be. There were supposed to be clues. Every night the good guys won and that made life bearable. Except that was a lie, too. It was fine with me if there was no justice among crustaceans, but it wasn't fine among humans.

"You should have slept with her when you had the chance," Ben said, sucking on the Fig Newton. "That's the only regrets I've got. No teeth and the things I could've done and didn't."

25

"Why are you so mad about your therapist saying be a person who writes?" the shrink asked.

"He wasn't my therapist," I said. "He was my wife's therapist."

"Your wife's therapist then."

"Because it's a fucking insult, that's why. You're with a group of writers and one says do you know Paul, and somebody says, sure, he's a writer, and another one says, no, he's not, he's a person who writes. Everybody knows what that means."

"What about your other accomplishments? You're a professor."

"Fuck being a professor," I shot back. The anger was starting again. The refusal to listen to what I wanted for my life. "Shovelling shit by any other name is still shovelling shit. I've got five classes of forty students writing essays on how they spent their summer vacation. Some of them don't know all the letters in the alphabet."

"There are lots of people who'd love to be professors."

"There are lots of people who'd like to be dogcatchers, so what?"

"How do you feel about your father?"

The question took me by surprise. "Quit wasting the taxpayer's money," I said.

He wrote that down. I hate that. I wanted to take his bloody pencil and shove it up his nose. Then he quit writing and sat absolutely still. I hated that even more.

"I love him," I said. "He's the greatest fucking dad in the world. If I got to be a kid again, I'd choose him three times out of four. The other time I'd go for somebody who'd die and leave me money."

"What do you like best about him?"

"He doesn't put up with shit from anybody."

"You said you used to hide behind the couch. Do you remember the couch?" That caught me from the side, head down. Bodychecked into the boards. The bodycheck knocked me right through the boards into another space. I ended up behind the couch. I could smell it. Dusty. Dry. The rough corduroy cover. Faded red. The pressure of the wall on one side, the pressure of the couch on the other. My legs jammed into the narrow space, just my head protruding. Me. Small. Little. A big purple four jumped into my mind. What can you hear? the shrink asked. Nothing, I replied. Nothing, there's nothing to hear but I was lying, the noise kept forcing its way into my head, like getting closer and closer to a noisy room. Somebody's shouting and something's breaking and men are yelling and swearing. I can hear them hitting each other and furniture tipping over and women yelling for them to stop.

"Drunk giants fighting," he said. "Do you feel scared?" And I did, I could feel it, not a thought, not thinking I'm afraid but my body shaking and me wanting to hide, wanting to make myself smaller, feeling like I'm going to shit my pants. All I do is nod and he says, "The night you had supper with the accountant and his wife, how'd you feel when they had predinner drinks?"

"Just social drinking," I said, shrugging it off but the noise is still in my head, and I hated that, the noise ricocheting around, crazy noise, making me feel crazy, like a ball bouncing around the room, everybody trying to catch it but it being unpredictable and everybody chasing it faster and faster, yelling and jumping and falling.

"At dinner," he said, "how did you feel? Let yourself feel that, when the liquor was being poured."

My wife's brother was pouring booze, whiskey, brandy. Handing out glasses. I had a ginger ale but I felt self-conscious about it.

And when I smelled the liquor, I felt so anxious I wanted to run away. I thought maybe I should say I'm not feeling well and excuse myself so I could go to my bedroom and lie down but I didn't. I felt weak inside. My chest was tight and my hands started to shake so I put my glass down. That way nobody would see. I put my hands on my knees and tightened my fingers every time they began to tremble. Then I started telling myself it was all right, take a deep breath, these people are just going to have a social drink. They aren't going to get drunk and fight. Nobody was going to kill anybody. Nobody was going to cry. Every time I felt the panic start, I told myself that.

It wasn't all bad when they were drinking. We'd have twelve or fourteen people over and set up the sawhorses and a door to add to the dining room table and cover them both with tablecloths. There'd be a card table at the end for us kids. Or we'd eat in the kitchen. My mother would cook a turkey or a ham and everything. When the guests came, the women would all go into the kitchen to help and the men would sit around and have a drink. Sometimes they'd push the tables aside so they could shoot craps. They'd form a circle and get out the dice and their money.

"C'mon, baby, c'mon, lady luck," they'd shout and sometimes they'd get me to blow on the dice to make them come up right and if they did, I'd get a nickel. That's how I learned to count. Before I went to school, I could count to twelve. I could add the numbers on both dice. Except the two was snake eyes and twelve was little sixes. But I had the idea. And I knew all the cards and the suits except I counted ten, jack, queen, king and got in trouble at school for it.

It was later, after supper, when there was more drinking, they'd sometimes give me a sip here and a sip there from their glasses and I'd feel real dizzy like I'd been spinning around until I fell down and everybody would laugh and get me to walk across the room. That's when they were still having a good time. It was later, after the laughing changed, when it took on a mean edge, that somebody would be insulted and push or threaten and somebody else would push back and I'd run and hide behind the couch. They'd start out pushing, then hitting with their open hands, then with fists.

Once I hid under the bed in my bedroom but everyone was fighting and there wasn't enough room in the living room and they spilled into the other rooms. Two of them were fighting in my bedroom, lunging into the dresser, over my toys, into the walls, onto the bed. I started to scream because I thought the bed was going to collapse on me. That's when my mother started to scream and she came in with a broom and beat them with it, shocking them into surrender and sheepishness with her anger. Even behind the couch wasn't always safe. One time I hid in the closet but someone fell into there, knocking down all the clothes with me underneath. For years I wished for a rope ladder. I wanted it so I could climb into the attic and safety when the fighting started.

They fought bitterly, with incredible violence. Nothing held back. They fought against outsiders, but that was away from the house, at the bootlegger's, at the country dances, in the beer parlour. At home they fought each other. Brothers, uncles, cousins, friends. After some fights, I couldn't recognize my father. This stranger with the swollen, blackened face would sit at the end of the table unable to eat, sipping warm milk through a straw. Gradually, the face would turn purple, then yellow while the swelling lessened until gradually it turned into my father's face again. During this transformation, my mother would gradually quit crying over the broken dishes or furniture and my father would promise to replace them.

There was a lot of puking. They all puked. For a long time I thought that was why people drank. So they could puke. I thought puking had to be fun. I even tried imitating them, leaning one arm against the wall and putting my head down and my fingers in my mouth until I gagged. When I finally did manage to puke, it wasn't fun at all and it really made me wonder about adults.

Mostly the women didn't drink. They cried. That was their role. The men drank and shouted and fought and the women screamed and cried. They scampered in and out of the kitchen yelling things like, "Oh, my God. They're fighting," as if it was a surprise, as if the whole ritual of the visit and the cooking of the food and the drinking of bottles of home-brew had some other purpose. Everything was so predictable that it was like seeing a play over and over again. Drink, eat, fight, scream, puke. Sometimes, for unknown reasons, the elements were alternated but they still were all there. Just as in any good drama there was exposition, rising action, climax, falling action, denouement. Lying behind the couch was where I learned dramatic structure. When I'm writing, I often think of the story like that. This is the puking part. The denouement always took place around the kitchen table with my father silent and my mother explaining who was guilty of what. Agatha Christie, I thought when I became older, must have come from a family like this.

One night, when I was behind the couch, there was no fighting. Instead, one of the women danced. Not with anyone. I was used to dancing. They'd push the furniture out of the way and someone would play an accordion and a harmonica and they'd all polka about the room, yelling at the top of their lungs. This was different. There was a record player and this woman who was drunk took off her shoes and climbed onto the dining room table. I remember thinking my mom's going to be mad at her. I'd got on the table once and got whacked all the way to the bedroom. Anyway, she got onto the table and just stood there for awhile and everyone was laughing and saying, "C'mon, Mabel, show us you're able." Slowly, she began to move. She had a scarf and kept holding it up with both hands. I squirmed to the corner of the room and settled between the chesterfield chair and the couch. I remember the base of that trilight. It was cream-coloured marble with wavy streaks of red. The upright was polished brass with a large salmon-coloured glass bowl on top. When I looked up, she was dancing, moving around the centre of the table, lifting her skirt a little, posturing. Someone started clapping, then others joined in and I thought it was great fun and I clapped as well. She reached under her dress and rolled down a stocking to her knee, then rolled down her other stocking. I'd seen my mother take off her stockings but she always sat on the edge of the bed to do it. Mabel took one stocking off and threw it in the air, then took off the other one and threw it in the air.

"Do you have parties like that at your place?" the shrink asked quietly.

"No," I said but my voice was far away. I was in the room with the music, with Mabel lifting her red silk dress then letting it fall.

"There are other ways of having a good time?"

I had to swim back towards the question, to catch hold of the words, but the current kept pulling me towards the room and the noise.

"It wasn't so bad," I said. "I survived. Other people had worse things happen to them."

"That's right," he said. "It can always be worse."

26

I'D JUST FINISHED CLASS and was putting in office hours when Karmen appeared. She was wearing a black beret, a black shirt that just came to her crotch and black leotards. The leotards looked as if they'd been painted on.

I didn't really want company. Things weren't good at work but they were worse at home so sitting with my feet on the desk was the best I could manage. We have to put in the office hours even though no one ever comes by except after grades are posted and then they line up and use two or three boxes of tissues. They've all got to have As. Nobody's a B. Or, God forbid, a C. There hasn't been a D or an F in at least five years. Since the administration has put in class evaluation forms, everybody needs to be popular and nobody's popular if they give Cs, Ds and Fs. In any case, I was happy no one wanted to learn how to write a parallel sentence. Ben had unsettled me so much I couldn't concentrate. I kept thinking of the lake being frozen over when I was a kid. A sheet of ice. Smooth. Complete. And then an unexpected wind from Hudson Bay and the ice breaking up, the sharp pans tossing in the waves. Ben had done that. The son of a bitch, I thought. I didn't need that. Let it go, walk away from it. Don't get involved. That's my way of dealing with things. Except I felt really bad, as bad as when I'd smashed the glass car. Lonely and filled with regret. There'd been no more glass cars. I wondered if there were any more Sharons and I knew there weren't. Women who were more beautiful, perhaps, women who were talented, woman who were kind, but not Sharon.

My office door was wedged open. Since the college changed its rules so that professors are guilty of sexual harassment if a student feels harassed, I never shut the door. If it wasn't for the local thief who periodically appears dressed in a suit and carrying a briefcase, I'd take the door off its hinges.

Karmen kicked the wedge out of the door. She took the books off one of the chairs, dragged it over to the desk and sat down, "My heart is broken," she said.

She's like that. No chitchat. She goes straight to the point.

My office is piled high with books, the shelves are full and there are books stuffed on top of the books and there are towers of books on any flat surface and towers of books on the floor. A lot of piles are precariously balanced, with notes to myself on the top of each pile reminding me what the pile is for. One pile is research into the lives of the saints. God only knows why. I don't operate logically. At some deep level something stirs and I need to know everything about that subject. Some piles begin but are stunted, abandoned. Nothing blooms. Like Ben's mummified plants. I used to uproot them, scatter them, giving up all the effort I'd expended hunting them through secondhand bookstores, at auctions, flea markets, but learned it was a mistake, like the gardener who uproots a plant too early, throws it on the compost only to have it grow to mock him. Indecision, my wife said. Any excuse not to make up your mind.

Karmen pressed the knuckles of her right hand against her teeth. She looked like a child who had lost her favourite toy. There's no word for it in English. The French must have a word for it. They are better at capturing emotion, a word that would mean beautiful and young and sad, as if a day bright with sunshine suddenly had a cloud cross in front of the sun.

"He's unfaithful," she said. "He promised he wouldn't make love to her and now she's pregnant again."

"The bouzouki player?" I guessed and she nodded. "They're married," I reminded her.

"Legally, but not spiritually. Spiritually he's married to me."

Tears dripped from her eyes. I handed her a Kleenex. She dabbed at her face and wiped her nose. Tears started to run in a stream and she leaned forward into my arms and then shifted, moving from her chair into my lap with her head on my shoulder. She was light and fragile as a bird. Her hair pressed against my face and the smell of her perfume made my chest tighten. It had been a long time since I'd felt like that. At first I thought it was a touch of asthma, then I remembered that constriction of my heart when I was a teenager. We sat for a long time, then she gave a sigh and snuggled against me.

"Make love to me," she whispered. "Making love always makes me feel better."

"Here?" I blurted out. The door was closed but unlocked. There was barely room to sit, never mind lie down. There was a colleague in the office next door. People were going by in the hall.

She kissed my neck and then my cheek and I kissed her mouth and she ran the tip of her tongue lightly between my lips and I cupped a breast in my hand.

I was thinking and not thinking. The thinking part of me was wanting to say I thought you didn't like bald guys, you've got a father fixation, but the not thinking part of me was running my hands over her breasts and back. The thinking part of me was thinking I'm an old fart. I'm neurotic to be doing this. But I was remembering Demytro saying what's the matter, the motives not pure enough for you? Not good enough? Is that what you say to them? They want to make love, they need to make love and you won't love them because their motives don't meet your high standards? I know priests who are more generous than you. And Ben saying how he regretted the things he hadn't done. I'd chastised him once, saying that he was taking advantage of all that loneliness. He'd been bewildered. "Taking advantage," he said, "They're grown up adults, too. They've got needs, too. Maybe they'd be better off if I said, bugger off with your loneliness."

I put my hand inside the hem of her top. Her stomach was silky and flat. Her breast fitted nicely into the palm of my hand. She stood up and rolled down her leotard. She wasn't lying. She didn't wear anything underneath. As soon as it was down far enough that she could sit, she eased back into my lap, lifted her legs up, bent her knees and pulled the leotard off. She handed it to me. I didn't know what to do with it so I dropped it into the top desk drawer with my cup of soup packages and my tea bags.

She undid my belt. I said, "The door's unlocked," and she got up, pushed the lock in, swivelled back and said, "Stand up so I can undo your pants." What, my thinking mind said, if she yells when she has a climax? There's a seminar on Romantic poetry just down the hall and they'll hear her. Maybe, I thought, they won't know what it is.

Hate fucking, I thought. Sex is supposed to go with love. But it didn't stop me from standing up so she could undo my buttons. At least she's not dressed like a nun, flashed through my mind. What if the secretary knocks and thinks I'm not here and lets herself in to drop off some papers? The rest of me was busy trying to get the chair out of the way so we'd have enough space to lie down. I was in such a hurry, I jerked the chair, hit a pile of books, knocked over the tower of saints, which toppled other piles like dominoes. Someone in American foreign policy was afraid of this, I thought, and nearly laughed out loud.

"On the desk," she said.

She had more experience with the creative use of space than I did. I shoved the papers off the desk onto the floor. I thought she was going to get onto the desk but, instead, she bent over with her hands on the desk. I put my arms around her waist and slipped into her from behind. I reached around and slid my hand over her stomach, then between her legs and started to stroke her with my middle finger.

Once started there was no stopping but I wasn't giving her my full attention. I was worried that if I pushed too hard the desk would rock. If a student was sitting in the hallway she would hear the rhythm. After a few minutes, Karmen twisted away, sat me down on a double pile of *The Books of Knowledge, circa* 1939, sat facing me, with us both absolutely still so as not to topple from our precarious seat, while she tightened and loosened some internal muscle until I came. At that moment, I didn't give a shit if the president, the chancellor, the entire feminist brigade smashed down the door. Somehow, her top had come off. I didn't remember it coming off. Now I knew what Ben meant about his wife's pants. It wasn't like they got taken off. They just fell down. She saw the sailor and they fell down.

After I had given her some Kleenex, we got dressed. Someone knocked at the door twice but I ignored it. We were still petting and I was wishing we were at a beach, under the palm trees, with no one around for miles and no need to put our clothes back on for the rest of the day. The knocking was probably the chairperson come to liven up my day by offering to take me for a tuna sandwich and tea.

"Don't look so guilty," Karmen said. "I feel much better. It was that or getting drunk. You wouldn't want to contribute to my drinking." She leaned over and kissed the top of my head.

After she left, I surveyed the wreckage. I'd never get the saints sorted out. They were mixed in with African tribal customs and books on dream analysis.

There was a knock at my door. It was unlocked and the chairperson let herself in.

"What the hell happened?" she asked. "It looks as if there was an earthquake."

"You know how it is," I replied. "Knock over one thing and it knocks over another. You change one thing and it changes everything."

"You're going to be months sorting it out." There are advantages to having a reputation for leading a boring life. She never suspected a thing.

"Yeah," I agreed. "Maybe a bloody lifetime."

27

"If the bastard had treated van Gogh, he'd have ended up being a bloody clerk."

"Dead people can't paint," the shrink said.

"If he ended up a clerk, he might as well have been dead. I can hear it now. Face up to reality, Vincent, you're not a painter, nobody wants your work. All you've ever sold is one painting. Give it up, Vincent. Adjust to reality. You're nothing but a mentally ill sponger living off your brother." I'd directed my anger at the wall but now I turned on him, feeling the rage, thinking somewhere in the back of my mind about Demytro and the charmed circle he'd tried to create with the café, of Gloria's shark constantly circling in the molten heart of the world, of Karmen's lovemaking, of the girl with the Botticelli face, somewhere beyond finding. "That's his reality, isn't it? He'd have smashed the little positive feeling van Gogh had about himself."

I was shouting again. I sat back and closed my eyes and began to breathe with my stomach, letting the air out through my mouth. I imagined a tail growing from my spine, down into the earth, locking itself around rock, holding me in place so I wouldn't go spinning away like a wheel made of knives.

"Would you like to try hypnosis?" he asked.

"No, I tried hypnosis. I let the m.c. hypnotize me. He started his pop psychology Disney World feel-good stuff and I jumped out of my chair. I didn't come for lousy bullshit mind games."

"How do you feel now?" he asked. He was very quiet, calm,

and it gave me nothing to fight against. Like being in a rage against the fog.

"I want to smash everything. I should have brought an ax. I want to chop everything to pieces."

"Whatever you have done, it couldn't be worth this much punishment. That Lutheran pastor was a fruitcake. What he was teaching had nothing to do with Christ." He leaned forward and quietly asked, "What of the sarcophagi?"

He did that to me, starting a hare in another direction, so I left one and pursued another, racing after it through mud and brambles. The sarcophagi.

"Two of them," I replied, suddenly remembering my dream. "On platforms of stone. In an abandoned graveyard where very poor people lived in shacks. I knew I should try to force them open but I couldn't bear the pain of what I would find."

That night, I woke at 3:00 A.M. I was lying on my side. I rolled over onto my back to listen. My entire body was tense. I felt ready to spring onto the floor. There was nothing making noise, not even acorns falling onto the tin roof of the garage beside my window. Maybe, I thought, a bit of branch had dropped, startled me from sleep. I held my breath. There was no sound of wind. The darkness was thick and soft and I was afraid. I got up and opened a window to let in fresh air, leaned out and breathed until my chest felt clean.

There was no going back to sleep so I put on my housecoat and made a familiar journey, inspecting each of the rooms, checking the windows and doors, trying the latches, refusing to give in to the fantasy that someone was following behind me, ready to leap onto my back and strangle me. In the past when I'd felt like this, I'd slept with a knife under the pillow, but the shrink said don't give in to the fantasy, stick with reality. I took my hunting knife with its razor edge from the workshop table drawer, carried it to my bedroom then, with great effort, as if I were struggling against an invisible tide, carried it back and put it away.

I made tea without turning on the light, watching the element turn red, then fade again. Weak tea with milk and honey. Sitting at the table, I thought about her, the dark-haired girl with the Botticelli face. I wished she was with me now, coming down the stairs, slipping up behind me, only the jingling of her bracelets announcing her presence. The smell of her perfume, faint and full of spring flowers. Putting her arms around me and pulling me close so that I could feel the warmth of her body through her white nightgown.

On nights like this, when I could not sleep, she would slip into her harem pants and her headpiece made of gold coins and dance for me, dance away the fear. She once told me she was taking belly dancing lessons at the Y. As I sat there, I imagined her dancing for me, raising her arms, pulling her hair high behind her head, letting it cascade down.

I shifted in my chair. The images excited me. Karmen had done that. Smashed something, a stone wall that had broken like eggshell in my office. Before that there had been a vast, high rampart, built of granite to hold back my wife when she attacked. And behind the wall, I'd created a vast expanse of scorched earth. Nothing she could attack there. Just a vast, burned emptiness. Beyond the horizon, in a small valley, I'd kept a secret oasis of green trees and flowers, with the sound of water running and a one-stringed instrument playing. I'd forgotten about this place, but now I remembered it, remembered the shrink counting me down the long flight of curving stone steps, the first tinkle of water over stones, the smell of jasmine and hyacinth, the cool shadows and the soft earth. Green palms and blue shadows and a tent with a floor of Persian carpets. When it gets too bad, he said, when you are pressed too hard, retreat here, no one knows of this place but you and I and no one can ever come here without your invitation. It was all right to risk having feelings here, to experience pleasure. I thought of the girl with the Botticelli face in this sanctuary with me, dancing to the music, and her face and the face of the dark-haired girl in my dreams ran together and I felt confused and fled back up the stairs to think about my wife who was in Vancouver, selling junk to antique junkies. Somewhere in the house, a great snake began to uncoil but then the image collapsed, crumbled into nothing but shadows. Instead, I thought about my wife as she'd been packing up to leave, the flesh around her eyes puckered and dark, the heaviness of her shoulders, the momentary uncertainty that flitted briefly across her face.

The Bitch of Buchenwald, I shouted, but the sound no longer filled up the house. Before, when I'd yelled like that I'd kicked the furniture, pounded on the walls. Now, it didn't seem worth the effort. Haul her in or cut the line, Ben had said.

Murder, I thought, I'll murder all of them. All the bastards and bitches in the world. The old rage surged like a tide through my body but then it began to ebb.

Everything seemed to be fading, all the old defence lines. All the barriers were crumbling and I felt like I had no shell, no skin. Skinned alive, like the people in the nut house, so that even the air hurt, a speck of dust was like a bur, a word, like jagged glass.

Buried in my great-aunt's back yard, I thought, my mind jerking away. Buried under the peas and beans, under the zucchini. And I was a child visiting, waking up with night terrors, so afraid that someone would discover the girl I had murdered that I could not move for a quarter hour, and when the paralysis was finally gone the shaking racked me like palsy. And crazy images falling one on the other like glass falling, splintering, so I couldn't hold them: the girl's bicycle she gave me, the pink room that was mine, the scissors and her voice saying if we just cut off those you'd be a cute little girl, of sitting before a mirror as she powdered my face and painted my lips and clipped earrings to my ears. Then everything, somewhere there, not here, but there, disintegrating and my killing the little girl with the dark hair, weeping as I did it, digging her grave deeper each time she came to life, rolling boulders and pouring concrete until she was completely entombed. When the night terror was finally gone, me creeping to the window, to peer through the venetian blinds, my lungs tight with the dusty smell of geraniums, looking to see if there really were people digging up the garden, dark men with shovels, digging for her body.

And remembering, I started to feel as though I wanted to run and hide, and I went to my study and dumped my credit card receipts onto the floor to see if there were charges for roses. I sorted through gas receipts and restaurant receipts but there were no receipts for roses, none for flowers of any kind but then I remembered Gloria said the flowers were paid for with cash in Regina. There were no credit card slips for plane tickets to Regina.

How, I wondered, did I kill her? More than once. In different places. Digging her deeper each time. Making the sarcophagus heavier, weighing it down.

I didn't want to be a girl but I didn't want to be a man, not like that, not if they did things like that to little boys. And then I was back, clinging to my mother's leg with shouting and violence all around me and they were pulling me into the living room and telling me not to be such a sissy. When I tried to run away, they caught my leg the way some people will catch a cat's tail and drag it back. Laughing, they rolled me around like a toy, tossing me back and forth, tickling me until I shrieked, until I no longer felt human, not even like a dog because no one was allowed to torment the dog until it howled, and I tried to bite and kick but they only laughed louder, amused by my impotent anger, rolling me over and over on the floor, all the time saying things, making things up until they found something that made me angrier, hurt more. Little girl, little girl, like a little girl, hiding behind his mommy, and once they found what hurt enough to make me scream with rage, they said it over and over, one and then another, and me screaming, I'm not, I'm not, I'm a boy. They'd pick me up by the straps on the back of my overalls and hold me at arm's length, me kicking and screaming, and they never stopped until I finally refused to respond, refused to laugh or scream or kick or bite, no matter what they did or said. I went limp, wandered away in my mind, somewhere far away, until I was on a beach by myself, playing in the sand.

One night when my mother was away, the woman who liked to dance on tables came back. It was poker night so no women were supposed to be there. She came with one of the men. Both of them were staggering when they came through the door. She danced and lifted her skirt while I hid behind the bedroom door and watched through the crack. She flipped her skirt up at the front, then at the back, showing her legs, even her red panties. The men cheered her on, raising their glasses. She'd stop to drink from someone's glass, then dance more suggestively.

"Show it to us, baby," someone cried and she undid her nylons and took them off. She danced fast and then slow and she reached up inside her skirt and pulled down her red panties and kicked them off. The next time she lifted her skirt she had nothing on underneath. That's when the noise stopped and there was just the men clapping as she took off her dress and then her bra. One of the men reached up and caught her around her hips and pulled her off the table and brought her into my bedroom and dropped her on my bed, then got on top of her. I hid in the closet and watched him going up and down in the light from the moon. Her white legs flashed and moved and they both groaned. He left and someone else came in and got on top of her and when he finished, someone else came. I got tired of watching and fell asleep among a pile of clothes.

The closet, I thought, exhausted. I could smell the closet. The freshly washed clothes. I could hear the sound of the bedsprings and, from the other room, the clink of the bottles. Remembering was exhausting. Was that the last time the dark-haired girl was killed and buried, I wondered, and I was overcome with tiredness, but it wasn't a good tiredness, not the kind that comes with hard work, but a heaviness, an aching, like having the flu, and I put my head down on the table and fell asleep thinking the sun will be up soon, the night will be over.

28

"ARE YOU HER FATHER?" Mrs. Sanders asked. She was in charge of the day care.

"No," I replied. "Just a—" I thought for a second, friend had a different meaning nowadays, then I remembered what Gloria had said to Joe "—cousin."

"It's nice to have family," Mrs. Sanders said. "Hardly any of our children's mothers have any family close by. No mother or grandmother to baby-sit. No family to provide support. Freedom has its price."

I was standing in the middle of chaos. Kids were banging nails into boards. running back and forth. They were getting ready to improvise a play about the Kurds. It was to help them try to understand what it was like to be driven from their homes, to be denied their rightful identity, to be turned into refugees. They were waiting for Sharon to turn up.

"I'm also a friend of Miss Dumbrowski's. I was hoping to see her for a minute or two."

"Miss Dumbrowski, I'm afraid I don't know any Miss Dumbrowski." Mrs. Sanders was tall and thin with untidy white hair, a silver whistle on a cord around her neck and a hint of hysteria in her voice.

Two kids ran up arguing about who got to hammer nails into a board. She divided the nails in two piles, then sent them back to screeching and pounding. She glanced at her watch for the fifth time.

"Sharon helps you with drama lessons and storytelling, doesn't she?"

"Sharon. Our Sharon? Her last name is Jones."

"Stage name. She didn't think Dumbrowski would make it on the marquee. Too long."

She quit watching the vortex of children and studied me. I felt like I was being checked against a file. "Is something the matter?"

"She lives in the same building as Gloria. That's how Gloria heard about the preschool and sent Melissa. Laundry room grapevine."

"Something's happened," she said, clutching her whistle with her left hand. "Something's wrong."

"I don't know," I said. "She hasn't been to work for the past week. She didn't tell anyone she was going anywhere. One of the waitresses thought she might have got a chance for a part in a play."

"You're a policeman?"

"No, just a friend. I've known her for a couple of years. We were supposed to go to the ballet a week ago today. She just disappeared."

She reached out and snagged a boy pelting by with a tent pole held like a lance. "I don't know anything about that part of her life. She's very private. She even has an unlisted number. She has them call an answering service. It's not good. The casting director doesn't get you in, she just goes down the list and rings the next person. I've told her that."

"What about her getting a part in a play or a movie?"

"Could be, I guess. It happens. There's nothing around right now. I know everything that's going on. A couple of things in Vancouver but it wouldn't require leaving instantly. Even if it was a rush job, there are telephones everywhere. She could have called. God, what am I going to do with them? She arranged all this the last time she saw them. She was always enthusiastic. Do you know anything about drama?"

"A little," I said, then grasping what she was suggesting, I added, "not much. Shakespeare. Aristotle. That sort of thing."

"It'll do," she said, grabbing my arm. "What did you say your name was?"

179

"Bob, but . . ."

She cut me off with a blast from her whistle. Nothing happened, except a few of the children paused to glance our way. "Class," she yelled, "this is Mr. Bob. Miss Jones can't be with us today. Mr. Bob is going to help instead. He knows all about drama."

This brought them to a pause, if not a stop. Melissa, though, froze where she was, staring at me as if she'd never seen me before. It was as if I was a Transformer. Common truck to space vehicle. At least that was the look on her face. I'd have begged off, fled, except for that. The rest, bless their black little hearts, were strangers but they'd all seen her bring me and I don't know the politics of preschool, but I'm sure it exists. If I finked out, it would cause her to lose face. There's a real pecking order at the sand table. I remembered that much from school.

Melissa had told me about the refugees on the drive over. Camels, and donkeys, and fighting, and little kids with no daddies because the daddies had been in the war. They all understood that, I expected. Oh, God, I thought as we all stared at each other, make me a better man than I am. For my sake and theirs. Normally, I can barely handle a classroom of reasonably civilized teenage girls.

"Okay," I said, "scene one. The fighting. You two, you're airplanes, you're a bomb, you three, you're tanks." I divided them up into the noisiest weapons I could think of. Anything to let them make as much noise as possible and to run around. When they'd exhausted that they got to be refugees. Some got to be camels and donkeys. There were dolls for babies.

We got the tent up. I got everybody sitting down, they still bounced, but they stayed in a reasonable sitting position. It was a bit like watching those movies of molecules banging against each other. I was making up a story about Ali Baba and the forty thieves, with lots of interjections from some of the kids about how to steal things, which I hoped they'd learned on TV and not at home, when Miss Sanders came in with milk and cookies. She'd even got into it enough to have pulled a colourful blanket around herself. She gave me milk and a cookie.

"Day old," she said, "but they're free. I mean, do you eat cookies the same day you buy them?" She motioned me out of the tent. "That was wonderful," she said. "Most of these kids have no male role model. Or terrible ones. You wouldn't like to help out on a regular basis?"

"I'd rather turn it back to Sharon," I said. "I think I'm past this. I'm older than their parents."

"Good," she said. "We always worry about people who are eager to volunteer. I mean, why would they do it if they weren't pedophiles?"

"Nothing under twenty-five," I said, "and only then if I can catch them."

"I called the answering service. I said someone was asking Sharon to try out for a part. They haven't heard from her since last Wednesday. They have a number of messages for her. She never told them she was going away."

A young woman in a green cape came in. Mrs. Sanders waved her over. "This is Sybil. She takes them now for art. She's very good. She got the newspaper to give us roll ends for nothing. They can paint on it to their heart's content. Bob here took Sharon's class. Something's wrong. She seems to be missing. Did she say anything to you?"

Sybil shook her head. "She was jumpy, though. You remember last year how she always checked from the upstairs window before she left. And she kept her bike inside. She got over it and then the last few weeks, she got jumpy again. Even when she was working with the kids, it was like she was watching the door."

Mrs. Sanders nodded. "I noticed that. And she never came or left at the same time. Sometimes she came early. Sometimes, she left a bit early or waited and left late. A couple of times, she didn't take her bike. She went out the back door and along the river."

"That," Sybil added, "was when her boyfriend couldn't meet her. Most of the time, he was right at the door waiting for her. You remember, he came and showed the kids mime."

"The government won't give us a cent," Mrs. Sanders said with a touch of bitterness. "Everything's volunteer. Volunteer food, volunteer teachers, volunteer space. But we're not doing anything important enough to get a lottery grant. Instead, it goes to improve country clubs."

The noise from the tent suggested that refugee food supplies were finished and that a riot was about to erupt. "I'd better go," Sybil said and hurried off.

"People go hungry," Mrs. Sanders said. "They have no place to sleep. They die from exposure. Here, not in Afghanistan. In this country. They kill themselves with drugs. And the government gives funds for improving golf courses. It's wrong."

"Maybe I could do storytelling now and again, when you're stuck for someone." I couldn't believe I was saying it. It probably had something to do with Melissa standing there watching me. This wasn't any good. I couldn't be her father or anybody else's father. I couldn't even father myself. I was nonfunctional most of the time. The crippled rescuing cripples.

Mrs. Sanders must have seen that expression before. "It's just an hour a week. We don't expect any other involvement. Everybody's got their own problems."

"Okay," I said, "But right now, I'm worried about Sharon."

"I don't know," she replied. "She kept her problems to herself. I could see that she was worried sometimes but you know, someone working as a waitress, trying to get work as an actress. But there was more to it than that. Sybil's right. I'd forgotten about that. She kept looking over her shoulder. I remember she used to go to the window. She was always casual about it but nobody else did it. I wondered what she was looking for. She wanted me to lock the door while she was leading her activity. She said it was so she wouldn't be interrupted. But I couldn't because of fire regulations. I remember thinking maybe it had something to do with drugs. There's so much of that sort of thing around. We've had two murders in our neighbourhood because of drug deals. And we're middle class."

"No drugs," I said, "she didn't use them." But I realized that I didn't know that. Maybe she did. Maybe she was a major distributor. Maybe anything.

29

THE TIDE WAS GOING OUT at the café. I could feel it ebbing. The sound of Pachelbel was thinner. Someone was occupying my table in the corner. I was forced to sit in the centre of the room.

"Any news?" I asked Evelyn.

The bones of her face stood out more. Her clothes seemed looser. Some people ate when things went wrong. She reverted to drinking water. Eat something, I wanted to say to her. It won't hurt you. You don't have to die to prove you're in control of your own life. Her parents sent her Bible tracts and crosses and bottles of holy water in hope that it would drive out the devil who was living inside her. The devil, they said, was like a tapeworm living inside her and her not eating was a holy act that would drive him out.

She went to get me a croissant with cheese and spinach. Demytro sat down.

"Where would we all go without you?" I said. "All the misfits."

He spread his large hands on the table. "Who's not misfits? Just the people you don't know. You drive through some little town and you say perfect. Everything is perfect. How beautiful. My brother is a doctor in such a place. Half have drinking problems. Violence. Incest. Here, this family," he said proudly, "we take care of each other. Protect each other."

"Was Sharon into politics?" I asked.

"No. No politics."

"Ethnic politics. You know. Croatia, Serbia."

"A Croatian flag on her jacket. She danced. It was nothing. No bombs. No guns."

"You're sure?"

"Her husband liked politics. He talked like a fascist."

"Nobody talks about her husband. Like he's a yeti or a ghost or something. He's there and he's not there."

"If she comes back safe, you'll have to marry her." He reached out and rested his hand on my shoulder.

The one time the m.c. had tried to put his hand on my shoulder, I'd gone rigid. Rather than knock his hand away, I had pushed the chair back with my foot so I was just out of reach. "Maybe," he had said, "that's part of your problem with your wife. People get married so they can touch each other all the time. Even when they're sleeping."

"It's okay for a woman to touch me. You're not a woman. It makes me want to throw up," I had snapped at the m.c.

Being touched was worse than meeting drunks on the street. If I saw drunks, I would turn around or cross the street to avoid them. My heart would beat faster and all my muscles would tighten. As soon as I was safely away, the symptoms would subside. Being touched made my muscles tighten until they cramped. It took all my self-control to keep from striking out.

Demytro squeezed my shoulder, then patted me. "You ask, she says no, how are you worse off? You ask, she says yes, then everything changes. But not," he said, "just for one night." He stopped patting my shoulder, leaned close. "Papa Demytro likes all his girls but this girl is special. Everybody loves her."

"Yes," I said, "life is too short to live so miserably. Better to take a chance."

Demytro looked serious. "Everything will be against you but so what? Lots of weddings, I hear people say look at such a beautiful couple, look how happy they are, they have everything going for them. A year later, they're separated. Life is crazy. Maybe having nothing going for you means success."

"And you?" I asked. "Why do you not take a risk?"

He smiled shyly. "I have my violets, my cat. Lots of people to take care of. Not much left over. I'm not unhappy. You are unhappy. So, you need to change."

"I can't just say, I've missed you. Let's get married. I'm not even separated."

"No," he agreed, "but you can make a start. Courting is fun."

Courting, I thought. I hadn't heard anybody refer to it like that in a long time. Screwing. Fucking. Getting laid. Scoring. That's what I heard. But not courting. I liked the idea of courting. It was filled with shyness and humility and a kind of innocence. Caring. Tentativeness. Risk. You could only have courting where something that mattered was at risk. Like a lobster without its shell. Out in the open. I wondered if I could really do that. Really care about what someone else thought or felt. And the image of frost on a windowpane sprang to mind. When I was a kid, on very cold days, frost formed on the inside of the windows and the sun shone through it, turning it to a glowing field of miniature diamonds and rainbows. At first, I wanted to grasp it, to hold it, but every time I touched it, I destroyed it. It turned to cold tears on my hands. I didn't want Sharon to be like that.

"In my village in old country," Demytro said, seeing my melancholy face, "there was older man married to a younger woman. The young men made jokes but she was happy. Not perfectly happy but happy. And he was happy. There were no problems with money."

"You are very serious about this," I said.

"Yes," Demytro agreed. "If she comes back safely, life cannot just be as it was. Sometimes, this happens."

I had taken out the ballet tickets and was holding them under the table, for good luck, for reassurance that, because something was not finished, she had to come back. Good-luck tokens. Like a friend who, for five years, had cherished a used airline ticket, in the belief that as long as he held onto it, somehow, magically, he would get from Moscow to Canada. It went everywhere with him. Once when he misplaced it, he was frantic. The more desperate we are, the more irrational our faith.

Demytro gave my arm a last pat, then disappeared into the

storeroom to get fruit and vegetables ready for the next wave of customers. Evelyn appeared with my croissant. As she put it down, she leaned close and whispered, "You can quit looking."

"What do you mean?"

"Shh," she whispered. "No one's to know. Don't keep looking. You'll just upset things." I caught her sweater and held it so she couldn't pull away. I felt that if I shook it, she'd collapse into a pile of bones. "She called. Everything's fine. She's got together with her husband. They're on a second honeymoon. She'll come back in a couple of weeks and get her stuff. Then she's moving to Saskatchewan with him."

"Her husband," I said. My voice seemed weak and far away.

"He's crazy about her. All he's wanted is to have her back. He'd do anything."

30

I WAS WANDERING AROUND the mall thinking about what damage a Kalishnikov could do. I didn't know how to load or fire one but the movies made it seem easy. Even the brain dead seemed able to make them work. Have you ever felt like that? Been so angry that you didn't know where to put your anger? Hand grenades would help. I could run down the mall throwing them into stores full of overpriced clothes. Except that the people going by were real, not actors. In the movies, no one has relatives, no one who loves them, no one who is scarred for life by murder or suicide. Real people. People like me who are hurt. People like me who spend hours wandering around malls just not to feel lonely, to be with strangers rather than at home. Because at least strangers are polite, even courteous. "Thank you" and "please" and "excuse me" exist.

But I knew why movies full of violence were so popular. The cry was, "Die. Die. I hate you all." I wondered if that's what it was all about. Ireland, Palestine, Yugoslavia, Spain, even in Canada— pain unheard. We didn't, I thought, stopping for another ice cream cone, need a God, we needed a world psychiatrist. From one o'clock to two o'clock five days a week, this half of the world lay on a couch and told their troubles to Shrinko in the Sky and twelve hours later, from one to two, people on the other half of the world lay down and unburdened themselves. That made me feel better. The idea of all the people in the mall, stopping where they were, lying down, customers, clerks, adults, kids, bag ladies, million-aires, and pouring out how they felt. Maybe, I thought, that's what

God's supposed to be but we've forgotten. Maybe that's what prayer is. Maybe Shrinko the Great had his shingle out but nobody was noticing. Maybe Christ wasn't a carpenter. Maybe the translators got it wrong. Maybe he was therapist.

Maybe, instead of killing people, I could kill people's pets. Late at night. After everyone was asleep. I could sneak into people's houses and murder their goldfish. Leave little fillets tidily wrapped in plastic in their fridge with a note saying fish is low in cholesterol. Or dismember turtles, or deleg frogs. Or someone would wake up to marinade of mutt. I could tell I was beginning to feel better. I'd gone through two chocolate cones, anger, philosophy and ironic humour. Defences, Shrinko would say, why not just admit you hurt?

The bouzouki player was dressing a mannequin. He looked different in a blue suit with a red hanky neatly folded in the pocket. I waited until he'd got the sports jacket and tie just right, then wandered into the store.

"You play in a band?" I said. His professional grimace changed to a smile. "At Harry's. You're the guy on the bouzouki. Hot stuff."

"Can't make a living, though." He waved his hand at the shop as if to apologize for what he was doing. "Gigs are okay but bankers don't lend you money on them."

"Good times, though. I was at the party at the mansion."

"That was good," he agreed. "Good food. Great perks. All the import we could drink." No mention of Karmen, though. Of the fifteen minutes in the upstairs bedroom. I wondered if she came under the same heading.

Playing the bouzouki, he didn't seem a suit man, a seller of shirts. Even now, in a creaseless suit, he seemed out of place, like a neighbourhood kid borrowed to serve dainties at a garden party. Good God, I thought, doesn't anybody get it right? Is it really true that we all spend our lives doing our second best thing, teaching instead of writing, waitressing instead of acting, selling instead of playing music? I felt sorry for him. And for me. I saw him years from now, older, heavier, balder, standing under the glare of the fluorescent lights, saying, "I have a fifteen and a half here, sir. These stripes are very in vogue." And me, greyer, sadder, barely visible behind stacks of term papers, my eyes shut, my hands automatically writing *faulty parallel construction, split infinitive, see rule for the semicolon.* And Sharon? Somewhere in Saskatchewan with two or three kids, baking cakes and reading movie magazines and getting drama lessons for her kids on weekends if they lived close enough to Saskatoon or Regina.

There were no other customers or salesmen and he was obviously bored so I asked him about the band and the gigs and the bouzouki and watched him transform from the inside out like someone was pumping blood into his body or putting flesh on an anorexic's bones. Then I showed him the picture of Sharon.

"The little Croat!" he said.

"She likes to dance."

"Lots of stage presence. Everybody knows she's there. She a friend of yours?"

"Sort of," I said casually, slipping the picture back into my shirt pocket.

"She used to come around a lot, then she got herself into hot water. You know how everybody gets up and dances at the restaurant? Nearly everybody is a WASP but they like to be ethnic for a night. She was always saying why do you play those Serbian dances, why don't you play Croatian dances?" Someone came in and the bouzouki player stopped talking to see if there was a sale but the customer wasn't really a customer, just a drifter, swinging through the store, touching things. When she left, he started again. "During the summer, lots of tourists come to the restaurant. One of the Americans asked who the dancers were. She heard him and she said, 'These are the Croatian Freedom Fighter Folk Dancers.' She gave him some bull about how they were all living in exile waiting to return to freedom in their homeland. You know Americans. They'll believe anything. They thought it was great stuff. The next week she came wearing a T-shirt with CFFFD. Harry thought it was terrific. He put an ad in the paper saying the CFFFD would be dancing every week. And then things began to happen. These guys with muscles and short hair turned up and wanted to talk politics. And then the Yugoslavian vice-consul turned up with some friends. A photographer from a famous magazine took pictures of the dancers but there were no pictures published. You know what I mean?"

While he was talking, I'd been sorting through a rack of sale ties. "You want that tie?" he asked.

I handed him the tie and took out my credit card. It was over the limit but for such a small amount they wouldn't check.

"And?"

"And nothing. They figured out it was just a joke."

"The Germans shot people who made jokes."

"The Germans are a serious people," he said. "No sense of humour." He was writing up the tie. The blood was draining out of him. He was becoming paler again. Emotionally malnourished. When he was talking about the music and the dancing, I could see him ripping off his clothes and jumping on top of Karmen, but now he looked like a man with a wife and a mortgage. His wife, Karmen had told me, wanted him to save enough to buy a clothing store franchise. Karmen wanted him to go with her to Europe and practise his music until the world wept when he played. He handed me the credit slip to sign. "Her husband was a German. Not a German German. A Canadian German. He didn't like the dancing. Inferior music, he told me. He wanted us to play waltzes and marches. He liked brass bands."

"What'd you think of him?" I asked as he handed me the bag.

"Unreasonable," he said.

"They're back together."

He shook his head but didn't say anything because someone had come in with a determined-looking wife and a suit that fitted him when he was thirty pounds lighter.

31

Karmen called.

"Your eternal love has an ex-husband in Saskatchewan," she said. "He's had three restraining orders against him. He's not to write, or phone, or put in an appearance. He's been charged with assault and he's not to leave his parents' farm unless one of them is with him."

I remembered the bruises. Sharon saying it was her problem and that she'd deal with it. Nothing catching.

"Is he there? On the farm. Have you got his name?"

"Frank Barnes. He's not there. I used my sweetest voice to ask if Frank was there and could I talk to him. She said he was there but he was busy and I said I'd wait and she said well, he wasn't right there but I could leave my name and he would call me back."

"He could be with his dad on the west forty."

"No," she said, sounding like she felt very clever. "The affidavit lists his father's name. Frank. A family with little imagination. I asked for Frank and she yelled, 'Hey, Frank, it's for you.' Then she asked me if I wanted Frank Senior or Frank Junior."

"Nobody's with him?"

"It doesn't sound like it."

I didn't know what to say. A court order would have been like a chain wrapped around my leg. But then I would have done everything I could to avoid a court order. But what, I thought, what if I'd been pushed a hairbreadth more, what if I'd gone over the edge and, when someone stirred the rage, I couldn't tell the difference between past and present? What if I thought the devil lived inside people's bodies like a tapeworm? What if I thought the snake slithering and sliding around the house was real and my wife was the fantasy? I remembered the m.c.'s nervousness when I brought the baseball bat, which he thought was real, and his relieved, nervous laughter when he realized it was foam.

"Bob," she said, "her divorce came through two weeks ago. I don't know if that means anything."

32

"Evelyn," I said, "I've got to talk to you." She was coming out of the storage shed. I hustled her back in and shut the door. "Sharon's husband. Do you know him?"

"No," she said but she looked afraid. As if she'd done something wrong. She was carrying vegetables in her apron. Her clothes looked like they might slip into a heap on the floor and she'd stand there naked, looking like an inmate of a death camp. She bit her lip. "Not really." She turned her head. "I mean, sometimes he came around. He liked lox and bagels. He had a yard of credit cards. He was always buying Sharon stuff. Flowers and chocolates. Sometimes he brought champagne when we were closing up. You know, for everybody."

"What kind of flowers?"

"Roses. Like you see in the movies. A long box. Sometimes, he'd have them sent during the day. We thought it was great."

"What about Sharon? Did she think it was great?"

"I dunno. I mean, she was funny about it. She said it was like he was watching her, letting her know he was around. I wouldn't feel like that if somebody sent me flowers."

"He used to beat her up." I said.

"Sometimes he'd lose his temper, but he wasn't bad or anything. He was always sorry afterwards."

"Is he back in town?"

"He couldn't be," she said, "he's in Saskatchewan. He's helping his folks with the farm."

"There's not much farming in Victoria."

"No," she said, "he was into computers but then business got bad. Too much competition."

"He's not in Saskatchewan. Somebody phoned and checked."

She let go of the corners of her apron. The green peppers and lettuce fell to the floor. "He's in Saskatchewan," she said. "The judge made him go to Saskatchewan."

I wanted to shake her but I was afraid she'd fall apart.

"Have you been talking to him?"

She started to cry. "Leave me alone. It's none of your business. It's their life."

The door opened. "What's going on in here?" Demytro asked.

Evelyn got down on her hands and knees and began picking up the green peppers and lettuce.

"She knows something. She's been talking to Sharon's husband."

"Evelyn," Demytro said. "You haven't!"

"He's okay," she said. "He was just phoning. That's all. He said he wasn't angry any more. He's getting help. He just wanted to mail her something to say he was sorry."

"You gave him her address?" Demytro said. His voice sounded hollow, like rotten wood when it's hit. He turned to me. "We told him she'd quit. She moved to a new apartment. She used another name."

Evelyn slipped to the floor, one leg under her, the other crossed in front. She might have been a broken doll or a puppet whose strings had been cut. A romance novel fell out of her pocket. On the cover a man and a woman were embracing on a cliff edge.

"Is he here?" I asked.

"He said maybe they'd get together again. Maybe if she could see how much he'd changed, they could start over."

"Evelyn. He threatened her with a gun."

"People deserve a second chance," she said.

"Oh, my God," Demytro said. "You didn't tell him where she lived? When she was working?"

"I didn't mean any harm," Evelyn cried. "She's okay. He was

just going to take her away for a second honeymoon. They were going down to California."

"What is it?" I asked Demytro but I didn't want to hear his answer, I wanted to turn the music up, to turn Pachelbel up until I couldn't hear anything he said.

Demytro grabbed my arm. "He said when she got the separation papers, that if she divorced him, he'd kill her."

33

"THE DARK-HAIRED GIRL," I said to him. "I keep dreaming about her but she's not there. It's always the same. The settings are different but there are always stone coffins I can't get open."

I didn't want to be here. I wanted to be out there, somewhere, searching for the green van with the Saskatchewan plates. But the police were doing that. This time, they'd taken Demytro seriously and sent someone to look in Sharon's apartment. Demytro did have a key and let them in. Everything looked fine until they pulled back the shower curtain. The tub had been cleaned but there was no mistaking the spray of dark blood on the wall.

"Why did she go away?" the shrink asked, and I felt momentarily confused. I had to pull myself back, away from images of Sharon, to the dark-haired girl of my dreams.

"I don't know," I said.

"Maybe," the shrink suggested, "you're looking in the wrong places."

"I'm looking everywhere I can think of."

"If you find her, will you love her?"

"Yes."

"Even if she's done things you don't approve of?"

"Like what?"

"You don't like being touched," he said. "You don't let anyone get close to you. You don't trust. Everything has a reason. We just have to descend deep enough to find it. Do you want to try?"

I had taught once in a mining town and, as he said this, I

remembered that year, the miners talking about descending in the cage, about the long ride into the darkness, about how, at one mine, something had gone wrong, the pumps had stopped working and the cage had descended into water and everyone had drowned. I could feel their horror, the desperate clawing, the inexorable quality of their death, the cage full of dead at the bottom of the shaft. The shaking in my upper arms started. It spread to my throat. Sometimes, late at night, it would be like this for me. Unable to stop the shaking, as if I had the DTS, my arms and my neck and my shoulders shaking uncontrollably and then the headaches like a band of fire inside my head, the vomiting and the slipping in and out of sleep for a day, or two days, until I was able to push it away, seal it, whatever it was, tight as Pandora's box.

I was shaking too hard to speak. I nodded.

"Good," he said. "Tip the chair back. That's it. Relax. No one's going to hurt you here. There's just me and I'm not going to leave my chair. Roll your eyes up. That's it. Relax. Count with me to three. As I count, let your eyes close. Good. Now, there's nothing to do but listen to the voices in your head."

I descended towards the dark-haired girl of my dreams, the one trapped somewhere inside a sarcophagus, lost somewhere on the ocean floor, but Sharon, laughing, handing me cappuccino, kept intruding, Sharon turned to the side, her hair braided, the skin of her upper arm curving into the smooth flesh above her breast, the smell of violets, and the warmth, like heat from a wood stove, radiating from her, soaking into me. Gradually, all the images faded away to emptiness. My head felt hollow.

After a while, I startled myself by saying, "You can make a little boy do anything you want if you just hurt him enough."

It was a strange experience, as if I was listening to a voice no one else could hear and was, a fraction of a second later, reporting what I had heard.

I heard the shrink's chair squeak as he shifted position. Outside the window there was traffic. I'm safe in here, I thought, nobody can get at me. They'll go to jail if they break in here. I let my breath out through my mouth and breathed with my stomach the way I had been shown. The room faded away.

"If you squeeze his testicle, you can make him do anything you want and not leave any evidence. A dead chicken," I suddenly said. Just like that, it was there. As plain as if it was happening again. "A white chicken with a red comb. Something drawn on the floor. I feel like I want to throw up." I retched after I said it and I felt him spread a towel over my lap in case I vomited. "They're arguing. The redheaded one wants to kill me. You wanted to do it, he's saying to the other one. You were always talking about it. Now you've got to go through with it. We can't have him telling anybody.

"No," I said, repeating what I was hearing. The images dashed and darted, veered at crazy angles, jumped up here and there, and the ferret was after them, twisting and turning. It wasn't like before, one word, one memory, one image, one something appearing and my chasing it through the landscape of the past. "No, we can't kill him. I can't do it. If his father finds out, he'll kill us. He won't care what happens."

"Who are they?" the shrink asks, and I'm not even sure it's his voice, it's so faint and far away, barely a whisper.

"Friends of my parents. Baby-sitting. Taking care of me. They said if I went with them, they'd have a treat for me. A nice surprise. I'd always liked surprises. My mother's surprises were cake and ice cream and jelly or going someplace to visit." And then it's like I'm there and I'm not there. I'm watching everything from outside with X-ray vision. I'm standing in the corner of the room, naked, so afraid I can't move, can't even try to run, know it's useless because they'll only catch me and drag me back. If I cry or scream or fight back, it'll only make it worse.

The redheaded one wants to kill me and stuff my body in an old icebox in the swamp. He's convinced it'll look like an accident, like I got in myself and then suffocated. The blond one's shaking his head, saying no, no, it won't work. I'll see that he doesn't talk. I'll make him so afraid that he won't tell anybody anything. He grabs me around the chest, lifts me up and carries me to a green washstand with a basin of dirty water. He grabs the back of my head and shoves my face into the water. I go limp. I've learned to do that to stop their teasing but this time it does no good. He doesn't stop and I can't remain limp, my arms and legs start to thrash and when the water sears up my nostrils, he lifts up my head, lets me breathe a couple of times, then shoves my head down and I piss on him. He keeps my head under, cursing as he does it, and this time when he lets my head up I'm choking so much that my whole body is jerking. He grabs me by the feet and hangs me upside down, shaking me over the dead chicken and the circle drawn on the floor with a star inside it.

He holds me over the water again. This time he shoves my face just to the surface and I'm trying to twist my head away but he's got a tight hold on my hair. You're not going to tell anybody, not anybody. If you do, we'll come into your house at night and we'll kill your mother and your father and your little brother. He pushes my face down until my mouth is on the water's surface. I start to scream and he lets me scream until everything goes away, everything except the screaming, and then they dressed me and took me downtown and bought me an ice cream cone.

"You do that to girls," I say but I can barely hear my voice, "not boys."

"Sometimes people do that to boys," the shrink whispers, and I'm twisting in my chair, grinding my body as if to escape from someone who is holding me in place. I'm gagging and my head is shaking uncontrollably. "The girl you locked in the sarcophagus is you. You don't really hate her. You buried her in a stone coffin. Like royalty."

I start shaking my whole upper body back and forth, denying what he is saying. "You promised," he said, "if she came back, you would love her. She saved your life. Don't reject her. Be fair. She's carried the pain all by herself. If she was your daughter, would you drive her away, or would you love her? What would you tell her? Would you say, you're not my little girl any more? Get out of this house. Or would you put your arms around her and tell her you love her and it's all over?"

"Not me," I said, "not me," but then she was there, in the darkness with me, I could feel her, awash in grief, standing on tiptoe, not knowing whether to reach out or flee, a little girl with dark hair, terribly alone, and I thought, *Me. She's me* and started to cry, hot, scalding tears, that burned their way down my cheeks and I put out my arms and pulled her close. I couldn't stop crying for a long time and then I heard his chair creak and then the traffic going by and I opened my eyes.

"A girl," I said, "with dark hair and dark eyes."

"Like Sharon?"

I nodded. I could see Sharon, like the lost part of myself grown up.

"Are you going to love her?" he asked and seeing my confusion added, "the little girl."

"Yes," I said but at the same time I was thinking of a green van snaking its way along country roads, somewhere out there.

34

THE DOOR TO THE CAFÉ was locked. The venetian blind was pulled down. I knocked on the door. There was no answer. I stood there, uncertain of where to go. I needed my table and cappuccino more than ever. I needed to sit a hundred feet under Pachelbel, backed into the safety of the corner. Shrinko had made me promise not to drive for an hour. We'd counted backwards from three twice. Drink two or three cups of strong coffee, he'd advised. I tried the handle again, as if somehow I'd just got door opening wrong and if I turned the handle the right way, the door would swing wide and everything would be all right.

There were no bicycles in the rack. Nearly all the waitresses rode bicycles.

It can't be closed, I thought. I looked across the street. The travel agency was still advertizing Costa Rica and palm trees and someone lying on a lounge chair sipping a drink from a coconut. The traffic was still going by. The traffic lights were still working. Nothing else had changed. I turned to the door. The sign said open. I tried the handle again, wrenching it back and forth.

I went to the next door entrance. There were ten buzzers for the apartments above the cafe. Demytro's was number eight. The fifth time I pressed it, his voice, sounding mechanical and fuzzy said, "Who is it?"

"It's me. Bob."

"She's dead," he said. "Leave me alone. Go away."

"What happened?"

"He killed her. He climbed up the balconies. He broke in through her patio door. I can't talk about it."

Up the balconies. In through the patio door. I had seen him. I knew for certain that I had seen him. In the pouring rain. He was climbing from patio to patio intent on murder. No face. Just a name. Frank Barnes. Intent on killing the girl with the Botticelli face because she'd divorced him.

It was starting to rain again. There was nowhere to go. There was nothing at home for me. Less than nothing. Nothing is just not feeling, not anything. What was in that house was pain and bitterness and suffering. The café windows were blank. I wanted to reach in and turn the sign around. At least be honest about it, I thought, at least keep it straight. The front needed painting, I realized. I huddled under the awning but it was torn and the water spiralled down over me and I knew I had to seek shelter somewhere else.

35

THE GIRL OF YOUR DREAMS, the m.c. said once, trying to keep me married. Just hope you don't find her. If you do, you'll fall in love with an image, not a person. Then you'll hate her because she isn't your ideal self. Be sensible. Remember that a man your age needs to think ahead. Marriage is a business arrangement. You should look for comfort, companionship. Social prestige. A good manager. With a little training and therapy, your wife can be someone who can have the dean over for supper and impress him no end. By that time, I didn't bother to explain to him that I wasn't interested in impressing the dean.

He was right, of course, I hadn't known Sharon. I'd fallen in love with her because she literally was the girl of my dreams, the part I'd driven away because of shame and fear. No wonder I had longed to put my arms around her, to have her make me feel complete. No wonder I'd come endlessly to the café, seeking and seeing the answer to an old mystery.

But it was equally true that I'd fallen in love with her little kindnesses, her moments of thoughtfulness, with the way she stood with her hand on her hip and the way she got onto her bicycle. With her self-confidence that let her ride a bike no street kid would be seen stealing.

36

He stabbed her, cut off her arms and legs and head. He put the pieces into garbage bags and sent them down the chute to the storage area. Then he put them in his van and took them all the way to Alberta before throwing them into a swamp. He threw the bags into a garbage dump somewhere outside Calgary. I don't know about the symbolism of that. The shrink would know. I don't care. I don't care what his motives were, either. I just know someone must have done some terrible things to him to make him that way. And I don't care about that, either. I just want him dead.

The trial was short. All the evidence was there. Blood in his van. He had in his possession a lot of items from her apartment. He insisted they belonged to him, as if, somehow, her having them justified what he'd done.

After he was convicted, I was standing at the front door of the courthouse when a reporter asked his mother why her son had killed his ex-wife.

"Because he loved her," she said. "He loved her so much that he couldn't bear the thought of being without her."

37

I CALLED IT QUITS AFTER THAT. No fireworks, no shouting or yelling, no arguing. I just walked in and sat down at the kitchen table and said, "It's over," and the way I said it, my wife didn't argue.

I got a pad of paper and went from room to room. At the top of a page, I wrote the name of the room, then listed everything, then did the same for the next room until I'd gone through the entire house. We went through the pages, putting our initials in front of the items we each thought were ours, then we went back and divided up everything else. Sometimes we had to stop. I'd go for a walk. She'd sort her flea-market goods. Then we'd start again.

All along, I'd been afraid of being on my own. I'd never been on my own. I wondered about that, about going to bed alone, waking up alone, eating breakfast and lunch and dinner alone. I made a list of our friends. If they were her friends, I put her initials beside them and, if they were my friends, my initials. They all had her initials beside them. The shrink had said if I was willing to like myself, I could be alone without being lonely. I hoped he was right.

She was going to move out immediately, but I said, don't bother, there's no rush. Now that the war's over, there's no hurry. Find a decent place to live first. For the next three months it was like sharing a house with another renter. We each did our own cooking, washed our own dishes, tidied up after ourselves. Sometimes, watching her, I wondered who is this person, as if some trick had been played on me and a stranger had taken the place of the person I'd married.

After she'd gone, I had a hard time sleeping. The twigs falling onto the garage roof, the furnace starting up, the crack of the house settling, made me wake with a start. To sleep, to really sleep, I went to the shrink's and slept in a storage room beside his office, not seeing him but knowing that he was there, that the secretary guarded the door, that no one would pounce on me in my sleep and kill me and all the people I loved.

After a time, I went up-island with a ground sheet and sleeping bag. I didn't need the noise any more, the TV, the radio, the surf. Instead, I slipped into second-growth cedar. The moss was deep and soft. Except for the sometime sound of the trees creaking in the wind, there was silence. I found an old stump, six feet across, five feet high, with the centre rotted out. Here, I laid out the ground sheet and sleeping bag and slept for fourteen hours at a time. Sometimes, I just sat, drinking coffee from my thermos, eating sandwiches I had brought in my pocket. The rabbits that sprang from the brush piles in my head ran less crazily by then. Instead of chasing them with a ferret, I whistled them to a stop, picked them up and studied them from every angle.

I took Karmen with me once. I planned it very carefully. I had a wicker picnic basket with everything in it. Matching plates, cups, saucers, cutlery. The basket even had space for a wine bottle. I bought hot smoked salmon and crackers. The deli made me fancy sandwiches. I picked strawberries and dipped them in Belgian chocolate. I took Blue Mountain coffee and four one-ounce bottles of brandy.

We had our picnic inside the hollowed out stump and made love twice on the sleeping bag. For me it was wonderful but I could feel that there was something missing for her. No intrigue. No excitement. No danger. Just us and the trees and the silence. Not the way it was in my office or, I'm sure, had been with Lazlo, in the washroom with his wife nearby.

For a time, I unplugged the phone. I didn't replace the TV or the radio. Now, I plug the phone back in when I'm willing to accept calls. Not a demand but a request, Shrinko says. You have the right to silence.

"What do you want to do?" he asked me. He was talking about the blond man and the redhaired one.

Kill them, I repeated over and over again, kill them, the sons of bitches, and he gave me a pillow to pound and kick. He didn't want me to do it, but I tracked them down. One was dead and the other was, I realized, an old man. I sawed the barrel and stock off my twenty-two so it would fit into my inside raincoat pocket.

"If you kill him, they'll have won. They'll have made you worse than them. They're guilty of sexual assault. You'll be guilty of murder."

"I want justice," I shouted.

"You'll get law," he replied. "We gave up on justice long ago. The best we can do is law."

I took my sawed-off rifle into the forest and emptied a box of shells into a stump, imagining myself at his door, ringing the bell, him answering and the look in his eyes when I told him who I was, the fear just before I shot him. I didn't want to kill him, I realized, it wasn't the killing, it was the fear, that's what I wanted, to make him afraid, so afraid that, like me, he'd piss himself, so afraid that he couldn't move, so afraid that until the day he died, he never slept a full night again.

"You'll find an answer," the shrink said. "Just as the garden looks like barren ground in early spring and then it rains and flowers appear," and I laughed with contempt but he was right. I was standing at the window, thinking of the sawed-off rifle, when I remembered my father saying, "The hardest thing is to walk away. You know you can win but you refuse to fight. Not because you're afraid. Because there's more important things in life."

I remembered how it was when he quit turning up at the kitchen table with his face swollen and battered and how glad I was when it stopped and the drinking stopped and the women quit crying and the drunks and fighters all went away and didn't come back. I didn't care where they'd gone, only that they weren't in our house or my room and I didn't need the space behind the couch or a rope ladder to the attic. I'll always love my father for that. For stopping the craziness.

"He isn't worth it," the shrink said. "He isn't worth a single day in jail."

38

A YEAR HAS GONE BY. It's raining again. A light drizzle. Jean called me. She and the Rocket are going to be selling at an antique show and she wants me to drop by.

When I arrive, she's standing behind the table, showing a Victorian side chair to a woman in a grey jacket. She's got rid of most of her secondhand junk and small antiques and used her half of our property to buy good quality furniture. There's a Georgian mahogany drop-leaf table, three Georgian side chairs and a Victorian slant-top desk. My son has told me that she's leased an old-fashioned building on the highway outside town and filled it with furniture, most of which is shipped from England in huge containers. She's talking in that intense way she has, like no one exists except the customer. It makes her a good saleswoman. She should have been in real estate or insurance or working for some big corporation. She should have had the chance, if she would have taken it, but standing there behind a Chinese screen, watching her, I doubt it. Other women a lot older than her did hustle, did grab for the brass ring, and like a lot of the men I know, once they got it, didn't want it. Still, she should have had a chance to be unhappy with success. But then there's me. I should have had a chance, too. Should have had a chance to make a life. That's us, two cripples sharing the same bed all those years. Maybe the m.c. was right about that. The holes in my head fit the rocks in hers. You want to have somebody less crazy, you've gotta get less crazy yourself.

Watching her this way, through the crack in the Chinese

screen, I'm shocked by how much older she looks. Older and smaller, as if some of the anger has leaked out and with it her ferocious energy. The circles under her eyes are darker and her face less defined, nearly puffy. If I hadn't been looking for her, I wouldn't have recognized her. Maybe she already looked like this and I just hadn't noticed. Sort of like an old sweater. You don't see how frayed it is until you haven't worn it for awhile.

She's got her hair tied back with a piece of pink wool like she used to when we were first married. Her hair is blonder than it used to be so she must be dying it. The grey streaks are gone. It looks rather good and seeing that, I feel sort of jealous and wish I'd bought a toupee and then feel guilty for being vain about my appearance. That's the hell of a church upbringing. You can't ever just feel. Somewhere, inside, there's a little pinch-faced minister second guessing and judging and making pronouncements. I always wonder about missionaries telling happy, naked natives to cover up and only have sex lying down and not, under any circumstances, to enjoy it. The natives should have discovered Europe and destroyed Rome. We'd all be better off.

When the lady with the coat leaves, I go over. The Rocket sees me and moves closer. He looks as if he's afraid I've come to take her back. I've never seen him when he isn't wearing a hockey sweater. Today, he's dressed for the occasion. A blue blazer, grey slacks, black loafers and a red hockey sweater with the number seventy-seven on it.

"How're ya doin'?" Jean asks. She talks like this sometimes, playing the country hick to hustle the middle-class matrons. It makes them feel they're getting a bargain from an ignorant yokel. Once she gets started, she has a hard time turning it off.

"You're doing your hair differently," I say.

"You don't like it."

"It's the new you. I'd have done something for the new me but painting my head didn't seem right."

She used to laugh at my jokes. She doesn't need to any more. She gets right to the point. "The painting you liked so much. You want it? I'm moving in with Ralph."

"Ralph?" I say.

She glances at the Rocket. He's off to one side showing a pair of hockey pants with a signature on them but his eyes keep flicking our way. I want to go over to him, put my arm around his shoulders like we're brothers and tell him it's okay, she's his, he's hers, whatever, and I really appreciate what he's doing for me. My worst nightmare has been that she might turn up at the door with a suitcase and say she wants to move back in. Instead, she's moving in with him. A good man in spite of the tattoo on his upper arm and the occasional wiping of his nose on his sleeve. Men should have some way of telling each other these things.

"He lives in a semitrailer. There's not much space. Would you like the painting back?"

"A house trailer," I say, correcting her.

"I know the difference between a house trailer and a semi. It's been taken off its wheels," she says. "It's on a barge on the Gorge. He's turning it into a houseboat. He's got a power line running to a repair shop. He has it fixed up with a couple of rooms. He's even got a bathroom installed."

I know the spot she's talking about. It's light industrial, with rusting heavy equipment, piles of wooden pallets, stacks of old bricks. Most of what's there is abandoned. There are some small floating docks with boats that are no longer seaworthy. A lot of rubbies spend the night there, sleeping in boxes or shelters made out of scrap lumber and tin sheets.

She sees the look I give her and says, "He's good with his hands. He's put in lights, a stove, a refrigerator. There's no rent, no taxes. People live on sailboats less than a quarter the size."

"How much?" I say, feigning indifference.

It's too much to hope that she might be willing to give it to me. When I first saw it, I nearly had a rear-end accident. I slammed on my brakes and the guy behind me screeched to within a millimetre of my bumper. Five minutes after seeing it, I was standing in the window display, pushing a hundred and fifty into the clerk's hand. It was a painting of a driftwood shelter on a West Coast beach. It's painted from inside so it's like you're looking out through an opening in the logs and there's a stretch of beach and then the ocean. When I moved into the guest bedroom, I took it with me, hung it over the head of the bed. It was three by four feet and covered with a sheet of glass. When things got really bad, I lay back and stared up at it, pretending I was there, inside the drift-log shelter, listening to the waves on the beach.

"Fifteen hundred."

It wasn't worth that. Maybe at gallery prices, but the gallery would take fifty per cent. She could let me have it for seven fifty and not lose any money. She knew that. I knew that. She knew that I knew that. She couldn't do anything without bargaining. She was the one person I knew who, when she went to a Mexican market, thought she'd died and gone to heaven. I hated the Mexican market and I hated this. The anger started. I'd found the painting. I'd bought it. I'd paid for it. Now I was going to have to pay top dollar for it again. The scales started to form on her hands and face but then the moment passed and she was just a middle-aged antique dealer. I know lots of middle-aged antique dealers. I don't expect any breaks from them. There's no reason to expect any from her. But seven fifty for the painting and another seven fifty for the anger is too much.

I understand about the anger. She has every right to be angry. Me, too. We both started out with hopes and dreams, Hollywood fantasies of happiness and success. She's hustling secondhand furniture and I'm teaching remedial English to twenty-year-old twits. Anything that's happened to her is matched by what's happened to me. Then I let it go. It's something about the Rocket, sneaking looks our way like a jealous teenager. Grow up, I want to tell him, people our age have histories. We make the Austro-Hungarian empire look simple and easy to understand. You can't wave away the past. You have a relationship with someone, you get into bed with their mother, father, kids, ex-husbands, lovers, snake-kissing, mice-eating relatives. You want a relationship, don't bitch about the crowd. When she was seventeen, she wouldn't have spoken to the Rocket if he'd followed her home on his knees. He has a ducktail instead of a fringe but I can't imagine his endless search through the locker rooms of North America for hockey memorabilia as being eternally interesting. He still carries an oversize wallet in his back pocket and uses a comb that flips open like a switchblade.

What, I wondered, was it like to be a woman, middle-aged, trying to be attractive and hoping desperately that somebody likes silver with a patina rather than new silver, as the m.c. said. We both knew it was a shit analogy in a society where being young is worshipped. In high school there had always been a kind of desperation among the girls who were unattractive, standing in a group, hoping that some guy would pay attention to them, would quit panting after the beauty queens who were busy collecting slavering males into obedient packs. It was the same game except now there was less to negotiate with. Lines and wrinkles and double chins and drooping breasts are devalued currency in a society where most males really want a virgin whore who looks fifteen. Since we'd split, I'd gone to a bar twice with friends. Fantasy night for troglodytes. No wonder they all have to use so much coke. The suspension of disbelief was more than could be managed unaided.

"Too much," I say, thinking about what was left in my bank account.

"You seeing anybody?" she asks.

"Too busy," I say.

"You haven't changed. Never tell the truth. Never say how you really feel. At least you're not so sarcastic."

"All right," I say, "the truth. I want the painting. I feel like shit about having to pay for it but that's reality. I hate it. I can't change it but I'm not going to be ripped off to get it. That better?"

She picks a silver candlestick off a side table and begins polishing it. It doesn't need polishing. She puts it down. "Business hasn't been very good. That's why we're moving in together. I'm selling my car. We can't afford to run two vehicles. Is that bad enough to make you feel good?"

"Oh, shit," I say, putting my hand on her arm. "I shouldn't have come."

She tells the Rocket she's going for a coffee and we walk to where the dealers have tables and a coffeepot set up behind some screens. Business must be off. Usually, they have china cups and saucers and napkins. Now, there's foam cups, plastic sticks and powdered whitener.

"You got half the house. Where'd the money go?"

"Stock. The lease. Equipment. Tourists are down. It'll pick up in awhile."

"Is he good to you?"

"No," she says matter of factly. "But he wants me."

"And I didn't?"

She doesn't say anything. And it's my turn to look away. She's right. Most of the time I couldn't bear to be touched. Once in a while, somehow, it was all right but most of the time, every time I was touched, I wanted to scream, wanted to say leave me alone, leave me alone, quit touching me, I can't bear to be touched, and not knowing why, thinking I was crazy, pushing it aside, trying to bury the child inside me screaming don't touch me, quit touching me, leave me alone, until my head and my body were separated, like my body was over there, disconnected, so everything was far away, so it wasn't happening to me.

Was I really so awful? I want to ask but, for once, I keep my mouth shut. I want to ask her about all those exciting men with whom she was going to have a real romance. That makes me feel even more mean-spirited and shitty. Now I know why people move to other cities after they split. Better to hang on to the way you remember your breakup, hang on to your hate, and your self-justification. Then you don't have to deal with the way it really is. You don't have to think about your own part in it.

Who was I fighting with, I wondered, when I had all those battles with the monstrous snake with the horrible fangs.

"Five hundred?"

"I can do better than that," she says. "I'm not trying to stiff you. It's just I need the money."

"I haven't got it," I say. "Even if you'll take seven fifty, I'll have to pay you a hundred a month."

"Deal," Jean says. "I thought you hated bargaining."

She takes her coffee and goes back to her antiques and the Rocket. I stand there mixing milk powder and sugar into a foam

213

cup and thinking that's how it ends, when it's all over and done, nothing dramatic, no epiphanies, in the middle of all the shufflers going by, fingering the secondhand goods, that's how it ends.

The coffee's just short of battery acid but I don't need the Divol anymore. I quit carrying Divol six months ago. She's not so bad, I think, not that I'd want her back, but there were good times, it all wasn't a waste. It's like my grandfather. After he retired, he voted for the Legion to accept German and Italian soldiers and when I asked him how he could do that, he said, "We went through it together, and after a while, after you get over the hate, that counts for more than who was on what side."

Printed in Canada